To Andy

To Serve Another

A Chris Lennox Story

By Ed Lane

With all best wishes

Ed Lane

http://www.fast-print.net/bookshop

TO SERVE ANOTHER DAY

ISBN: 978-178456-485-8

Most characters are fictional.
Any similarity to any living person is purely coincidental. Conversations, attitudes and actions of historical persons are works of imagination.

A catalogue record for this book is available from the British Library

First published 2017 by
FASTPRINT PUBLISHING
Peterborough, England.

Full length Novels by Ed Lane:

(All titles are available in all ebook formats from Amazon).

The 'Going Dark' Series

A Circling of Vultures	ASIN: B005DHYG3C
Terrible Beauty	ASIN: B006ZDE2QE
The Lunatic Game	ASIN: B00ABL7L5K
A Circling of Hawks	ASIN: B00H7HDXJY

The following are also available:

The 'Fields of Fire' Trilogy

Blood Debt	ASIN: B00KXJ62Y6
Dragonfire	ASIN: B00Q1OPUX6
Dust to Dust	ASIN: B00V45GOS2

Chris Lennox stories

To Fight Another Day	ASIN: B01HFBT070

Find Ed Lane on Facebook:
https://www.facebook.com/ed.lane.3

Visit his website for the latest news:
www.edtheauthor.wix.com/the-books-of-ed-lane

Email:
edtheauthor@gmail.com

Acknowledgements

In memory of my old friend
Sergeant Roger Biggin,
Royal Regiment of Fusiliers
who passed away on May 12th 2017.

Once again, I would like to thank my beta reader, Veronica Stonehouse, for suggesting improvements and finding and correcting my errors.

Spartan-Warrior is a non-profit organisation that helps sufferers combat Post Traumatic Stress Disorder (PTSD).
As they say, they are large enough to matter
but small enough to care.
You can check out their website at
www.spartan-warrior.com
I will be making a donation towards the charity from the proceeds of this book.

Introduction

From the pen of George Lennox

Let me explain.

I'm a 21st century soldier living at the turn of the 18th and 19th centuries.

That's right, I'm living more than two-hundred years in the past.

I'm writing this with quill and ink and it will be left in an airtight stone jar buried in the centre of Stonehenge for future generations to find... if I don't make it back to dig it up myself.

How did I get here? That's as much of a mystery to me. It involved being struck by lightning one morning while I was clowning around at the centre of Stonehenge in a thunderstorm. That strike took me back to 1799 and the birth of my own regiment, The Rifles, (then known as the Corps of Riflemen) in which I played some small part. Or was this scenario all a coma-induced and very detailed dream based on my knowledge of Regimental history?

I wasn't sure and this is where things got even more complicated. Back in 1799, I fell in love. Totally, utterly, completely, in love with the most beautiful young woman I'd ever seen. I was on the verge of marrying her when, once again at the centre of Stonehenge, in the middle of a duel, I was struck by lightning a second time and thrown, near to death, back to the 21st century.

The medic who saved my life that morning was the spitting image of Catherine, even down to her name, which decided me that my year in the past was nothing but ten minutes of intense imagination fired by high voltage and the vision of beauty before my semi-conscious eyes. Except . . .

Except that two of my Glock pistol magazines were half-empty. I'd dreamed I'd used them in battles against the French and Spanish, but in real life, each should still have been full with the sixteen rounds I'd loaded prior to a live field-firing exercise.

The medics sent me for an MRI scan at the hospital which caused excruciating pain in my head and the next thing I knew I was back in the year 1800 with my head resting in Catherine's lap.

By the way, my name is Lieutenant Chris Lennox but in this time I'm known as Lieutenant-colonel George Lennox. All of which is another story.

When first I was thrown back in time I assumed it was for a purpose, to facilitate the raising of the Corps of Riflemen and the introduction of the Baker Rifle to the British Army. Once that had been achieved, I believed my mission to the past was completed and that was why I was returned to my own time.

I have no idea what is now expected of me, or what, if any, my new mission will be. I have long imagined that my every act was guided by an unknown force but now I have a sense of aimlessness and I wonder what the future will bring.

Only time can tell.

Chris (George) Lennox,

September, 1800.

1

"George, dearest, speak to me."

Chris forced open his eyes just as sunlight seeped through the clouds above Stonehenge and shone on Catherine's beautiful face. She had his head in her lap and he could see tears streaking her cheeks.

He raised one hand to wipe them away. "Don't cry, Catherine … I'm back."

"Back from whence. You have been struck by a lightning bolt and cast to the ground. It is a miracle and God's mercy that you still live."

Chris looked at the shattered remains of the duelling pistol still clamped in his other fist and grimaced. "Henry's pistol did not fare so well it seems."

Henry Wadman's blurred face hovered into Chris's field of vision. By god, sir, you are but the luckiest man alive to be struck down twice by lightning and yet survive both assaults. The devil must be kind to his own."

"Chris managed a stiff smile. "Hah, Henry, you were merely hoping that the gods would do the work for you today."

Henry was Chris's duelling opponent and Catherine's brother. They had come to an agreement one night over glasses of Madeira that their quarrel would be resolved amicably and Henry had shot wide of Chris's head. It was as he was raising his own pistol to shoot skyward that the lightning had struck. The gods it seemed did not relish the weapon fired in their direction.

Henry prised the heavy pistol from Chris's grasp and grimaced in turn. "The Guards Officer's mess will be in need of some replacement pistols I fear."

"The gun makers will be happy with the business, I daresay," Chris said and levered himself into a sitting position.

Catherine tutted. "Do take care, dearest. Your seconds have ridden for father's carriage to bear you to Imber Court so be at ease ere it comes."

Chris turned his head to look into her blue-grey eyes. "Catherine, you mustn't fuss over me. I'm a soldier and should take these happenings in my stride. I have no need of your father's carriage. I can ride back to Imber Court."

"I have seen lightning cleave a majestic oak and you are but flesh, George Lennox. You must not exert yourself unduly until Doctor Hawking has examined you."

Chris's vision was clearing and he could see that he was still wearing his anachronistic combat suit and Kevlar vest. It wasn't that he distrusted Henry's shooting ability but with his recently agreed engagement to Catherine uppermost in his mind he had taken the precaution of wearing the armoured vest and had brought his Bergen back pack with his trauma kit inside it. It was standing where he had left it propped against one of the monolithic stones. It puzzled him as all he had been wearing when rolled into the MRI scanner was a T-Shirt and jeans. Whatever had caused his return to the past had dumped him back exactly where he had left it three days earlier. He resolved, should he ever get back to the future, that he would bone up on Einstein's Theory of Relativity.

He put his left hand to his head. The excruciating pain he had felt had eased to a dull throb but he could barely move his right hand. He tried closing the fingers but could manage only a claw. He pulled up his sleeve and saw that the Maori-like tattoo tracery on his arm was as vivid as ever, proof, if he ever needed it, that water running down his arm had earthed the electricity and saved his life. Those slight movements tired him and he groaned. "I think you're right, sweetheart. I'll take the carriage and let Hawking mutter and rub his chin over me.

"Now what are you doing here, Catherine? The duelling ground is no place for a lady."

"I could not bear the thought of you facing such danger with me left in ignorance of your plight for even one second. I had to be by your side whatever the outcome. Amelia and I rode out but minutes after your departure to be here."

"Then both of you are inordinately courageous and foolhardy in equal measure but I thank you both for your concern. But where's your sister now?"

"She is returning to Imber with your brother officers to rouse papa with the news. She is unaware of your good fortune and may believe you be struck to death, so still did you lie for so many minutes."

Henry returned from dismissing his seconds and nodded. "Yes, sir. Like a corpse, with barely a breath taken and a pulse as weak as a day old kitten."

Chris noticed for the first time that the storm had passed. He and Henry were soaking wet but Catherine had the good sense to be wearing a riding cloak with hood. Chris's combat suit was weatherproof but the coolness of the rain-slicked earth was beginning to seep into his bones, bones still tingling from the shock.

"Henry, you will catch *your* death," Chris said. "You'd better get out of that soaking uniform quickly. Ride on to Imber while we wait for the carriage."

"Tush, sir," Henry said. "I have been in worst plights and survived the rigours. I too am a soldier of long service. These privations are nought to concern me, nor should they concern you unduly, though I do thank you for your courtesy. I will wait here with you and Catherine.

"I have noted your forms of address between each other, is there something of which you should apprise me."

"George and I became engaged to be married last eve," Catherine said. "We are to be wed by special licence as George is due back to his duties at Shorncliffe in but a few days."

"Then my hearty congratulations to you both. May I be the first to wish you long life and happiness. But the colonel is not destined to return to Shorncliffe. I have despatches from Horse Guards that order him to attend His Royal Highness the Duke of York at his earliest convenience. I am to escort him back to London forthwith."

"But surely, Henry, George cannot be expected to travel in his weakened state. He must have sufficient leave to recover his health fully," Catherine said.

Henry's careworn face broke into a brief smile. "That is perhaps the silver lining to this sorry cloud. I shall send a despatch back to Horse Guards with the news of what has occurred. Enough time will be granted for your nuptials to take place, I am certain of it, for I shall word the letter with great care."

Catherine stood and kissed her brother on the cheek. She had a tear in her eye. "Oh, thank you, Henry. What should we do without your kind offices?"

Henry took her hand. "You have had enough tragedy to blight you in recent times. Losing your husband, Anthony Dean, so soon after you were wed and in such circumstance as an accident with a pistol after his return from long absence fighting against the French whilst serving under Lennox here. You deserve some happiness, dear sister, albeit it must be brief on this occasion as His

Royal Highness has need of Lennox's particular services once again."

"Anthony was my friend and I feel his loss as deeply as anyone," Chris said. "He asked that I should take what care of Catherine I could. I'm sure he suspected that I held her in the greatest regard and any duty he may have put upon me was an exceeding kindness on his part. I'm just happy that Catherine agreed to accept me as her husband."

"You did save my life, sir and my honour when I was assaulted by highwaymen. For that I will be forever in your debt," Catherine said.

"Tush, that is enough of this," Henry said with a twinkle in his eye. "The pair of you have been in love from the beginning. I may be an old soldier, I may be absent from Imber for many a day, you both may have tried to hide your affection from each other but there is no hiding it from me, nor from Amelia, I'd wager."

Catherine's cheeks turned pink and she turned her eyes away. "You must think me horrid that I did marry Anthony even though I did love him more as a brother."

"Not at all," Henry said. "You stood by your honour as a Wadman. It was exceeding bad timing that Lennox happened upon you in your time of distress so shortly after your engagement to Anthony was announced. You did your duty, Catherine and I admire you for it. I'd wager that you and Lennox will make an excellent match."

Chris had been listening to the exchange with a worried look on his face. "Perhaps it would be best if your parents, Sir George and Lady Isobel, were kept in ignorance of that, Henry. I know how quickly rumour spreads in the villages and tongues wag so easily. The Deans are still in mourning and I would hate to have anything said that would open divisions between your families or cast Catherine in a bad light in the community."

"Fear not, sir. This will be kept between us. I would leave mama and papa in happy ignorance and the rest of Imber too."

"Papa has not yet been informed of our engagement, Henry," Catherine said. "Colonel Lennox was to inform him this morn, after your duel had been settled and the colonel could once more be welcomed into Imber Court."

"Then he will be doubly pleased that a son and a prospective son-in-law did survive both a duel and the wrath of heaven.

"Come, I can see the carriage approaching. Give me your good arm, sir and I will assist you to your feet."

Henry pulled Chris up and wrapped an arm around his waist. Chris's legs were like jelly and he clung onto Henry in turn. Catherine walked away to wave to the coachman and Chris took the opportunity to whisper in Henry's ear. "What does His Royal Highness want with me, Major Wadman?"

Henry grimaced. "Do not get too comfortable in your marriage, sir. I do believe the Duke has plans to put you back into the teeth of the enemy."

2

Four days after the experiment at the Fast Hadron Collider, buried beneath the Swiss/French border outside Zurich, had been concluded, the top scientists and engineers from seven countries were gathered around a conference table, each with a wide area network connected laptop open and gently whirring as data trickled up the screens.

"As you see, gentlemen," Dr Max Bruckner said, "the Atlas computer has thrown up some very interesting data. During the recent experiment to create dark matter, the streams of protons exceeded all known parameters and reached a combined speed of 18 Tera-electron volts. There was also, for an infinitesimal period of time, a variation in the voltage and two magnets in the containment field registered a less than one micro-second drop in power.

"I am not sure that anything conclusive can be assumed from this current data until it has been extensively analysed but, strangely for a scientist, my gut feeling tells me that we did indeed create a minute quantity of dark matter."

"The figures will bear this out when we have them, or not, as the case may be but I cannot see how you can arrive at this conclusion, Herr Doktor, without positive proof," Professor Johan Schmidt said.

Bruckner took off his rimless glasses and polished them with his tie. It was an old trick that gave him time to think. "There are a series of coincidences which of themselves mean little, Herr Professor, but when added together may give us some cause for optimism. As well as the incidents I have already mentioned, the unexplained increase in TeV speed and the loss of power to the bending magnets, there was also a minor disruption in the ionosphere, or the Heaviside Layer if you prefer, picked up by orbiting satellite, and a quantum surge in the power output of an electrical storm on the planet's surface in southern England, in Wiltshire, I believe."

"And how does this inform your deduction," Schmidt asked.

"All of these occurrences happened within less than one microsecond of each other. It seems to me that the increased velocity of the proton streams as they collided together caused by the power surge that also weakened the containment field produced a microscopic particle of dark energy that escaped the containment field at the point where the two magnets were weakened, flew up to the Heaviside Layer, ricocheted off a particle of ionised energy and was drawn to the magnetic disturbance on the earth's surface where it caused a quantum surge. Our Astral physicists have determined that a trajectory from here to Wiltshire via the Heaviside Layer is perfectly feasible due to the height of the layer above the earth's surface over Europe at that time."

Schmidt shook his head. "It is pure conjecture, Herr Doktor. As scientists we cannot accept anything but the absolute certainty that dark matter was created. We have no idea how such matter would behave within our own parameters of physics. Surely there would be some manifestation of dark matter, somewhere, if it existed."

"You are quite correct, Herr Professor. It is conjecture but we do not know what the half-life of dark matter would be. It may have been consumed in the quantum surge, at this point it is impossible to say without thorough research but I would ask you gentlemen to keep your minds open to the possibility that somewhere on this planet is proof of the creation of dark matter. We are hoping to recreate the exact conditions within the collider to reproduce a further sample but my engineers tell me that the power requirement needed to emulate the 18TeVs is beyond our present safe capability. We are working on increasing our power options but this will take some time as we would also need to bolster the strength of the containment field to ensure that no more dark energy could possibly escape."

Chris still had a buzzing inside his head. He could not know it but the particle of dark energy lodged in his cerebrum was the cause of it. He assumed it was a result of the trouble with the MRI scan.

He finished writing a note to the future and admired his penmanship. His claw of a right hand made writing difficult but he managed to lodge the quill between his thumb and first finger. It had taken him some time on his previous visit to the past to master the quill pen and ink without major blots on the paper but he was pleased with his effort and sanded it carefully. He rolled it into a heavy stone jar taken from the kitchen and heated it over a candle before ramming in a wooden bung and completely sealing it with wax. It was as airtight as he could make it. He planned to ride out one early morning to bury it beneath a central stone at the henge, where he could be sure to find it, if he ever got back to his present time.

It was his way of testing whether he was truly back in 1800 or whether he was back in dreamland. If the jar *was* there it would be proof of his current reality. He wrapped it carefully in a plastic bag from his Bergen, cushioned it with straw so that it would have a reasonable chance of surviving more than two hundred years in a hole that was unlikely to be disturbed due to its hallowed location.

On the other hand, he was more than content with his lot. He was to marry the love of his life as soon as the special licence was granted. Sir George welcomed the news of his and Catherine's engagement and lady Isobel almost danced with delight. She had always had a soft spot for Chris after he saved Catherine from a fate worse than death. The Dean family too had given the announcement a cautious welcome. Anthony's brother Charles, who now owned the house Catherine and Anthony had lived in, was more open with his good wishes. Chris had the thought that Charles, who had kindly let Catherine stay on in the house after Anthony's death, would now have more opportunity to propose to Amelia and have more chance of the proposal being accepted. Chris knew that Amelia had no intention of marrying while Catherine lived in the house that she herself would occupy once married to Charles. Chris had to smile at the machinations but Charles had a good heart and he knew that Amelia did care for him.

His plea to Henry to keep his and Catherine's feelings for each other prior to Anthony's death had an ulterior motive. Anthony had committed suicide in Chris's presence due to his incapacitating injuries and the onset of Post Traumatic Stress Disorder. Chris had put the word around that it had been a terrible accident with a Dragon pistol. Suicide was an illegal act and viewed by both the civil and ecumenical authorities as a sin punishable by eternal damnation.

There was no way Chris would let his friend's reputation be tarnished and invented the story. Now he was concerned that a different interpretation might be applied in the light of his and Catherine's feelings for each other. He was being ultra sensitive but he did not want the thought that he had killed Anthony, in order to claim his wife, to gain any credence amongst the gossipmongers. Luckily, both he and Anthony were held in high regard in Imber but others further afield would relish spreading malicious gossip given the chance. It was a small worry but a worry nonetheless.

A knock brought him out of his reverie. He made sure the plastic bag was tucked out of sight and opened the door on the smiling face of his borrowed valet.

"We, Mary and me, are right pleased of your news, sir," Matthew said. "The whole of Imber be agog with it, sir."

Chris smiled back and beckoned Matthew in. "Thanks, Matthew. And how is Mary?

"Well, sir, thankee, sir. You did save her from the unwelcome attentions of Mr Foxley and she is assuredly most grateful and will never forget your kindness."

Chris nodded. It seemed he was destined to save the womenfolk of Imber from sexual predators. "Wish her well for me, Matthew. I was pleased to help."

"That you did cuff Mr Foxley, sir and put him on his arse, pardon my language, Colonel, did have us all in fits once we were sure that Mary was unharmed." Matthew lowered his voice and glanced around as if he were afraid of being overheard. "It is also said that you did defeat Mr Foxley in a duel and avenge us of the traitor."

"Foxley went over to the French and brought them on us in Portugal. It gave me no pleasure but you're right, I was forced to duel with him and he lost."

"He were the finest swordsman in Wiltshire and in the 62nd regiment, tis said by those who ajudge such things, sir.

Twould have been something to behold, of that I am certain."

"Taking a life is no easy thing, Matthew. Even someone as black-hearted as Foxley has a right to trial but this is a desperate age where life is cheap and it is an unfortunate fact that killing is taken so lightly. I wish it were otherwise."

"You are a true gentleman, Colonel Lennox, I'll not have it said that you are not."

"That's very good of you, Matthew. Now what is it that brings you to my room?"

"Oh, begging your pardon, sir. Mrs Catherine Dean requests your presence in the withdrawing room as soon as you are able."

"Inform Mrs Dean that I'll be with her shortly."

Matthew left but the conversation had brought back the memory of the duel with Foxley. He tried to clench his right hand but could not close it completely yet. He was an Olympic standard pentathlete in his own time but preferred the sabre over the foil used in the pentathlon and, because of that and his need to concentrate on his military career, had disqualified himself from qualifying for the Great Britain team. He wondered if he would be able to hold a sabre again.

3

Catherine was waiting for him in the drawing room and she rose to greet him and took both his hands in hers. She stood on tiptoe to kiss him then stepped back and eyed him with a concerned look. "You are still limping somewhat, George and your fingers are clawed on one hand. Are you in pain?"

He gave her a reassuring smile in return and led her back to her seat. "It's just a little numbness that's slow to wear off. I expect it will cure itself in a day or so. Doctor Hawking could find nothing physically wrong with me, all the bits are in the right place."

She tapped lightly on his arm with her fan as he sat beside her. "You are making merry with me, George Lennox, I am far too concerned for your health and I am not amused."

Chris grinned. "I do believe that phrase will become famous one day. But please don't worry unduly. The effects of the lightning strike will wear off. It jangles the nerves in the body and excites the muscles so they seem to have a mind of their own but it is purely temporary."

"I bow to your superior knowledge in things medical and I do declare that you have eased my mind on that score. However, Henry tells me that you are summoned to His Royal Highness the Duke of York's presence as soon as may be."

"Sadly, that's so. I've no idea what the duke has in store for me but I owe him my rank and my income. I'm not so naïve as to assume there would not be some form of repayment due and I'm honour bound not to delay my departure to London for long. I'm sorry, sweetheart but I will have to leave you far too soon."

"You will be careful. After that which befell Anthony I am greatly disturbed by your ever closer relationship with danger."

Chris raised her chin and looked straight into her eyes. "Please don't concern yourself unduly. I'm a trained soldier and Anthony was a civilian in uniform who purchased his commission so that he could repay a debt of honour to me. He was not prepared, physically or mentally, for the rigours of a soldier's life nor his awful experiences in Portugal. He was a gentle man who did all that was asked of him but it was too much for him to bear after he sustained his injury.

"I once asked you if I frightened you, dear Catherine. I was concerned in my turn that you would find my character far too audacious for you to like, let alone love. Be assured, with my loved ones and my friends I am as gentle as can be, as gentle as Anthony was, but should any person threaten them or put them in jeopardy of any sort, then I'm a force to be reckoned with. It is the same with the King's enemies and they should be fearful of my capabilities. I have a guardian angel called St Kevlar and I will always return to you, Catherine, safe and whole."

"I do believe you will, dearest George, but what of us betwixt times?"

"I had thought to rent a house in Shorncliffe or Folkstone for us but I don't know where the duke will order me or for how long. Perhaps your father, Sir George, would agree to you living here at Imber Court until things become settled and I can send for you."

Catherine gave a sober nod. "You may enquire of him for I can see no alternative for the present. I shall be comfortable here but with a lonely heart whilst you are away."

"I'll make sure you have an income," Chris continued, "so that you won't be a burden on the household finances with enough to buy whatever you need. I'm assuming you would wish to keep your maid, Esther, in employment."

"Of course, dearest, she is an able companion and I would be at a loss without her. I was so wondering how you would view my need of her."

"Where I'm from women have as much right to their own life as we men. You can have whatever you need to give you independence. The income I'll give you is yours to do with as you wish. I'll cover any household bills and Esther's wages separately. I would not want you to feel beholden to anyone."

Catherine put a gentle hand on his cheek. "You will find me an extraordinarily fine housekeeper and I will live well within my income for I do not believe in profligacy. We have always lived a simple but pleasurable god fearing life here at Imber and I cannot see the need to change the habit of my twenty-three years."

Chris took her hand and kissed the palm. "Apart from your extraordinary beauty, I also fell deeply in love with your courage, your loyalty and your intelligence. The lady who saved *my* life in turn from a highwayman's bullet. I have complete faith in you, Catherine."

"Then it will indeed be a match made in heaven."

The door opened and Henry Wadman came in followed by Amelia who gave a graceful curtsey.

"So I am to be your sister, Colonel Lennox. How shall I rise to the occasion?"

Chris laughed, stood and bowed. "I do believe you are more than capable of rising to any occasion, Miss Wadman.

But have you forgotten our vow of friendship so soon? You must call me George. You too, Major Wadman. I would deem it an honour if you would favour me with your friendship."

Henry held out his hand. "So be it, George. I should be proud to call you friend. Now, many apologies in interrupting the love birds but I have news from Horse Guards. The duke insists that you be in attendance three days hence. We shall take the post coach at noon two days hence in order that we should be punctual."

"The special marriage licence? I've heard nothing about it," Chris said, consternation on his face.

Amelia gave a small delighted laugh. "Then it falls to me to be the bearer of glad tidings for the vicar is in receipt of the said document which came with Henry's despatches from the Archbishop of Canterbury himself on the good offices of the Duke of York. The Vicar is preparing for your nuptials on the morrow."

Catherine gasped and put a hand to her mouth. "Then I must make haste and prepare. You must not see me hereafter until the morrow, George Lennox. Tis said to bring bad luck. Come Amelia, we have much to do. Oh, what time is the ceremony? I must hurry Esther to lay out my gown. Excuse us, Henry and do excuse us, dear George."

She and Amelia curtsied and left giggling and chattering to each other. Both the men watched them go with smiles on their faces. Chris indicated a chair.

"Do sit, Henry. What further news do you have?"

"Some welcome news indeed. Our friend, William Stewart, is making a good recovery from the Spanish ball that laid him low. He does say that much is due to your ministrations and the native concoction that you have which staved off infection."

Chris gave a strained grin as Henry's remarks brought back a memory of the story he had concocted of coming from the unknown island of New Zealand with strange native medicines such as Baneocin powder and the self-injecting morphine ampoules which he carried in his trauma kit and which never seemed to run out; another foible of his time travelling where anything metallic did not regenerate but almost everything else did. The cover story also went some way to explaining his odd accent, strange vocabulary and phrasing. Although he tried hard to mimic local usage he often fell back into 21st century idioms.

The long pause in his response had Henry looking puzzled. He gave him a reassuring smile. "That's good to hear. I'm sure Colonel Stewart will have a bright future ahead of him."

Henry grunted and looked Chris square in the face. "You may well be part of it, George. The duke has also summoned Stewart from his sick bed. I do not yet know the reason but I have heard of grave tidings from abroad and you must be prepared to travel."

4

Under the provisions of the special licence the wedding could be held in the afternoon so Chris had time to ride into Salisbury to buy rings for himself and Catherine. It wasn't the fashion for men to wear them but he was the product of another age and felt beholden to have one. He gave the jeweller a sovereign his own father had given him as a gift on his graduation from Sandhurst to set into his ring. He also found time to bury the jar with his letter to the future inside it under a stone at the very centre of the henge.

The ceremony itself was drawn out by the vicar enjoying his moment in the limelight and proud of the document signed by the archbishop. There were few people inside the church, Sir George and Lady Isobel, Henry who acted as best man and Amelia who was Catherine's bridesmaid for the second time. Charles Dean was also in attendance with two captains from the 62nd Regiment billeted outside Salisbury who were acquainted with Chris. He had issued the invitation that morning and the two men had detached themselves from their duties for the occasion. They added splashes of colour with their red coats.

Chris had worn his Rifleman's green and looked dull by comparison. Catherine, in silver, shone beside him in the light that cascaded through the one stained-glass window that the small church possessed. He had never seen any woman look so radiant.

With the register signed and witnessed the small group made their way out to be welcomed by what seemed like the whole of Imber's population of over two-hundred.

Chris knew very few of them but recognised the smith and the seamstress who had worked for him on a previous occasion. Shoes were thrown for luck as they made their way back to Imber Court for a late wedding breakfast.

It was afterwards that was giving Chris butterflies. He had little idea what was expected of him in the bedroom with his new bride. The morals and mores of the times seemed shrouded in mystery as far as ladies of good birth were concerned. He knew Catherine would come to him in his room from hers, dressed for bed. He was no prude, he'd had his share of girlfriends all of whom disrobed with abandon, but the last thing he wanted was to make Catherine feel uncomfortable or even worse, insulted, by his behaviour.

The thoughts circled his mind as Catherine departed to retire and he was left with the men finishing their brandies and cigars. He did not want to leave in an unseemly rush, neither did he want to leave Catherine waiting for too long. The two soldiers were smiling and casting sideways looks in his direction and Sir George was fiddling with his cravat and hurrumping to himself.

Charles Dean looked across at him, winked and cast his eyes at the ceiling.

Chris stood and bowed. "If you would excuse me gentlemen, I have an important assignation."

Sir George stopped fiddling and cast a hard stare at him. "You will treat my daughter with great care, sir. She is most precious to me."

Chris bowed. "And to me, sir, more than you can know."

In his bedroom Matthew had already laid out his kit and left. Chris pulled off his tunic and boots but left his linen shirt and breeches on. He was wearing 21st century briefs with the word 'Gant' printed on the waistband and he had to grin at the memory of the character in the film *'Back to the Future'* who found himself in a similar situation.

He sat on the bed and twiddled his thumbs, then stood and counted the number of paces back and forth across the room. He sat again. His heart lurched as the latch on the door clicked up and the door swung slowly open.

Catherine came in dressed in a night cap and a low cut nightdress that almost reached the ground. She held her eyes on the floor but walked slowly towards him and stopped just short. His heart was thumping like a jackhammer as he reached out and took her hands.

"Anthony told me that he was unable to consummate the marriage and that you still have your maidenhead. I will be as gentle with you as I can. If there is anything you don't wish me to do you only have to say so and I'll stop. I sincerely hope you will remember this night with joy in the days to come."

Catherine looked up now and had tears on her cheeks. "You have already made me the happiest woman in the land, dear George. Do with me as you will for I am a woman of the country and there is nought that will offend me or cause you to desist from your husbandly duty."

He ran his hands gently up her sides, down her back, across her thighs and up to her small breasts. She was breathing heavily as he kissed her neck. "May I leave a candle burning. I'd like to see you as god intended."

She bit her lip and her voice quavered. "You may leave all the candles burning if that is your wish, sir."

"And what is your wish, darling Catherine?"

"To see you too as god intended."

"Then perhaps I should put them all out."

She shot him a hot look and pulled at his shirt. "You are making merry again, George Lennox."

"I have much to be merry about, Mrs Lennox. Now help me out of these damned breeches."

They spent the whole day together in Chris's room. It was their only honeymoon. Matthew and Esther brought them refreshments throughout the day and they had everything they needed.

After the initial pain, Catherine had taken to intercourse with joy and abandon. They made love several times throughout the day and rested between times on the goose down mattress propped up with pillows. As the day wore on both their minds turned to Chris's imminent departure.

Catherine rolled to him and put a small hand on his chest. "Will you write often, dearest?"

Chris put his arm underneath her shoulders and pulled her to him. "As often as I can but don't be alarmed if you don't hear from me for some time. It means nothing except the difficulty in getting despatches delivered."

"Within England?"

"You are too clever by half, Mrs Lennox. I don't yet know the circumstances of my deployment but yes, there is a chance I will be posted abroad."

"Into mortal danger?"

"When we sign on for a military career we do it in the knowledge that we may have to put our lives on the line for our country. It comes with the territory."

"Then I shall pray every day, dear husband, that God may keep you safe and that the seed you have planted within me shall ripen into the sweetest fruit."

"Children? Oh my lord, I'd never considered that might happen."

"What is wrong, George? You have no wish for a family?"

"Yes, of course, the thought of having little Catherines is a joy but …"

"That is a momentous *but*, George."

"What will happen to the future?"

5

The coach journey to London was uncomfortable in more ways than one. The turnpikes were bumpy in places and the seats hard but that was the least of the worries on Chris's mind. He had left Catherine inconsolable at his departure and he felt the wrench badly. She had always been so strong but he knew that the memory of losing Anthony in a similar fashion played hard on her mind.

Then there was the thought of having children and the effect that could have on his own time. How would that change history? Nothing noticeable had changed on his previous return but that was not to say it would stay the same this time. He came from an age of prophylactics and birth pills and had not considered the possible result of his lovemaking with Catherine until she had mentioned it. The vicar had droned on about procreation but he had been too engrossed in Catherine's lovely face to pay much attention at the time. He was, he considered, totally besotted with her.

Then there was another thought. If he was really dreaming this, what kind of a mess would he be in back in his hospital bed?

He had been silent for some time and Henry, seated opposite, tapped his shin with a boot. "You are unusually silent, sir."

Chris gave a gesture of resignation. "I have much on my mind, Major." There was little else they could say as the two other passengers in the coach, both heavily veiled women who had been on the coach when they boarded, could overhear.

"Indeed, sir. May I say that I have every sympathy, having to drag you away at such an inopportune time."

"Thank you, Major. That's most kind. The situation is not what I would have wished."

"Your wife did not come out to bid you farewell. All is well there, I hope."

"We said our goodbyes much earlier and she retired to her own room as I made my preparations to leave. I said there was no need for her to accompany me to the coach but now I have some regret that we didn't pass our last minutes together and I could be sure she was in good spirits."

"I thought as much. You do not need to fear for her, sir. She is in the loving bosom of her family and will be well cared for."

"I take some comfort from that."

Henry straightened his back and eased his belt with a grunt. "Tonight we will stay at my club in St. James's Street. The morrow will bring much to take your mind from your domestic thoughts."

"With that in mind, I have sent for Serjeant-major Biggin to come up from Shorncliffe," Chris said. "He returned with me and Colonel Stewart from Ferrol on the *Aquilon,* although I had no time to converse with him during the voyage. He will be lodging in Ye Olde Cheshire Cheese in Fleet Street at my expense. One hopes in not too thirsty a mood. I daresay I'll have need of Biggin's services before long."

"Dash it, sir, you have an admirable way with organisation, to think such in advance of any instruction."

"Forewarned is forearmed, Major and if the hints you have been dropping are anything to go by, it is as well I'm prepared for any eventuality."

*

Chris stood rigidly to attention as the Duke of York sat at a desk and sanded a document before handing it to his private secretary. He glanced up and waved a languid hand. "Be at ease, Lennox."

Chris relaxed and glanced around. There were two other men seated in the window that overlooked the Horse Guards parade ground but he recognised neither. Henry had disappeared as soon as he announced Chris's presence and had not returned.

A flunkey came in and spread charts across a side table in good light.

"Ah, capital," the duke said. "Come forward Lennox and study these."

"What are they, Your Royal Highness?"

"Charts of course, supplied by the Admiralty ... charts of Copenhagen."

"Copenhagen, sir?"

The duke tutted. "Yes, Lennox, the capital city of Denmark. You *have* heard of it?"

Chris gave a rueful grin. "Of course, sir. Even in the South Pacific the name of Denmark is well known."

"Then what you may not be privy to is the machinations of its current government in collusion with Tsar Paul of Russia and if intelligence is to be believed, the damned Frogs."

"I do seem to recall our Plenipotentiary to Tsarina Catherine was summarily dismissed by her successor, Tsar Paul, but I cannot remember the details."

The duke waved a hand and a tall, handsome and distinguished man in his fifties rose, walked to the table and bowed. "Your Royal Highness."

The duke put a hand out. "Permit us to introduce Baron Charles Whitworth. Whitworth was our Plenipotentiary to the Russian court at St Petersburg until, as you rightly thought, he was dismissed by Tsar Paul who has taken up with Bonaparte. Whitworth, this is Lieutenant-colonel Lennox of the Corps of Riflemen of whom we have spoken."

Whitworth bowed to Chris who returned the compliment.

"It's a pleasure to meet you, Baron. I remember reading of your exploits."

Whitworth raised one eyebrow in mild surprise. "The devil you say, sir. I was not aware that my fame was heralded in the common news sheets."

"Hah!" The duke said and guffawed. It appears to us that your reputation as friend and confidant of the queens of Europe has spread far and wide, Whitworth. We hear tell that both Marie Antoinette and the Tsarina were eating out of your hand."

"You do honour me too much, sir, with your praise."

"Not praise, sir, merely observation. Now let us get down to business. Lennox, Whitworth is sailing to Copenhagen as our Plenipotentiary Extraordinaire. One of the Danes' ships, the *Freya* and its convoy, was taken by *HMS Nemesis* and her squadron for interfering with our right to search ships on the high seas. It is Whitworth's task to smooth over troubled waters."

"And what then is my task, sir?"

"You will accompany Whitworth with whomever you see fit to serve as protection for the Plenipotentiary."

"You want me to be the baron's bodyguard?"

"Despite your extraordinary terminology you seem to have grasped the essence of your task, Lennox. We have a fleet under Admiral Dickson sailing from Yarmouth six days hence. Make your arrangements swiftly for you must be aboard with your chosen men with the evening tide."

Chris nodded and took a smart step back before bowing. "I'll leave at once, sir."

"We hear you are lodging at Boodle's. We shall have your orders despatched to you there. Good day, Lennox." As Chris backed through the door the third man rose from his seat in the window.

"Have you chosen well, sir?" He said to the duke. "I hear both the Russians and the French have an interest in Whitworth's envoy coming to nought."

"Be at ease, Mr Pitt. We have every faith that Lennox will complete his task with due rigour. Whitworth is in safe hands or you may call me Frederick."

"I do hope you are correct, sir," William Pitt said, "for much is riding on these *Freya* negotiations. The Russians and their French allies are dead set against them as they wish to persuade Denmark to join the northern powers to combine against us. I fear Colonel Lennox may be biting off a rather large mouthful."

6

Chris found Biggin at Ye Olde Cheshire Cheese in Fleet Street and sat him down in a quiet corner away from the inky scribes and storytellers who frequented the place. Doctor Johnson was reckoned to have visited there as he had lived close by and in later years, Dickens would cast some of his darker characters from denizens of the place, to be followed in turn by Sir Arthur Conan Doyle and P.G. Wodehouse.

Chris cast an eye around the room but could see no one who looked vaguely like a famous author but did notice one or two of the patrons eyeing his and Biggin's green uniforms with interest bordering on rudeness.

Biggin had ordered two tankards of ale which sat on the circular table between them. He raised one now. "To the Corps of Riflemen, sir, beggin' your pardon if I should make so bold."

Chris raised his in turn with a half smile on his face. "The Rifles, long may they continue."

"Is there any word, sir on how we may look to our future?"

Chris took a sip of the warm beer and nodded. "I have heard it said that, in time, the Corps of Riflemen will become the 95th Regiment and form part of the order of battle. But first we must prove our mettle once again."

Biggin's round face split into a wide grin. "About time, sir, beggin' your pardon, that we did give the Frogs another bloody nose."

"Steady down, Serjeant-major. It's not the French this time, although I have my suspicions that they may be involved somewhere in the background. This time we are to face the Danes at Copenhagen."

Biggin frowned. "The Danes, sir? Are we not at peace with the Danes?"

"It is a tricky situation. The Danes have a large navy that rivals our own Royal Navy in size and power. They have been flexing their muscles in the northern seas and we have taken one of their navy ships and the convoy which it was escorting. His Royal Highness the Duke of York is concerned that things may well get out of hand so is sending a diplomat to smooth over ruffled feathers. We are to accompany the diplomat to ensure he comes to no harm.

"To that end, Serjeant-major, I require you to return to Shorncliffe as soon as you can take the post coach. I need nine pairs of Riflemen armed with their rifles and sword bayonets, two pistols each and the iron faced weskits we used in Portugal."

"We have those put away for safety, sir. I know where they can be found."

"Good. Issue one to each man and one for yourself."

"What of you, sir, beggin' your pardon, do you not require one?"

Chris shook his head. "I have my own. Now you and the men will meet me at the docks in Yarmouth, in five days time. Do you have any questions?"

"May I have permission to finish my ale, sir?"

Chris laughed. "Of course but make sure it's your last. Have you settled your account?"

"Aye, sir, twas half a crown."

Chris fished in his pocket for some coins. "There's ten shillings. It should cover your expenses and your journey back to Shorncliffe."

"Thankee, sir," Biggin said and picked up the coins with a show of reluctance.

"Do you have anything on your mind, Serjeant-major?"

"No, sir, beggin' your pardon."

Chris didn't push it but something was bothering Biggin. He put it down to worry about leaving his family again so soon after their battles in Portugal and Spain. The man's face was transparent, it showed his every emotion. Despite all his years in the army Biggin had not learned to lie with any credibility and was usually more honest than most because of it.

"You will tell me if anything worries you, Biggin. I'm here to help."

Biggin shuffled in his seat. "All's well, sir. I shall look to my orders as soon as may be."

"Very well. I'll expect you in Yarmouth in five days. Choose your men wisely and take them from the training cadre that accompanied us to Portugal. They are all good trustworthy fighting men."

"That twas my intention, beggin' your pardon for making so bold, sir. I will do as you ask."

Chris nodded and passed over a sealed package. "Those are the orders from the duke himself. It is my authorisation to act as I see fit with the men from the Corps of Riflemen. I have been informed that Lieutenant-colonel Stewart has been ordered to resume command of the Corps and you must hand them to him so that they may be expedited with all speed. Give the colonel my compliments and my regrets that I am decimating his training cadre for the foreseeable future. I have included a personal note to that effect. There is also an order from the Admiralty for him to commission a Frigate from Dover to transport you and the men by sea to Yarmouth. It will save your boot leather and much time.

It is well over one hundred miles from Shorncliffe to Yarmouth on the west side of the Isle of Wight and the voyage should ensure you're not late."

"As you wish, Colonel Lennox. And may I say twill be a pleasure to be at your side again, sir."

"Thank you, Serjeant-major. I have just one thing to add and that is to be careful and guard those orders with your life. There may be spies around who would be pleased to discover their contents. I've noticed we have caused something of a stir amongst the clientele in this tavern which may or may not be innocent curiosity. Be on your guard."

"Aye, that I will, sir. I have my trusty Dragon in one pocket and a cudgel in the other which will give any rascal cause to desist."

Chris gave him a taut smile of appreciation. The Dragon was a mini blunderbuss of a pistol and much favoured by the Dragoons from which the cavalrymen had derived their name. "Just be careful."

Chris stood and turned for the door as a man approached. He had a disreputable look but the ink-stained fingers of his right hand gave away his occupation as a correspondent.

"Can I help you, sir?" Chris said as the man blocked his path.

He bowed. "If it please you, sir, may I ask your regiment? Green is an unusual colour for the soldiery."

"What concern is it of yours?"

"There be rumours of a new weapon, the Baker Rifle and of a body of men trained in its use. I hear that the men wear green and that they fight like the devil. I hear that the French had cause to confront them and rued the day."

"You hear a lot of things, sir. Who may you be?"

"Lloyd of the London Gazette, sir. You will agree that any news of the military would be of interest to our readership."

"And of interest to others who may not be loyal to the Crown, Mr Lloyd. I can't confirm your rumours."

"You bear the demeanour of an officer, sir but you wear no epaulettes. May I ask your name?"

Chris had no intention of ever allowing his name to appear in print anywhere in this time but he surmised that, if snubbed, Lloyd would continue to dig on his own accord and he would have to give him an answer. "Lieutenant-colonel Stewart of the 62nd Regiment of foot. Now I wish you good day, sir."

"Wearing green, sir?"

"On occasion, Mr Lloyd, on occasion."

7

The tavern exited onto a narrow alley between two buildings and Chris turned right towards Fleet Street when a hand caught his arm. He stepped smartly aside and the wooden cudgel aimed at his head glanced off his shoulder. He twisted and put a knee into the man's groin. As he doubled over Chris drove his clawed right hand under the man's chin and into his eyes in a jab that snapped his head back and stunned him. A second man tried to join the fight but could not pass the falling body in the narrow alley. Chris pulled his infantry sabre in the hope it would scare the man off. It worked, he put away a long butcher's knife and backed up into Biggin who had followed Chris out. Biggin clouted him with the barrel of the Dragon and the man joined his companion in a heap on the dirty pavement.

Chris slid the sabre back into its scabbard and turned the first man over. He rifled through his pockets in search of a clue to identity but could find nothing but a few coins.

"They be footpads, sir. Biggin said. Maybe they saw the ten shillings you did pass to me and thought you rich pickings."

"Perhaps," Chris said. He flexed his fingers. They were easing and nearly back to normal but he would have had a hard time using the blade with any strength. "Thank you, Serjeant-major. Your intervention saved the day."

"That's as maybe, sir but you did have the blackguard at your mercy."

Chris grimaced. He wasn't at all sure the two were just thugs out for easy pickings. Most would not have taken on an armed officer in daylight. They were either desperate or there was an ulterior reason for the attack and from the look of their soiled but good quality clothing and well fed faces, desperation did not seem a likely motive.

"Tie them with their own belts, Biggin. We'll leave them for the constables to deal with. Take the second man's knife too and check his pockets for any evidence of their identities."

By now a small crowd had formed, Lloyd amongst them, smiling to himself and leaning on the tavern's door post.

Biggin finished his tasks and beckoned to a small boy. "Here, lad, run for a constable and I'll give you a ha'penny on your return."

"A farthin' now, mister and a farthin' when I gets back."

Biggin grinned at the cheek and tossed the boy a tiny coin. "Be quick now, lad."

Chris left Biggin to it and shouldered his way through the crowd to Lloyd. His smile faltered a little as Chris approached.

"Do you know these two men, Mr Lloyd?"

Lloyd shook his head. "They be strangers to me, sir. Tis the first time I ever clapped eyes on them but I did notice they surely took much interest in your conversation with yonder Serjeant-major."

"Which gave your own interest cause, I suspect."

"Indeed, sir. I have a reporter's thirst for knowledge and an eye for the odd."

"And a nose for a story I don't doubt. There will be a story here but not yet for publication. I would ask you to find out as much about these two men as you can. Do it quietly, so as not to arouse their suspicions. I daresay the magistrates will be having words about their futures but it's their pasts that most interests me."

"And why should that be, Colonel? A pair of footpads can be of little interest to a military gentleman."

"That's what I'm trying to discover. Are they just footpads or did they have another motive in attacking me? There's a sovereign in it for you."

"Very generous of you, sir. Now my interest is truly piqued. And how shall I forward such intrigue to yourself?"

"Despatch it for the personal attention of Lieutenant-colonel Stewart at Shorncliffe camp. It will reach me there. Should anything come of it I will give you the details for your publication in due course."

"As I am to be employed by you, sir, perhaps I should inform you of another matter which has come recently to my attention."

Chris cocked an eye. "Which is?"

"Immediately prior to your arrival at this tavern the Serjeant-major was in earnest conversation with a woman."

"What the Serjeant-major does in his own time is his own affair, though I am surprised as he is happily married."

"No you misunderstand me, sir. This was not a whore and perhaps, for a journalist, I may have chosen my language with more care, this was a well-born lady of some refinement. She was cloaked and veiled but could hide neither her beauty, as on occasion the light did penetrate her veil, nor her hauteur. She did appear somewhat out of place but previously acquainted with the Serjeant-major, I am sure of it. Do you wish me to ascertain her identity also? I do believe she and her maid have taken rooms here for the night."

"No, thank you, Mr Lloyd. I have an inkling who she may be and you shouldn't concern yourself over the matter."

"As you say, sir. Now I see the constable has come and will be constraining the miscreants and escorting them forthwith to the magistrates' court. I shall follow in their footsteps. Rest assured I will be reporting in due time. Good day, sir."

Biggin walked over dusting his palms. "That is done with, sir, beggin' your pardon. There were some witnesses to the assault and I paid them a sixpence each to testify to the magistrate on our behalf. The constable did require a written statement but another shilling did persuade him twas unnecessary as we are taking ship abroad. We are free to leave."

"Come back inside, Serjeant-major. I have to pen another despatch for Lieutenant-colonel Stewart to warn him of further despatches from a Mr Lloyd."

Biggin quickly found him a quill, ink and paper and he scrawled a quick note, sealing it with wax and impressing it with the image of St George and the Dragon from the front of the sovereign inset into his wedding ring. It had become his personal coat of arms and Charles Stewart would recognise it immediately. He handed it to Biggin with some more cash.

"Be off now and see to your duties."

Biggin stood and put on his cap. "Aye, sir, with all possible speed." He knuckled his forehead and marched out, leaving Chris to discover the reason why Biggin had been so disturbed earlier and to confront the lady of good breeding in the rooms above whom, he suspected, was the cause of it.

8

"Bless you, sir, the lady has been left not these twenty minutes past, whilst the fracas did occur in the alley. She and her maid took sedans from the drayman's door," the landlord said.

Chris bit his lip. "Did she leave a name?"

"Twas not my place to enquire, sir."

"And no idea where she was going, I assume."

"I believe I did overhear the maid direct the sedans to the nearest post coach inn, which I know to be situated in High Holborn."

Chris thanked the man and tipped him sixpence. High Holborn was a short walk away and he checked his Breitling wristwatch, kept hidden from 18th century eyes beneath his cuff. It was ten minutes to noon and he had a feeling that all the post coaches left the inns together every midday to get to their various destinations. He doubted he could make it to the inn in time to confront the lady but may get an idea where she was heading.

He found the answer at the Bell and Crown where the landlord remembered two last minute passengers, resembling a lady and maid, who bought tickets for Dover on the noon post coach.

Dover? Just a short ride away from Cheriton to the east of Folkstone and the location of Shorncliffe Camp. Why would the lady be heading there? And why the earnest conversation with Biggin which appeared to worry the serjeant-major so much? Chris scratched his head. He had his suspicions but they weren't making much sense. It was a mystery for another time, he had to make arrangements with his bank to set aside £1,000 for Catherine's allowance in a separate account and then to borrow one of Henry's horses for the ride to Yarmouth. He made a mental note to buy two good geldings himself on his return from Denmark and have them stabled in the cavalry barracks at Knightsbridge. He had the feeling he was going to spend more time in London at the duke's beck and call than he would with the Corps of Riflemen at Shorncliffe.

The duke had given him his rank and an income of £5,000 per annum with which he was supposed to support himself, clothe, feed, pay and arm almost fifty men of the training cadre. Luckily he had come to an agreement with the Duke of Devonshire who would cover that cost in return for some insider knowledge on the procurement of the Baker Rifle for the army. The thought made Chris grin as he made his way towards Coutts Bank in the Strand. It would take William Cavendish some years to recoup his £1,500 per annum outlay but the man was an inveterate gambler and on Chris's recommendation had invested in Ezekial Baker's business which was set to boom for the next forty years or so as the army bought more and more Baker Rifles.

He was uneasy about depending on the Duke of York's largesse. Something easily given could easily be taken away and he would need to determine ways of supplementing his income. He had no land, as yet no property of any kind and would need to rent a place for himself and Catherine until it could be organised. He guessed Catherine would be happiest at Imber, near to her family but that would mean long absences from him. London was more expensive but he would be able to see her more frequently. Many of the upper classes had both town and country houses and maybe that was the way forward for the future. £5,000 was a good income for the times but it would soon melt away if not managed carefully. The thought made him stop suddenly and the man walking behind almost collided with him. He apologised but chided himself. *He* was a man of the future, making plans as if he would live in this century for the rest of his life, knowing that he could be catapulted back to the present at any time, leaving Catherine bereft of husband and any way of supporting herself. From his history studies he knew that the life of a destitute lady could be a hard one. Time travel was the problem but also a possible solution. He had ideas in his head, ideas from the future and knowledge of what was going to happen over the next two-hundred plus years. Somewhere in amongst all the historical detritus he had picked up from his parents' love of the subject and his own education there must be a way to secure Catherine's future.

The reality of what he had done was dawning on him. He had been seduced by the love of an unattainable woman into behaving without a thought for her. If he was really in the past he could be thrown back to his own time, presumably leaving a giant hole in Catherine's life that would leave her baffled and bereft. In all conscience he did not know how he could have been so blind as to not see the awful consequences of his selfish actions.

The journey to Yarmouth took Chris two days on horseback and he was stiff and saddle-sore when he eventually rode off the Cowes ferry and made his way to the naval dockyard.

He found Biggin and his eighteen riflemen lounging on sacks on the quayside, smoking and laughing together. He was spotted and the men jumped to their feet and shuffled into ranks.

Chris ran his eye over them and recognised all the soldiers from his Portugal expedition. He remembered all their names. Biggin brought them to attention and knuckled his forehead. "The chosen men are ready for your orders, should it please you, sir."

Biggin looked shifty again and Chris wondered why. He dismounted his tired horse and gave the reins to a rifleman he knew as Jed Carter. He looked Biggin in the eye and the man cast his gaze onto his boots. "Anything to report, Serjeant-major?"

"No, sir, all is well, sir. We have been arrived this past day and was wonderin' on our further orders, sir."

Chris counted heads. "Twenty of you? I asked for eighteen riflemen and yourself."

"Tis the bugler boy, sir. The men be lost without him blowing them to their duties each day, sir. Beggin' your pardon if I did overstep my authority, sir."

"There'll be no need for bugle calls on this expedition, Biggin. The boy will have a wasted journey. How old is he? He seems quite small in stature and his face is masked, I can't make out his features."

"He be older than his size portends, Colonel Lennox, and he has a pox-scarred face and fair skin much prone to the ravages of sun and wind so does keep it covered."

"I have no need of him but I can't send him back to Shorncliffe alone. He'll accompany us and he can work as my servant to keep him from harm's way. Some of the tars have a taste for young boys and he will sleep next to my cabin on board the ship. I'll inform the Master at Arms when we embark."

"Thankee, sir, that is most generous but the men will care for him. He is their mascot and will not let any harm befall him."

"Don't look so worried, Serjeant-major. He will be safer in my care."

Biggin knuckled his forehead but looked no less concerned. "As you wish, Colonel."

A coach and four clattered to a halt further along the quay and Chris spotted Baron Whitworth seated inside. He turned to Biggin. "The Ambassador has arrived and we'll be taking ship shortly. I'll pay my respects and you make sure that the men are ready to leave. Have Corporal Carter and the boy find a livery to stable my horse, I passed one nearby, and make sure it is well cared for until we return. Take charge of my pack and don't let it out of your sight."

The harbour master was fawning over Whitworth as Chris strode up and saluted. "Good day, Baron, I trust you had a comfortable journey."

"Indeed, Colonel Lennox. The harbour master tells me that Admiral Dickson's flagship will be sending a longboat to fetch us aboard. Tis *HMS Monarch,* a seventy-four of the line, anchored in the roads and preparing to set sail on the tide. You have made your own arrangements, I trust."

"As much as I'm able, sir. My men are all excellent soldiers, experienced in battle and as well prepared as any for your safety."

Whitworth sniffed. "I doubt they will be necessary. His Royal Highness and First Lord of the Treasury Pitt are prone to see dangers where none exist. I am sure that my personal safety will be secure in Copenhagen."

"Let's hope you are correct, sir," Chris said, but personally, he had his doubts.

9

HMS Monarch was a Ramillies Class two deck third rater of the line armed with a mixture of 32 and 18 pounder long guns on her two main decks, eight 14 pounders on her quarter deck and two 4 pounder chasers on her bow. The ship and her crew had seen plenty of action in the preceding years in the Americas and the Caribbean and had been commanded by several captains during that time.

The present incumbent was Captain James Mosse who had recently succeeded Sir Archibald Dickson on his promotion to Rear Admiral. Mosse met them at the side as Whitworth clambered aboard with Chris and Biggin in close support and touched his cap as the bosun piped them aboard. Chris and Biggin saluted the quarterdeck and then the captain in turn.

Mosse smiled. "Tis good to see that lubbers know the ways of the navy. Welcome aboard, gentlemen. My Lord Whitworth, tis a pleasure to have you aboard my ship which carries Vice Admiral Dickson's flag. He will receive you in the captain's day cabin should you please to grace him with your presence. The ship's master will escort you."

Mosse waved the ship's master mariner forward and indicated for Whitworth to follow the man aft before turning back to Chris. "Lieutenant-colonel Lennox, I presume, sir. I have heard something of your exploits in Both Portugal and Ferrol and am pleased to make your acquaintance."

"Likewise, Captain Mosse. But might I enquire how come you know of me?"

"A fellow officer and friend, Captain Charles Cunningham of the *Aquilon* speaks most highly of you and of your greenbacks."

Chris laughed. "And how does the good captain fare?"

"Well, sir and once the news of your presence aboard spread amongst the northern fleet he did bid me to wish you good health and success for your duty."

"He has been promoted then? Not before time."

"Indeed, sir. He still commands the *Aquilon* whilst he awaits appointment to a third rater. His Frigate will accompany the fleet to Copenhagen."

"Then I shall make it my duty to pay him a visit soon."

"Enough of the pleasantries for now, sir. We may gossip in the wardroom this eve, for now I must prepare to depart these shores. You, sir will occupy my cabin. The Master at Arms will quarter your greenbacks below deck with the marine detachment."

"I will need to quarter my bugler with me. Can a cot be made available outside my door for the duration of the voyage."

Mosse raised one questioning eyebrow. "A bugler, sir to billet in the officer's quarters?"

"He is my servant and will run errands and messages for me. It is more convenient to have him close by."

"As you wish, sir. Tis damnably unusual and the Rear Admiral will surely frown upon it but I can see no reason to deny your request. He must stay quiet and be respectful at all times or I will needs to remove him to the gun deck with the tars."

"I shall hold myself responsible for his behaviour, Captain."

"Very well, sir, so be it. Now if you would be so kind as to follow the bosun, he will lead you and the boy to your quarters. I will send the ship's carpenter to prepare a cot inside your cabin where it will not cause inconvenience."

"I'm most grateful for your compliance, Captain and for the no doubt inconvenience to which I'm putting you. Where will you sleep?"

"In the first lieutenant's quarters, he in with the junior lieutenants and so on down the line of command. Tis the usual arrangements when the admiral flies his pennant and there are honoured guests aboard. You may repay me and my officers by entertaining us with your exploits against the Frogs at dinner this night."

Chris grinned. "I'll do my best, sir." He followed the beckoning bosun beneath the quarter deck and into the cabin the man indicated. The small bugler followed dragging Chris's Bergen as well as his own kit, large pack and rifle, making a clatter that drew an oath from the bosun.

"Belay that racket, you lubber. Did you not hear the captain's orders that you be quiet?" He raised his hand to swipe at the lad with a length of knotted rope but Chris caught it.

"I'll deal with the boy, bosun. His discipline is my concern and I will not have my men struck."

The bosun glared but bowed and touched his forelock. Chris dropped his wrist and the man backed away. "As you say, sir but this be a man's navy and the end of a rope can learn young whippersnappers to be more seamanlike in their duties."

"Speaking of which, you'd best be about yours."

The man touched his forelock again and turned away but not before he had shot the boy a calculating glare. Chris saw it and was glad he'd had the foresight to billet the boy with him. He cocked a thumb at the cabin. "You'd best get the kit inside, bugler." He grinned as he watched the slight figure struggle to get it through the narrow cabin door. He grabbed his own Bergen by the straps and lifted it from the boy's back. "In you go, rifleman. Drop your kit in the corner. I'll take care of this."

The boy nodded mutely, laid his rifle against the bulkhead and shrugged out of his own pack. Chris followed him in. "What's your name, lad?"

"Eli, sir." The voice was a little high pitched and muffled by the mask that obscured the boy's lower face.

"How old are you, Eli?"

"Thirteen, sir?"

"Thirteen, eh! And how long have you served with the Corps of Riflemen?"

The boy coughed. "Not long, sir."

"And yet the men treat you as a mascot and are reluctant to leave without you. Strange, don't you think?"

"They be good men, sir."

"Indeed they are, Eli. Good men, true and faithful to their officer. They would do almost anything for him, don't you think?"

"If you do say so, sir."

"Perhaps they would do favours that they would not do for anyone else."

"I daresay that is true, sir."

"Do you understand where this conversation is heading, Eli?"

"The boy giggled, it was almost feminine. "Yes, indeed I do, sir."

"Then perhaps it's time you removed your disguise, Catherine. You could not change those beautiful eyes, no matter how much you covered your face."

Catherine unwound the scarf, removed her cap and gave him a chastened look. "How long have you known and have you been making merry at my cost?"

"I would think it amusing if it wasn't so serious. You have come aboard one of His Majesty's ships by subterfuge. You have coerced my men into giving you help in your plan at great cost to themselves, you have attempted to make a fool of me and most serious of all you have possibly put yourself in mortal danger should this expedition prove hazardous. What do you have to say for yourself?"

"Oh, George. Twas not my intent to make you look foolish. I could not bear to be away from your side so soon after we were wed, not after Anthony's sad fate. I did plot with Esther to be on the coach when you did depart for London and I overheard you say that the Serjeant-major would be lodging at the inn in Fleet Street. Until then I had thought only to surprise you before you embarked on your foray to parts unknown but, as I did think on it, a plan came to mind that I could accompany you and be with you in any danger that may befall you. I did compel the serjeant-major with most forceful argument. He was most unwilling but did comply once I had opened my heart to him that I could not bear your loss if so far away from me."

"I shall speak to Biggin in due time. But Catherine, dear, had you no concept of the problems that you would cause? The anchor has been raised and we are under sail on a ship of war. Many seamen believe it to be unlucky to have a woman aboard since in 1795, the *Royal George,* full of visiting wives and sweethearts, sank. Hundreds died.

"Others below decks think if a woman is of low birth she is fair game which can also be the fate of young boys preyed on by men of warrant or officer rank."

Catherine's hand went to her mouth with shock. "Surely not, sir. Could a British sailor sink so low; the idea is an abomination."

"Nevertheless it is the case and life in this man's navy is often characterised as 'rum, sodomy and the lash'.

Catherine appeared even more shocked. "Really, sir, your language leaves much to be desired."

Chris gave her a tight smile. "You will hear far worse between decks, my dear, so you must steel yourself for it. It is one of the reasons Admiralty rules forbid women to be aboard and although it sometimes occurs, the senior captains frown upon it and I daresay that Captain Mosse would be of a similar mind. That is why I have ordered you to sleep in my cabin but as you have come aboard as a bugler and have been entered in the ship's manifest, you must continue to be a bugler of the Corps of Riflemen with whatever hardship that may entail for you personally.

Catherine dug into her tunic pocket. "Fear not, George, for I have taken all precautions. See, here, I have also borrowed father's Wheeler pocket pistol should any soul take undue liberties with my person. The serjeant-major and the riflemen will have a care for me when I am with them."

Chris took the small pistol from her hand. It was barely seven inches long and over half an inch in calibre. "I daresay that would make a nice hole in someone but having a pistol and being prepared to use it against a living person is another matter entirely and the consequences may be even more tragic for the shooter."

Catherine pulled herself up to her full sixty-three inches. "Do not misunderstand me, sir. I am of country stock and well used to fending for myself. I have no qualms on shooting blackguards."

Chris smiled and gripped her hand. "I don't believe you do. Now put your disguise back on, I believe I hear the ship's carpenter coming to make your cot and there is no way he could mistake those rosy lips for a boy's.

"And keep away from the bosun or I fear there may be trouble."

10

It was a slow voyage as the warships had to tow four slower ships carrying heavy mortars but for Chris the voyage passed all too quickly with Catherine sharing his narrow bunk each night. During the day she would exercise with the riflemen on the main deck as Chris ran them through procedures and actions-on when on body-guarding duties. It was new work for the soldiers, never before had they been called upon for close protection roles but they readily took to the skills and the drills.

The sailors watched the routines with mouths agape, especially when Catherine played Lord Whitworth's part as the man himself roundly refused to lower his sense of dignity and be manhandled by rough soldiery.

It was in the wardroom one evening, over the sherry that Chris challenged him on his attitude to his own survival.

"Come, sir," Whitworth said, "I am His Majesty's Plenipotentiary Extraordinaire, I cannot be seen to be dragged into the dirt in the face of the enemy. I must stand with dignity."

"And risk a ball in the chest? There is little dignity in death, my Lord, and probably a lot more trouble to be had diplomatically if it is found that the Danes allowed your assassination in their capital city."

"Stuff and nonsense, sir. I have immunity from harm. I cannot see King Christian's government colluding in my demise."

"It's not the Danes who worry me but the French and Russians. It would be in their interests to see your mission fail."

"I cannot see Tsar Paul's hand in any action as low as murder."

"Yet he did order you out of St Petersburg when the French persuaded him it was in his interests to do so. Do you have the same regard for Bonaparte?"

"There you may have a point, Lennox, but dashed if I can allow the thought to be father to my actions."

"His Royal Highness, the Duke of York bade me to ensure your safety and it's a duty I do not take lightly. I would be grateful if you were guided by my advice when we are out and about in Copenhagen."

"I know the duke holds you in some regard, Lennox but, tush, man, you are seeing shadows where none exist. I do not fear to tread where there be dragons for they be nothing but idle imagination."

Admiral Dickson had been listening to the exchange and now he stirred in his seat. "Twould seem we are at an impasse so let us not dwell on the subject further. Colonel Lennox, Captain Mosse tells me that you have experience in seeing off the Frogs. Let us hear of it, sir."

For the next hour Chris regaled them with the story of his expedition to Portugal and the fight against the French Grenadiers and cavalry regiment which ended in their withdrawal from the Algarve and ended Bonaparte's plan to infiltrate Portugal from the south. Some of the officers roared with laughter and banged the table as he told of the damage he and his fifty greenbacks wrought on a battalion of Napoleon's finest soldiers.

"And it is all down to tactics and this Baker Rifle, sir," Mosse said. "I did hear that your greenbacks fought well when the Aquilon took the French frigate *Hercule* for His Majesty's navy. Took down the Frog officers and marines with fire from the rigging."

"That's so, sir," Chris said. "Captain Cunningham was kind enough to remark that it turned the tide of battle on that day and I would recommend the tactic in any future engagement that the Corps of Riflemen is aboard ship."

"We near the Skag on the morrow and the glass is dropping we may anchor up for the duration of the blow before venturing ashore," the admiral said. "Let us have the offices of the monkey's orphan for I do declare some music from his fiddle will lighten my mood."

The fiddler was summoned, brought by the bosun, and duly ran through his limited repertoire twice before the admiral waved a hand to silence him. "Perhaps I was sorely mistaken for I feel my mood is now darkening. Have we no alternative to these interminable capstan turners?

"Lennox, you have travelled I am told, is there nothing fresh with which you can regale us? You have a pleasing baritone, let us hear it."

Chris thought hard. He felt that some of the boy band music of his youth wouldn't be well received but he had a fall back position. "There's a song I picked up in the Americas when passing through. It is performed a cappella but if the fiddler can play by ear he may well pick up the tune as I sing."

The admiral sat up in his seat. "Very well, sir. Have at it with a will."

Chris cleared his throat and looked around at all the expectant faces in the wardroom, some with slack-mouthed wide grins from the wine they had imbibed but still in good humour.

Chris started slowly.

"A life on the ocean wave! A home on the rolling deep! Where the scattered waters rave, and the wind its revels keep!

Like an eagle caged I pine, on this dull unchanging shore.
Oh give me the flashing brine! The spray and the tempest roar!
A life on the ocean wave! A home on the rolling deep!
Where the scattered waters rave, and the wind its revels keep!
The wind, the wind, the wind its revels keep!"

Just for a moment there was a stunned silence and then everyone cheered.

The admiral was on his feet, bent forward under the low headroom. "By god, sir, where did you learn of that? Tis a song to gladden the heart of any seafaring man."

Chris grinned. He could hardly admit that the song was written by an American in 1853, still fifty-three years in the future. "Perhaps His Majesty's marines could find a use for it, sir."

The marine captain gurgled a laugh. "Tis a catchy ditty but I fail to see how the marines could make a use of it."

"Maybe in time," Chris said, knowing full well that the marines would eventually adopt is as their signature tune.

"Again, then. Let us hear it again," Mosse said. "I find it much to my liking."

As he waited out in the companionway the bosun had a different thought in mind as he listened to the merriment from the wardroom. The lickspittal greenback boy was close by in the greenback colonel's quarters. He had bided his time but now a golden opportunity had presented itself. With all the noise no one would hear the boy's squeals as he took him.

He eased open the cabin door and looked inside. The cabin was lit by weak lamplight which showed the boy asleep on his cot, his face to the wall. He was still fully dressed apart from his shoes which were neatly placed beside the cot. Small feet but then the lad was small in every respect, much as he liked them, without the strength to repel him.

He pounced on the small form, pulled the legs from the cot and held the boy face down, his hand and forearm pinioning the boy's head in the bedding. He pulled a knife from his belt and cut through the back of the boy's pantaloons before pulling them down.

"By god, that's a peach of an arse, lad, smooth as a baby's head."

Catherine was now fully awake from a deep sleep and began to struggle against the weight pressing on her neck and back.

"You wriggle all you like, boy," the bosun, said, "twill add to the pleasure of it." He began to undo the cord that held up his own loose seaman's trousers.

Catherine began to twist in an effort to shake him off and her hand felt inside the pocket of her tunic for the Wheeler. Her hand found the butt but the pistol was on half cock.

The bosun's trousers dropped to the floor and he used his free hand to pull Catherine's rear around towards him. "You'll be sayin' nothin' o' this to anyone, lad. No one will believe it and you'll have me to answer to. Tis easy to disappear over the side in foul weather with no one knowing the why of it."

Catherine pulled the pistol part out of her pocket in desperation. She tried to scream but could not. The man was doing something behind her and she dared not think what it might be or what indignity was about to be perpetrated upon her. She straightened her arm, the hammer snagged on the pocket lining and cocked itself. She pulled the trigger and the gun exploded.

11

Chris was in the middle of a rousing chorus when the crash of a firearm had him spinning towards the door. He knew immediately what it was and feared the worst.

He reached his cabin, reeking from the smell of gunpowder and burning cloth. The bosun was leaning against the bulkhead keening, a bloody foot in his hand and the knife on the deck by his feet. Catherine was quickly beating out the flames from her pocket and holding up her pantaloons with the other hand. One glance at the bosun's trousers around his ankles was enough to tell the awful story.

Chris scooped the knife from the deck, pushed his forearm across the bosun's throat and the knife blade against his naked testicles.

"He hissed in the man's ear. "I would cut your balls off with a blunt and rusty knife for what you've done tonight."

The man gurgled against the pressure on his throat. "The little bastard did blow my toes off, sir."

"That's not all the body parts you're about to lose," Chris said and jerked on the knife.

A hand came on his arm. "Desist, Lennox, I beg," Mosse said. "The captain of marines has sent for the sentries to carry the man away."

Chris glanced across at Catherine who had had the coolness to cover her face. He nodded at her. "This man did attack my bugler with evil intent as you can see from his state of undress. Whatever has happened to him is no fault of the boy's and I will not see him punished for protecting himself in self-defence."

"Mosse walked inside and closed the cabin door. "This should not go beyond this cabin, Lennox. The knowledge that a warrant officer of the crew did salaciously attack a boy would bring irreparable harm to the reputation of this ship and of its crew. I beg you do not call for a court martial. We have our own ways of dealing with such matters and the man will be gone from the service as soon as we reach home port. Do not sully yourself with his filthy blood.

"If the boy is in agreement and there is no court martial there will be no need for his testimony to describe the sordid affair in a manner which must surely try him also."

Chris still had fierce pressure on the bosun's throat and the man was going red in the face for lack of oxygen and swivel-eyed with fear as he felt the sharp blade cutting into his groin. He gave the blade a final flick and threw it to the deck. "As you say, Captain. Eli will listen to my advice on the matter and I will leave it in your hands. However should I see this villain's face anywhere near the boy or any other of my men I will personally castrate him and toss him to the gulls."

"Have no fear, Colonel. He will be kept in the brig or under marine guard for the duration of the voyage. Once the surgeon has done with him he would be hard pressed to stir his bones from his hammock this side of Christmas."

A clatter from outside announced the arrival of the marines. As Mosse opened the cabin door Chris spun the bosun into their grip. "Take him away, men and get him to the surgeon's tender mercies."

"I shall make it known he was wounded by his own pistol discharging carelessly but I daresay word of the truth of it will spread between decks and he will get little sympathy from his shipmates," Mosse whispered. "Now see to your bugler, Lennox, and if he wants for ought you have but to ask."

Chris thanked the captain and closed the door on him. As he turned Catherine catapulted herself into his arms. He kissed her face and hair as she sobbed.

"Are you hurt? Did he violate you in any way?"

Catherine shook her head and her tears sprayed in fine droplets onto his tunic. She took a deep ragged breath. "No, sir. I did heed your warning and kept the Wheeler about my person as I slept. I did discharge it before he could have his way with me."

"At the cost of a perfectly good tunic pocket." Chris made light of it but the thought of what might have occurred cause his heart to thump against his ribs.

Catherine felt it and raised her face to him. "Did I not inform you that I am perfectly capable of protecting my own honour? Do not punish yourself over what may have been for I am whole in body and in mind."

"I know that you are a woman of great courage. I knew that the moment I laid eyes on you as the highwaymen attacked you that day on Salisbury Plain."

"The day that I did fall in love with you, the green-faced goblin who did save me from being robbed and ravished."

"Green camouflage cream. It has a way of charming the ladies."

Catherine sniffed, wiped her eyes and smiled. "You are making merry again, George Lennox."

The next morning as the ships anchored in the Skag to ride out the storm Chris was called into the wardroom by Admiral Dickson who rose to meet him.

"I did hear from Captain Mosse of last eve's troubles, Colonel Lennox. Is the boy sound?"

"If you mean will he remain mute on his experience and is he a good and trustworthy soldier, then yes, Sir Archibald, he is sound."

"I am pleased to hear it but it is of concern to me that he was in your cabin in an officer's quarters. Mosse did explain the circumstance but it is unusual practice, sir, highly unusual, the boy is older than some of Mosse's midshipmen and should take his place with the soldiery."

"I do have my reasons, sir. One of which being the boy's family have applied for his commission as an Ensign and the money has been paid for its purchase. Unfortunately we had to depart before the commission could arrive and I have taken it upon myself to properly instruct him and to keep him from mixing too readily with men he will soon command before his posting to another regiment. You will have noted that they treat him with respect. He is from a good family and ran away to join the Corps of Riflemen as a private soldier but was found out and his promotion secured."

Chris took a deep breath. It was as good a cover story as he could concoct on the spur of the moment and hoped that the admiral would swallow it.

"Ah, I see the way of it. Very well Lennox, you may continue your instruction and have the boy billeted with you. I have watched your manoeuvres on the gun deck and see that you are a diligent instructor; the boy could not have better. I also have cause to wonder why he covers his face so completely."

Chris fell back on Biggin's explanation. "It's due to smallpox, sir. The marks are recent and livid and he has my permission to cover them to escape embarrassment."

The admiral gave a wry smile. "I see you have an answer for all, sir. Very well, if that is your explanation I will accept it as the word of an officer and a gentleman. None will question it aboard this ship. Now away to your duties. Lord Whitworth is making his preparations as we speak and will be disembarking once the storm eases. You and your greenbacks must be ready to accompany him as will I on this occasion."

"Your presence will be most welcome, Sir Archibald. Your wise counsel will be invaluable."

Chris took a smart step back and saluted. He breathed a sigh of relief as he left the wardroom. The smile on the admiral's face hinted that he suspected there was more to the story but Catherine's cover was still intact.

Now he had two VIPs and a wife to watch over on their trip ashore and his difficult task had now become much harder.

12

The man known as James Grant snapped closed his telescope as the longboat rowed the nautical mile from the British ships at anchor in the Sund opposite a row of Danish and Norwegian warships that guarded the entrance to Flaadens Leie. The boat made its slow way towards the quay opposite the Christiansborg Palace on the islet of Slotsholmen inside the massive outer curtain wall of Copenhagen's defences.

He pulled a thoughtful face. He stood on the ramparts of the Citadel that overlooked the Sund and measured distances and timings in his mind's eye. It wasn't going to be easy, that he knew. He could not attack a long boat on the water but would need to arrange an ambush on dry land, somewhere before the palace gates were reached.

He knew that the Danish King would send a coach and horses to greet the visiting British plenipotentiary, to remain for his use for the duration of his embassy and perhaps that was where the strength of a plan would lie.

He snapped open the scope again and watched. He could now see a second longboat behind the first filled with red-coated marines and an officer in blue and gold. There was no such protection in the first long boat but the plenipotentiary's vivid gold-fronted garb stood out amongst drably dressed men and sailors. Grant wondered idly why a naval officer demanded an escort but the envoy did not. The marines were of little consequence as they would be unable to influence the outcome of the assassination if he had his timings worked out correctly. He would earn the money from his French paymasters and retire back to London to spend the proceeds.

He had left England via an overland route through France as soon as the news of the British envoy had seeped out from the Danish court to a French agent who notified the French Directory which in turn informed Coileán Leech, the man who led the United Irishmen's Grey Wolves. He had hurried a despatch to Grant with instructions that the meeting at the Christiansborg Palace be prevented by the most extreme measures. He had gathered a dozen men of the United Irishmen secret society to travel with him and these now awaited his instructions at an inn off the Øster Voldegade. He knew from his own enquiries that no business would be conducted this day, just the presentation of documents of accreditation and that the real negotiations would begin the following day. Which gave him time to plan.

Chris viewed the coach and four on the quay with a vague sense of unease. He wasn't sure why but at the back of his mind was the possibility that it could hide an assassin. He shrugged off the thought and ordered the cox'n to hold water while the second longboat with the admiral and ten marines landed. Only then was he happy to let Lord Whitworth ashore. Four riflemen landed first and set up a perimeter. He handed Whitworth out of the boat and held onto his arm while six more riflemen disembarked and formed a protective square around him.

Whitworth clucking in disapproval at what he saw as arrant nonsense, shook Chris's hand off his sleeve. The remaining riflemen fanned out and kept watchful eyes on nearby alleyways and rooftops as Catherine walked inside the comforting screen of the close protection detail where Chris had insisted she position herself. Biggin gave her a crafty wink as she took her place. All the riflemen wore the iron-faced weskits beneath their tunics that Chris had designed to prevent chest wounds. A poor version of his Kevlar body armour but better than nothing. It was too heavy for Catherine to wear and he thought inside the close protection squad but well away from Whitworth the safest place for her.

He had instructed the marines before leaving the ship. They had checked the coach and were standing at ease on either side of it. The admiral was already reclining inside as Whitworth and Chris climbed in.

It was a short journey to the palace and it was passed in silence as Whitworth contemplated his audience with the king and the admiral seemed engrossed in the antics of the marines and riflemen as they kept pace.

The gates were guarded by Danish soldiers wearing uniforms similar in colour to that worn by British line regiments but with shorter tunics, broad white cross belts and bearskin caps. They allowed the coach through but stopped the marines from entering. The riflemen had melted away and took up covering positions in the corners and niches of the outer square. Their green uniforms blending into the moss covered walls in the shadows of a lowering sun.

The admiral cleared his throat. "Stopped my marines at the gate. Damned unfriendly."

Chris gave a tight smile. It was what he would have done under similar circumstances. He would never let armed troops of a potentially hostile nation anywhere near the Queen. "They are doing their duty, Admiral, as I hope our own Foot Guards would."

"You are correct, Lennox, of course, my apologies but it is this damnable feeling of mistrust that irks me."

Whitworth raised his head. "Tis why I am here. There will be a conciliation in the coming days, you see if there is not." He put on his bicorn hat with its rich ostrich feather plumage, straightened his ornate gold-embroidered blue coat and took a deep breath. "We have arrived."

The coach door was pulled open and a set of folding steps rolled down for Whitworth to descend in an appropriately pompous manner as befitted an emissary of King George III. As had been discussed previously with the admiral, Chris exited next to be at Whitworth's elbow, his sabre tucked tightly against his side with one hand on the scabbard. He also had his Glock 17 stuffed into his waistband in the middle of his back where no one in this age would think of looking for a weapon. He saw the two statue-like sentries at the door swivel their eyes towards him but neither made any attempt to move.

They were ushered inside by a major domo and shown into a large reception room where they were bidden to await the king's pleasure. When the call came Whitworth was allowed in alone and Chris fretted and paced the floor.

The admiral had found a comfortable bench to sit on and watched Chris with some amusement. "Be at ease, Lennox. There will be no attempt on His Excellency's life whilst between these walls. Lord Whitworth will be safe here."

"I know that, sir. It is what might happen once we leave. I have studied a plan of the city given to me by His Royal Highness. Later, we have to travel to the charge d'affaires residence on Kastelsvej, some distance away and then return tomorrow along narrow roads with side alleys and blind corners. There is a lot to concern me."

The admiral pulled a face. "Is his Royal Highness so certain that there will be an attempt on Lord Whitworth's life?"

"My orders were to take extreme care and the most prudent precautions. The French are known to have agents in this city. They and the Russians are intent on drawing Denmark into a league of armed neutrality aimed at frustrating British mastery of the northern seas and is designed to be a brake on our ability to control contraband shipments. As you know, sir, it was for that very reason *HMS Nemesis* had the *Freya* taken, as she was attempting to prevent our ships from searching Danish merchantmen trading to French ports. If Lord Whitworth can draw the sting of this situation, Denmark will be less likely to join the French and Russians in their design. At least, for the time being."

"And His Royal Highness does believe that the Frogs would stoop to assassination to prevent this from happening?"

Chris nodded. "Yes, Admiral. The French are not alone in having spies in Copenhagen. Our charge d'affaires has his ear to the ground and his agents have reported that the French have paid a group of Irishmen, part of a secret society, who style themselves 'Grey Wolves', after the name of Wolfe Tone, an Irishman who served in the French army. He was known for his anti-British sentiment and was executed for his part in the French invasion of Ireland which fostered the rebellion of '98. These Irishmen are implacable enemies with fingers in many plots, so I've been told. Men who would stoop to any atrocity and of whom I should be most wary."

13

The British charge d'affaires lived in a large house backing onto parkland. The roof had a parapet running around it and Chris positioned two riflemen there to watch over the perimeter on a two hours on, four hours off, guard rota throughout the night. As he gave his orders he pulled Biggin to one side.

"You have allowed my wife to be brought into danger, Serjeant-major. I can understand that she was most insistent but it was a lapse of good judgement on your part. To make amends you will ensure her very safety every hour of every day that we're in this situation. If any harm becomes her I shall make it my duty to drum you out of the Corps."

Biggin hung his head and mumbled an apology.

"I haven't yet decided what disciplinary action I will take over this. It will depend on the outcome of this expedition. I no longer have to worry about only Lord Whitworth but now also Vice Admiral Dickson and my wife. You've probably no idea what stress is, Biggin, but believe me you will soon feel the effects of it if Mrs Lennox comes to harm."

"We will take all due care of her, sir, beggin' your pardon, that I have distressed you so. It did seem such a simple favour to grant, allowing your lady to dress as a boy so that she may be near you to say farewell and surprise you at Yarmouth. But once the charade was begun it did take on a different aspect over which I had no say."

"You were reeled in, Serjeant-major, like a fish on a line and I can see how it did occur. That is not to say your part in the deception is any less mitigated."

"I am yours to command, sir. You did save my life at Ferrol and I will be forever beholden to you on that score. I will take whatever punishment you see fit with a soldier's dignity."

"Allow Mrs Lennox her privacy from the riflemen and from the marines who are billeted with them. The riflemen know her secret but the marines do not and I want it kept that way. She is a lady of good birth, the daughter of a knight of the realm and the granddaughter of a duke. She is used to cleanliness and abhors soldierly language. Ensure the riflemen know of it."

"It will be as you wish, sir. The riflemen do have great regard and respect for your wife, sir. They have already made it known to the marines that their corner of the room will be curtained off with blankets and no marine would be welcome beyond them. They will fraternise in an open area so that good relations may be kept but that they may also know their place. There will be no strong drink on your orders."

"Very good. Keep the sentries alert. I don't think there will be an attempt while we are at this house but I want no risk taken that an assassin can sneak in undetected.

"Have the marines post guards outside Lord Whitworth's rooms. If you need me at any time send a runner to my room on the first floor. I'll sleep in my uniform so do not hesitate to call for me."

Biggin knuckled his forehead and turned away. Chris had repeated his orders several times and knew that the experienced soldier would do his duty to the letter. He watched the man go with a wry smile. He had made much of the punishment he might administer but he in his turn had a high regard for Biggin and, provided Catherine returned to England in one piece, he was determined to let the matter slip his mind.

He found Whitworth and the Admiral in company of the charge d'affaires in the large drawing room. Sir William Drummond was an aesthetic looking thirty-year old with receding curly hair and mutton chop whiskers that tended to age him more. He rose to greet Chris with a bow.

"Lieutenant-colonel Lennox. Welcome, sir. Will you partake of some Madeira?"

Chris shook his head. "I've banned strong alcohol for my soldiers, Sir William. It would ill become me to do otherwise and I need to keep a clear head."

Drummond gave him a quick smile and continued in his soft highland accent. "Then please be seated. We have been discussing the political and military aspects of the case here at Copenhagen and would welcome your opinion."

Chris sat on the edge of a chair, leaned forward and clasped his hands together. "I've travelled widely and on those travels I learned much from listening to people of all ranks in many countries and I hope that has given me an insight into current affairs and military adventurism around the globe. We are fighting wars and insurrections on four continents. On the Indian sub-continent, in the Americas, Egypt in North Africa and here in Europe where Bonaparte is flexing his military might. My understanding is that we will eventually lose control of America, not for a few years to be true but the problems in Europe will take precedence for our government who will see the American Revolution, not for what it is but as merely a trade war which no doubt will be exploited by the French.

"Bonaparte is our biggest problem. He is growing and training his armies and it is my opinion that he will soon attempt to conquer the Iberian Peninsular. I was down there last year and saw that he has designs on Portugal which we managed to thwart for the time being."

"Yes, I did hear from His Royal Highness, the Duke of York, of your exploits, Lennox," Whitworth said. "And you were instrumental in the founding of the Corps of Riflemen of which his Highness is so fond. The generals, it seems, are not so taken with the notion of such independence of action. General Sir David Dundas has written his eighteen manoeuvres, based on the Prussian school, which the army must follow and he sees large scale skirmishing as a great danger with possibly fatal consequences."

"You are well informed, my Lord, but as a mere Lieutenant-colonel, I must hazard that General Dundas is wrong and that regulated obedience, volley fire and packed formations will be proven costly in both lives and treasure. The tactics of a light brigade will bear fruit in the coming years, of that I'm certain."

Drummond put down his glass and gave Chris a shrewd look. "You yourself seem well-informed, Colonel. Of what do you make of the current position here in Copenhagen?"

"Given that I believe there will be an attempt on His Lordship's life which I will d o my utmost to prevent, I also believe we have the upper hand in negotiations on the *Freya* incident."

Whitworth snorted. "So you say, sir. I do believe you have overstated the dangers and I see little reason to be dragooned like a puppy in its kennel. And I fail to see how you can be so certain on the *Freya* subject as negotiations have yet to begin."

Drummond crossed his legs at the ankle and sat back. "I believe that you would be wise to take heed of Lennox, my Lord. Word is abroad that a group of Irishmen have recently arrived here in the city."

"What have the Irish to do with this? There is nothing here to concern them," Whitworth said.

Drummond gave a sage smile. "They are allied with the French and are in their pay. Their leader is rumoured to live in Paris and has taken up the gauntlet cast down by the traitor Wolfe Tone. They are a menace, sir and one should be wary of them. Now, come, I am interested in the colonel's opinion on the *Freya* matter."

"Whilst we were anchored in the Skag I took the opportunity to study the city's fortifications," Chris said. "They are incomplete and the large batteries not yet in the emplacements. We have with us four ships with heavy mortars aboard which would cause untold damage if used. I am aware that the Admiralty included those ships deliberately to focus Danish minds. It's good that Admiral Dickson will accompany His Lordship during negotiations for a threat of using the bombards can be implied without being voiced, that should we not agree on a solution regarding the *Freya,* retribution may follow without effective retaliation."

Dickson slapped his thigh. "By god, sir, I believe you may have hit upon a scheme that we may utilise. What say you, My Lord?"

Whitworth nodded. "I am not so hidebound that I cannot recognise a good ploy when I hear it. Your notion may prove useful, Lennox. It would needs be tempered with diplomacy and mayhap to concede relinquishing the Danish frigate and its convoy but it may well bear fruit in keeping the Danes out of the clutches of this mooted league of armed neutrality which the Russians and French are prognosticating."

"The Russians should learn to deal with the French at arm's length. I can foresee a time when Bonaparte might cast his gaze eastwards to St Petersburg and Moscow."

Drummond laughed. "You are a remarkably fey fellow, Lennox. One could almost think you have an eye in the future."

Chris gave what he hoped was a confident smile. "That is not the first time I've been accused of that, sir. However it is merely an opinion formed of Bonaparte that he has a hunger to conquer all of Europe, especially as his foray into Egypt did not end so well for him. He grasped power from the French Directorate on his return from that country, which rejuvenated his confidence and whetted his appetite for repairing his reputation. He is a single-minded despot who will not negotiate or take counsel."

"A man who will not listen is a fool. A man who cannot listen is a slave," Drummond said.

"Ah, philosophy," Whitworth said. "I did hear you were something of a philosopher, sir. A reputation that you bear well it seems."

Drummond laughed. "Perhaps those words will need a little polishing with time but I daresay there is a modicum of truth in them."

Chris stood. "You will have to excuse me, gentlemen. I have much to prepare. We will need to borrow your carriage and four tomorrow, Sir William."

"We have the one His Majesty King Christian has provided," Whitworth said.

Chris gave him a grim look. "The one may not be enough."

14

James Grant had a plan. It was simple and effective. His men had watched the British charge d'affaires' house and knew that the Ambassador had stayed the night. They had also reported on the sentries and the lookouts on the roof which had made his fall-back plan of attacking the house impossible.

There was only one route that a coach and four could take through Copenhagen's narrow streets to reach the Christianborg Palace and he had placed his men well. One was in an overhanging gallery with a good view along the street. The back wall of the gallery had been sheeted off so that the man's outline would not show as he aimed his French fusil de dragons musket. The cavalryman's weapon, shorter than the Charleville musket and easier to conceal beneath a cloak, had a fore sight but no rear sight and was inaccurate above fifty yards. Grant consoled himself with the knowledge that the distance from the gallery into the coach was less than twenty feet.

Others were hiding in alleyways with pistols and knives hidden beneath their cloaks to stop the coach and then finish the work that the musket would begin.

Dawn was lightening the sky and the street was beginning to fill with people going about their daily grind. Some were certain to be injured in the attack but it was a price worth paying if it hardened the Danish government's resolve and besmirched the name of England. The inevitable clamour in the Danish newssheets would be directed by friends of France and point the finger of blame at the British for their intransigence.

A white kerchief fluttered at the corner of the street and Grant tensed. It was the signal that the house gates had opened and a carriage was departing. Not one carriage but two if he had interpreted the signal correctly. He had not foreseen this turn of events and he had a momentary chill run up his spine. He shrugged it off, however many carriages there were made little difference, the Ambassador would be in one and impossible to mistake in his finery. He turned and waved to the musketeer to be ready.

The first carriage turned into the narrow thoroughfare, moving slowly to avoid pedestrians walking along either side of the road. Red coated marines kept pace with the conveyance, four on either side, their muskets held at the trail. Grant let his breath out with a hiss. This was not the ornate carriage lent by the Danish king but an altogether plainer vehicle with dull-coated posterns and driver. It would contain the British admiral, of that he was certain; the same arrangement as came over in the longboats.

The second carriage followed behind the first moving at the same sedate pace with two liveried footmen seated in the rumble and on the perch and a pair of coachmen on the box with whip and horn.

Grant slid into a dark alley and ordered his men to cock their Duval pistols. These men would stop the coach by catching the horses' bridles, then shoot the coachmen to give the musketeer the brief seconds he needed to assassinate the Ambassador.

The first carriage rumbled slowly past and he could see the top of the Admiral's bicorn hat worn front to rear with its gold braid. Nowhere near as ostentatious as the Ambassador's fine headgear adorned with ostrich feathers from Africa. The marine guards did not even turn their heads to see into the alley but kept their eyes straight ahead in disciplined military fashion. It brought a smile to Grant's thin lips. The British soldiery were so predictable.

Grant gave a warning growl. "Be ready men. Two to the far side o' the street and await the carriage until it is abreast o' this alleyway. You all know the plan be sure you follow it to the letter."

The four men gave nervous nods. One licked his dry lips. Nerves were taut but none doubted that this would be a fine hour for the Grey Wolves and the United Irishmen.

Two slunk from the alley but straightened their backs and strolled across not fifteen feet from the approaching carriage. The horses were skittish, lifting their hooves and snorting at the two figures draped in grey cloaks that crossed their eye line.

The coachman clicked his tongue to soothe them and pulled back on the reins to slow their already slow pace. He silently cursed the thoughtless pedestrians who gave no heed to the rigours of his task. He decided to give them a hard stare as he passed as they were standing with their backs pressed against the wall, looking at him from inside their cowls.

"NOW!"

The scream echoed and the two men leapt at the horses. Two more jumped from the alley, pistols in their hands. There was a thunderclap of noise and a scream. Pistols and rifles exploded together. The two men holding the bridles were punched over. A third spun under the horse's hooves. The fourth man raised his pistol and shot the coachman through the head before he too was punched flat by a .53 calibre ball.

Grant's head spun his men had gone down like skittles at a country fair. The musketeer had fired his weapon and there had been a scream from inside the coach. He raised his own pistol and leapt onto the coach's running board to ensure the kill. The Ambassador was slumped in his seat and he thrust the pistol at his head. He did not see the fist that punched his face from out of nowhere. He fell backwards and the pistol fired into the carriage roof. Flat on his back in the muck of the street, through watering eyes, he could see his remaining Grey Wolves rushing towards him waving urgently. He turned his head towards the rear of the first coach with its boot canvas rolled up and two men in green leaning out. More had appeared from above; the coachmen and posterns all dressed in dull green, their weapons shrouded in smoke. Two had jumped from the coach and were running towards him. He rolled to his feet and screamed, waving his arms in great windmills. The horses took fright and bolted, scattering people like wind-blown leaves. It gave him time to dart for the alley.

Chris had Catherine by his side as the carriage gathered speed towards them. Pedestrians were screaming. If the carriage was not stopped it would collide with the other, still blocking the street ahead, with calamitous results.

The dead coachman had fallen from his box and his companion, fearful for his own safety had jumped clear. The carriage was out of control.

Chris gave Catherine a look and she nodded. No words were needed. As the horses clattered past he picked up her light frame and threw her bodily onto the driver's box. She slipped, feet scrabbling for purchase, sliding towards the flailing hooves and carriage wheels but clung on, pulling herself headfirst to safety. The front carriage was just thirty yards away as she heaved on the reins.

One of the footmen, braver or more foolhardy than the other, slithered along the roof of the rocking coach to the box and pushed his foot against the brake locking the wheels. The snorting horses came to a stop a bare yard from the rear of the forward carriage.

The door slammed open and Biggin's head came out.

"Take care of the bugler, Serjeant-major." Chris yelled. "Six men stay with the first carriage and the marines, the rest with me."

Catherine had slid from the box and caught his sleeve. "Where ...?"

"In pursuit of the assassins. Stay with Biggin and look to the Ambassador and the Admiral." He took her hand away as gently as he could. He wanted to kiss her for her courage and hold her tightly in his arms as the thought of how close she had come to death made him shudder.

She was an accomplished carriage driver, as he knew from their first meeting on Salisbury Plain, but the risk to her life on this occasion had been monumental, outweighed only by the risk to the lives of so many civilians and soldiers had the carriages collided. Yet she had acted unhesitatingly. He wondered if he deserved the love of such a woman.

The crack of a rifle brought his mind back to the chase. A rifleman was down on one knee, a smoke cloud drifting away from the barrel of his Baker rifle. There was a huddled grey-clad shape on the ground two hundred yards away.

Corporal O'Dell pointed and spat. Five did go that way, sir. Four now that Matthews has taken one down. One went into yon alley running as if the hounds of hell were a-snappin' at his heels."

Two men with me then, O'Dell. You take the others in pursuit of the four but take care you aren't surprised in turn."

O'Dell knuckled his forehead and spat again. "Aye, sir but *they* best have the greatest care. There was one up in yonder gallery that took a ball. I do believe he went down for certain but best you know of him, sir."

Chris gave a grim nod and waited impatiently as his two riflemen jogged over to him. There was now to be a chase through the unfamiliar back alleys of Copenhagen in pursuit of possibly two armed and dangerous men.

15

Grant ran. There was the pounding of feet behind him and he turned, Duval pistol raised as a club but it was his own sniper, blood smearing his face and half an ear missing. A rifle ball had creased his cheek and smashed his teeth and blood bubbled from his lips as he fought for breath.

Grant gave him a slit-eyed look. The man spat blood and enamel and pointed to Grant's own head.

He put a hand to his nose. It too was dripping blood from the blow to his face and his eye was beginning to close as his cheek swelled. He gave it a gentle touch and winced. He felt that the bone had been fractured below his eye socket. He took the sniper by the sleeve.

"Was your aim true? Did you hit the bastard?"

"Aye, that I did, dead centre. He'll be takin' his last breath, so he will."

Grant grimaced. "So will we if we do not make haste away to the rendezvous. I hear boots on cobbles, the enemy does pursue us with a vengeance."

The man nodded. "I know these alleys, James, from last I was here. There are places we can shelter and reload our weapons. We will give them something more to consider before this day is out."

"Lead on, Daniel. All I need is a quiet niche and a few seconds to reload this Duval."

They ran in silence, the sniper occasionally spitting blood onto the cobbles. Danes in their open doorways slipped inside and slammed shut their doors as they passed, terrified by the guns and the blood soaked visages.

As fast as they ran, they could still hear boots pounding the cobbles behind them and sounding louder by the minute.

"Here," the sniper yelled and ducked into a deep embrasure. Grant squeezed in behind him and ripped the end off a powder cartridge with his teeth, pouring the gunpowder first into the priming pan and then the barrel, ramming wadding and ball in place. The sniper was doing likewise with his fusil and they both finished reloading together.

Grant, breathing heavily, peered around the stonework. The pounding of boots had stopped and he wondered why. Then it came to him. As they had heard the boots of the pursuers, then the enemy soldiers in turn had been following the sound of their own frantic footfalls.

"They are wary," the sniper said.

"And cunning, damn their eyes.

"As we may be. Leave me your Duval, James and run for the corner up ahead. The sound of your feet will draw them out and I will take two of them down ere I follow."

Grant nodded and handed the pistol over butt first. "Make both balls count. We will await you at the inn as planned."

"The blessin's o' the Virgin Mary go with ye. Offer up a prayer or two for me besides."

"To be sure," Grant said and ran.

Chris stopped. The echo of running feet has faded and that could mean an ambush. The alley curved in a graceful arc at this point and he could see only thirty feet ahead. The doorways set into the walls were closed and bolted, as they had been along the full length of the alley. It was unlikely that the fugitives had found a house in which to hide. He removed his cap and took a brief glance around the curve. The alleyway ahead was empty as far as a junction a hundred yards further along where the alleyways split into four at a crossroads. Could the fugitives have reached that far? It was possible, sound echoed and carried between the narrow walls and the runners may have seemed closer than they really were. In which case they had to hope that they could still follow a blood trail as there was only a thirty-three percent chance of choosing the right branch to follow. And time was wasting. There was only one way to find out.

He stepped out and risked another glance. Still nothing visible. He had an advantage in his rubber soled combat boots that made little sound. He signalled for his riflemen to stay put and inched around the curve, following the tighter side of the arc with his back to the wall and his sabre in his hand. The path was littered with debris and rubbish and he trod cautiously, rolling his foot like a tiger. As the alley straightened out he thought he could hear voices, low and indistinct, coming from somewhere ahead.

There was an explosion of movement and a cloaked figure hurled itself from inside the wall and ran pell-mell for the junction.

Chris yelled and another man, brandishing a musket leaned out and fired. The ball hit Chris squarely in the chest and he fell on his back. Thick powder smoke blocked his view but he could see a pair of legs emerging. He rolled onto his knees, lashed out with the sabre and felt the tip bite into flesh and the musket clattered to the ground. He lunged forward but the man had turned away and the sabre punched through air. The smoke thinned and he could see his opponent clawing a pistol from his belt. He jumped to his feet, slashed backhand and caught the man on his neck with the flat of the blade. The pistol was still rising, the man's left hand reaching to pull the hammer off half-cock. A rifle cracked and the man spun back against the wall but there was still fire in his eyes.

He raised the pistol at Chris's head. "Die now, spawn o' the Devil."

Chris pushed the pistol skyward and punched the man with the hilt of his sabre. The Duval exploded and the ball ricocheted from a stone windowsill.

Matthews arrived at Chris's side and plunged his sword bayonet into the man's guts before Chris could stop him. "That will be one less to bother with, sir"

Chris pulled him away. "He's still breathing. He may know where the other assassin is heading."

"He is not long for this world, sir, you'd best be quick to ask him your questions."

"Go to the alley junction. See if there's any indication which way the other man ran. Look for blood on the pavement."

Matthews nodded and went away. Chris could see the man staring at him. He pulled him into a sitting position against the wall.

The man coughed up blood and stared again. "The ball hit you fair an' square. Tis the Devil's work."

Chris knelt beside him. "No, just armour. He pulled aside the tunic to show the canvas weskit with its iron bands. The ball is lodged between the bands. I'll have a sore and bruised breastbone but little else to concern me."

The man coughed again and gave a slack grin. "Tis my ill-fortune."

"Where is your companion heading for?"

"I'm no clat. I'll tell ye nothin'." He groaned and clutched his wounds.

"You're dying, man. You should go with a clear conscience."

The man's voice was growing weaker and his eyes were misting over. "All I done, I done for Ireland. Killin' one or two protestants will not damn my soul. You harken to yours, a time of reckoning is nigh."

16

The man was dead. His lungs collapsed and his last breath bubbled through his lips but his words left a chill on Chris's spine. Would a dying man engage in bravado with his last breath or was he hinting at some tragedy to come?

Matthews loped back shaking his head. "I lost the spoor, sir. I do believe he was not bleeding as heavily as this devil and left no trace."

"Very well. Wrap this man in his cloak and carry him back to the carriages. The Danes won't thank us for leaving a corpse on their doorsteps."

The scene around the carriage was manic. Danish soldiers had arrived and were attempting some sort of order as civilians milled around trying to peer into the regal carriage. Catherine met him with Biggin by her side. A quick glance around showed that the charge 'd'affaires' carriage had driven away and he breathed out in relief. "The Ambassador?"

Biggin grinned. "Mightily upset at having to don the admiral's cap, sir, but mightily relieved that he was not travelling in this 'ere carriage."

"How is the marine who was wearing the charge d'affaires' spare tunic and cap?"

"He is well, sir and grateful for the loan of your native cloth, sir. It did stop the ball with a mere cracked rib to concern him."

"Kevlar, yes, it's remarkable material. I shall advise the captain of marines to put the man on light duties and a double ration of grog when this excitement is over as reward for his bravery."

"Your plan did exceed all expectations, sir," Catherine said. "But your tunic is holed at the breast."

Chris smiled and shrugged. "Par for the course but I've come to no harm."

"By the grace of God, sir. You must take more care."

Chris gave her hand a quick squeeze. "I take every care that I can but I've chosen a hazardous career and you must be prepared for anything that may come at me."

The Danish soldiers had restored order, moving the people away from the carriage and their officer was listening to a man and looking around. The man pointed at Chris's group and gestured.

"I think we're about to get some unwanted attention. Serjeant-major, collect the riflemen still here from their piquets and march on to the palace. Some of the attackers are still on the loose and may make another attempt. We will continue to watch over the Ambassador on his return. Take Mrs Lennox with you and guard her well."

"I will not be dismissed in such cavalier fashion," Catherine said. "I will stay by your side, sir, as it seems you imperil yourself with impunity, I shall join you in whatever danger you may face. You may command the Serjeant-major but I will defy you in this. It is my final word on it." She folded her arms and her eyes above the black face veil challenged him to argue.

Very well, I don't have time to argue. Away to your duties, Mr Biggin."

"The Danish officer approached and saluted. "Godmorgen hr. Har jeg forstå, du har en vis viden om, hvad der skete her til morgen?"

Chris shook his head, apart from the salutation, he had no idea what the man had said.

Catherine interjected. "Pardon, Monsieur, en Francais, sil vous plait."

The Dane smiled. Pardonnez, moi. Est-ce que je comprends que vous avez une certaine connaissance de ce qui s'est passé ici ce matin?"

Chris gave Catherine a questioning look. His French had not passed beyond GCSE level.

"The officer is asking if you are aware of the circumstance of the happenings here this morning."

Chris drew himself up to his full six foot height and put a stern expression on his face. "Please translate for me, Bugler. I am Lieutenant-colonel Lennox of the British Plenipotentiary Extraordinaire's personal guard. This morning an attempt was made on His Excellency's life." Chris waited for Catherine to translate in her gruffest voice before continuing. "This was allowed to take place on Danish soil, in your very capital city. I demand both an explanation of how this outrage was allowed to occur and to have every assistance from the Danish military in tracking down and apprehending the remaining assassins."

The Danish officer's mouth had dropped open and he took a step back. He replied in good English. "My apologies, Colonel. Has His Excellency come to harm?"

"Due to the diligence of his guards, thankfully not but that is no thanks to your government, sir."

"I do beg your pardon. I will send a messenger to my commanding officer immediately. If what you say is true diplomatic immunity has been disregarded and there shall be a full enquiry."

"As you can see from the bodies here in the street, these assassins wear grey cloaks and call themselves the Grey

Wolves. They are Irishmen and one still at large has a facial wound."

The officer relaxed a little. "Ah, Irishmen, not Danish citizens."

"That does not alter the fact the attack was made on Danish soil and the British government will hold the Danish government to task over it."

"I am not attempting to belittle the significance, sir." He beckoned over a soldier, whispered in his ear and the man scurried off. "I have sent a messenger to my colonel. The search for these Grey Wolves will begin immediately."

"Thank you, sir. What's your name?"

The Dane sprang to attention and clicked his heels. "Captain Agnar Sturlusson, Colonel."

"I have to make haste to the Christiansborg Palace, Captain. Make arrangements to report to me at the British charge d'affaires' residence in Kastelsvej this evening with results of the hunt, if you please."

"As you wish, Colonel Lennox. My men have cleared the road of the dead and the king's carriage may proceed. The assistant coachman will convey you at your convenience."

"The man deserted his post. My bugler has the skills, he has most surely proved his worth in preventing an even bigger disaster and he will drive the carriage with me beside him on the box. The head footman however is to be commended for his bravery and quick thinking. I will ensure he is rewarded."

"As you wish, sir. Your bugler is very well skilled for one so young … and." He waved a hand around his face.

"The lasting result of smallpox, Captain. Despite his suffering he has been a diligent student. He is soon to be promoted to Ensign and posted to another regiment. I shall sorely miss his bravery and companionship."

The captain bowed and turned away so did not see the kick that Catherine aimed at Chris's shin. "Ha! Miss my companionship will you, sir? We will think on it," she hissed.

Chris gave a small hop as the pain spread up his leg. "You are becoming most unladylike, madam. Mixing with rough soldiery has not improved your manners."

"Nor reduced my love for you and concern for your well-being. I wish to be at your side, always."

"That can't be so. You cannot continue with this charade for much longer. I won't have you sailing home in rough company. You must buy a wardrobe here in Copenhagen and sail by packet boat back to England. I insist on it."

"Very well, sir, if that is your wish. However, it is my intention to accompany you where ere I may 'til I am with child."

Chris smiled and it broadened into a grin as the ramifications of her statement hit home. "Then I suppose we'll just have to try harder."

17

Whitworth and the admiral were in a jubilant mood at dinner that evening, reciting their discussions with the Danish First Minister, Christian Günther von Bernstorff, and the success of the negotiations which had taken just the day to reach fruition.

Sir William Drummond seemed delighted with the result and passed the port round again. "So, gentlemen, we have an agreement and the Danes will resist the French and Russian entreaties to join their northern alliance."

"Pro tem," Whitworth said, sounding a note of caution. "If it was not for the abortive assassination attempt on my life and Admiral Dickson's veiled threat to bombard the city if all came to nought we might have another outcome to report. Von Bernstorff was rightly apologetic and ashamed that the attempt on my life should be enacted on Danish soil and was more than ready to come to some form of agreement on the *Freya* issue but I did sense a marked reluctance to make an agreement in perpetuity over the freedom of the Royal Navy to police the illicit trade in contraband that so many Danish ships are engaged upon."

Chris moved uneasily in his seat. "I've a feeling the navy will be back again, possibly next year and some time thereafter. I can't see the French and Russians giving up so easily and the Danish reluctance to come to a permanent agreement is worrying."

Whitworth nodded. "I agree, Lennox. This is but a mechanism to allow the Danes to reinforce their fortifications against us, and to gain the time to seek an arrangement with the Frogs."

"But for Lennox's greenbacks and his stratagem this day may have ended on a tragic note," Dickson said. "I did see your bugler play a most effectual part in the drama, sir. But for him the carriages would have collided with a disastrous outcome. I trust you will see him suitably rewarded."

Chris gave a slight smile. "I will see the bugler has a just reward, Admiral. I am sending him back on the packet to Dover with my Serjeant-major as escort. The memory of what occurred aboard the *Monarch* is still fresh in his mind and I felt it best he should join his new regiment as soon as possible."

"A gutsy lad, Lennox, if ever I saw one. What is his name?"

"Eli Dean, Admiral, or so he said. The Deans are a family of some substance in Wiltshire with whom I have a slight acquaintance but had no knowledge of young Eli until this trip."

A servant entered and whispered in Drummond's ear. He put down his glass and looked over at Chris. "There is a Danish army captain by name of Agnar Sturlusson at the gate who wishes to speak with you, Lennox. Shall I allow him entry?"

Chris stood and threw his napkin on the table. "Of course. I'm awaiting his report on the rest of the Grey Wolves to hear if they have been apprehended."

Drummond signalled his servant. "Have the captain shown in and bring another decanter of port for our guests."

The port arrived before Sturlusson who was shown in by a suspicious looking rifleman.

"Captain Sturlusson, come in and take a seat," Drummond invited. "Never let it be said that the British charge d'affaires cannot treat his guests civilly. You will take some port with us, sir."

Sturlusson clicked his heels in teutonic fashion, bowed and took Chris's vacated seat. "I thank you, Sir William. The port would be most welcome."

"I trust you have some good news, Captain," Whitworth said.

Sturlusson shook his head slowly from side to side in a pantomime of sorrow. "Alas no, Your Excellency. We have soldiers searching the city inn by inn but have yet found no trace of the blackguards who did assault you. We had news of them at an inn off the Øster Voldegade but they did vacate their rooms this morn and did not return. We have the port watched for any sign of men of their description taking ship but alas a grey cloak can be removed and other than a story of a man with a wounded face we have nought else to direct us."

"Perhaps they could have taken horse south or west," Drummond said.

The Dane nodded. "It is a possibility they could ride the fifteen English miles south to Krǿge or ride the fifty miles west to Korson to catch a ferry to Funen. It is also possible that they still hide in Copenhagen. We have no way of knowing."

"But you will keep looking," Chris said.

"Of course, Colonel, but we cannot give guarantees that these men will be found."

Whitworth put down his glass with a bang. "Or that they will not strike again."

After Sturlusson had left and Whitworth had retired for the night, Chris sat with Drummond and Dickson with their feet up around the fire. September was drawing to a close and the nights were getting a definite chill to them. It reminded Chris to make sure his riflemen were kept warm and that the guard was rotated every two hours in Biggin's absence. O'Dell was the senior corporal and had charge of the men. He was a good soldier but liked a drink and needed to be watched to ensure he carried out his duties efficiently.

Dickson coughed and brought his attention back to the conversation. "Did you perceive that our Dane was somewhat more pessimistic in his opinion of locating these Grey Wolves than is the case, Lennox?"

Chris grimaced. "I had the same thought, Admiral. I was also most impressed that he knew Sir William and Lord Whitworth's identities without having previously met either of those gentlemen. It seems our captain, of whom I had thought better, has been briefed on his duty and perhaps some pressure applied from above that he relax his diligence in the search. It's just my opinion but it would not surprise me."

"Which would intimate a degree of collusion from the Danish government, either in the knowledge of the assassination attempt or in the escape of these Grey Wolves," Drummond said.

"I do not believe that First Minister von Bernstorff had prior knowledge," Dickson said. "He did seem mightily surprised at the news and quite distraught that a British diplomat had been attacked by renegades."

"I agree," Drummond said. "It is unthinkable that a man of honour like von Bernstorff would be complicit in murder but I do see a desire to appease the Frogs in this reluctance to apprehend their agents. The Danes are riding two horses in this race."

"And hedging their bets," Chris added. "I can't say I fully blame them but the upshot is that we have a dangerous cadre of assassins on the loose with no knowing where they may strike next."

18

Grant was seething. The pain in his cracked cheekbone did not help his mood. He had lost half of his twelve Grey Wolves in a few minutes, most taken down by such accurate musketry as he had never before witnessed. Four men smashed to the ground in seconds and another, so he had been informed by a survivor, taken down at over two hundred yards whilst running away.

Daniel O'Rourke had not joined them at their refuge although they had waited for him. He too was added to the list of the claimed. Six martyrs for the cause of a free Ireland.

At least they had struck a blow. He had seen the hole in the British Ambassador's breast for himself. The man could not have survived a .54 calibre ball at that close range. It had been an all too brief a vision as the hard fist had hurled him from the step but he had seen enough to convince himself that the French money was well spent.

Now they had to leave the island and make for Hanover on the first stage of a journey to Paris and thence to London. The grey cloaks had been discarded and his surviving Grey Wolves had split into three groups to attempt the journey without raising any suspicion. His own face was badly marked and the bruise was beginning to form but he planned to keep it covered and his hood raised as he rode. It was not an uncommon sight on an island that could be bleak and inhospitable.

For some reason he could not fathom, the Danes had sighted their capital city not in the centre of the country but as far east as they could place it. Copenhagen sat opposite the coast of Sweden on the island of Zealand on the sound between the Kattegat and the Skagerrak. The only place closer to a hostile Sweden was Elsinore to the north. The geography made his life difficult as he had to travel fifty miles to Korson on the west coast to catch a ferry to Funen and then a ride of over two-hundred miles south to Holstein and the port of Hamburg where he would take ship for France. It would be easier to take ship immediately but he feared that the ports at Copenhagen would be watched. It was important for him to keep his freedom as, the head of the Grey Wolves, Coileán Leech, had plans, big plans and would need him, James Grant, to ensure their success.

He gave a small grunt of satisfaction at the thought as he headed his horse out of the western gate of Copenhagen with barely a second glance from the soldiery stationed there. In fact one waved him adieu as he passed then turned back to tending the brazier lit on a chilly and dull afternoon with the smell of a fast approaching winter on the wind.

Grant relaxed the shoulders he had not realised were tense and with that movement his mood lightened and he laughed. The Danes were not on alert. The alarm had not been raised so they would perceive the danger to be at an end with the death of the British plenipotentiary. Their guard was down and his luck was in. There would be no negotiation over the *Freya* affair, no weakening of the Dane's stance on the issue and the likelihood that the Danish government would throw in their lot with the Russians and the French in forming the area of armed neutrality in the northern seas that would stymie the British and keep the trading routes to France free from British interference. Coileán and their French paymasters would be pleased with the outcome and perhaps his success would secure additional funding for the United Irishmen in their fight to oust the English from Ireland once and for all time.

The voyage back to Yarmouth was uneventful but Chris missed Catherine's warm body next to him in the bunk and regretted his decision to send her back on the packet with Biggin, although he knew it had been for the best.

She had an amazing pull on him. The attraction was almost magnetic and his lightning tattooed arm tingled whenever he was close to her. He had thought it was brought on in his dreamlike state when he was first struck by the bolt at Stonehenge, when the electricity was still throbbing through his body and the lovely image of Cat Dean, the army medic, hovered in his field of vision as she worked to save his life but now he wasn't so sure.

He knew that Cat was at the hospital when they had put him into the MRI scanner, she had been in the control room with the technicians, keeping a military medic's eye on her military patient. When his body and mind were returned to the 21st century, would he still feel the magnetic attraction, the pull, that Catherine had on him or would he feel that way about her doppelganger, Cat?

Like almost everything to do with his journeys to the past it was an enigma; one that he was glad of in Catherine's case for he was determined he would enjoy her company to the full, as much as he was able, for as long as he remained in this time.

All this passed through his mind as one calm day, after he persuaded Captain Mosse for the loan of his jolly boat, he was rowed over to the *Aquilon*, the frigate commanded by his old friend Captain Charles Cunningham, with whom he had shared a wardroom and battle against a

French fourth rater on the voyage to Portugal the previous year. Cunningham was pleased to see him and they exchanged gossip in the captain's day cabin.

Cunningham poured Chris a good Madeira. "Word on the decks is that you have become hitched, sir."

Chris grinned. "Is nothing to be sacred in this man's navy?"

Cunningham gave a rakish smile in return. "You know all seafarer's are inveterate gossips, Lennox, worse than washerwomen, and your name is known amongst the crew so any word of you is digested and repeated until the original meaning is lost in the telling. By all accounts, the lady is of becoming beauty and good birth and you fought a duel for her hand."

"One half of the story is correct, sir. She is the most beautiful woman I ever laid eyes on and she is of good birth. As for the rest, it makes a good tale but it has been misconstrued in the telling."

"Ah, so no duel then to add spice to the story."

"Not as such, not for her hand as we were already engaged to be married. The duel was with her brother, Major Henry Wadman."

"My god, sir, you must give instruction on how to impress your wife's family. Did the major object to your union?"

"Not at all, sir. There was another argument behind it which was settled amicably and we are now good friends."

Cunningham topped up their glasses and sat back. "Is this the same Major Wadman who did litter my desk with despatches prior to our embarkation to the Portuguese Algarve this last year past?"

"The very same. He is an aide de camp to His Royal Highness the Duke of York and much exercised in His Highness's employment."

"Which would, no doubt, explain this despatch ..." Cunningham waved his hand over a paper on his table "... that came from the *Monarch,* along with you in the jolly boat."

Chris raised his eyebrows. "From Henry Wadman?"

"Indeed, sir, on the instruction of His Royal Highness a fast sloop brought the despatch. We are to embark your greenbacks forthwith and make for Dover. We are to disembark your men there for their return to Shorncliffe and then make all sail for the Thames and London. It seems your presence is required at Horse Guards at your earliest convenience."

19

The *Aquilon* could not pass under London Bridge, so Cunningham made the ship fast to Custom House Quay on the north side of the Thames, browbeating the customs officials who complained they needed the space for merchant vessels to moor prior to having their cargoes assessed and taxed. The quay had long been known as Wool Quay although now it dealt with all kinds of cargoes from all over the known world.

Chris had to smile on overhearing the captain unrepentantly pulling rank and putting his marines ashore to give weight to his argument. He boarded Cunningham's pinnace and was rowed upriver as far as King's Reach where he disembarked at Whitehall Stairs just a short walk from Horse Guards on the far side of Whitehall.

18th century London always amazed him with its vibrancy and complexity. Downing Street was there, with the Inigo Jones designed Palladian style Banqueting House which had been the scene of King Charles's execution but no Edwin Lutyens Cenotaph which wasn't completed until 1920. To his right, where Nelson's column would, in future, command Trafalgar Square, there was just Charing Cross and the beginning of the Strand.

It was the seat of government with the First Lord of the Treasury residing in Number 10 Downing Street and the road was busy with horse drawn carts, carriages and riders, interspaced with men carrying Sedan Chairs to and fro. The smell was of manure and horse sweat rather than diesel and petrol fumes and he thought he preferred it to red buses and black taxis.

He dodged across Whitehall, past the saluting guards in their boxes and into Horse Guards proper. Henry Wadman's room was on the first floor adjacent to the Duke of York's own offices. Chris rapped on the door and entered. Henry was bent over his desk with quill in hand. He looked up in vague annoyance at the interruption until he recognised his visitor and his face split into a weary smile. "Ha! So you have arrived at last, sir. I had decided you to be at the bottom of Davy Jones' Locker with your tardiness."

Chris held out his hand to his brother-in-law. "No, Henry, it's the cursed slowness of His Majesty's navy. I sometimes dream of a land where distances can be covered in the blink of an eye."

Henry guffawed. "And men could fly, no doubt."

"Perhaps not so far fetched. I did hear that the French Montgolfier brothers have succeeded in untethering their hot air balloon and flying some distance."

"I did also hear of such but they were driven by the vagaries of wind at less pace than a man walking. A carnival trick, sir."

"As always, sir, you have arrived at the nub. I don't foresee much future for the balloon except as a passtime, other than perhaps as a viewing platform to keep an eye on enemy formations that manoeuvre out of sight of scouts on the ground."

"And as is also usual, sir, you have hit upon a notion that may bear some investigation. Perhaps His Royal Highness will take a fancy to it and pursue the matter.

"Now, how did you fare in Copenhagen and do you have despatches from Admiral Dickson."

Chris delved into his leather satchel and pulled out several sealed documents. "These are from the admiral and two of my own. I spent some time while we were anchored in the sound studying the fortifications which may be of use for future expeditions."

Henry took the papers and laid them on his desk with a thoughtful expression. "You believe another expedition to Copenhagen will be necessary?"

Henry rang a small bell on his desk and a footman came and gathered up the papers to take to the duke.

Chris waited for the door to close behind the man before continuing. "Another expedition is almost inevitable and possibly as early as next year. My mission was successful. An attempt *was* made to assassinate the ambassador by the Irish band of cutthroats who call themselves the Grey Wolves. The duke was correct that Lord Whitworth was a target for French inspired murder. But for my riflemen they would have succeeded. Lord Whitworth resolved the *Freya* issue to our advantage but he, as do I and Admiral Dickson, distrusts the result and believes that the Danish government will fall into the Franco-Russian alliance and pursue their policy of armed neutrality to prevent the Royal Navy from intercepting contraband."

"Ah! Good news spliced with bad. The duke will be delighted to hear of Lord Whitworth's success but I fear he will view the prospect of further intervention in Denmark with some dismay. He was hoping for a more lasting agreement which would take his attention from the northern seas and to watch events in France and the Americas more assiduously."

"He's wise to keep a close eye on events in France. Bonaparte is beginning to flex his muscles and will grow in strength over the next few years. The Americas are perhaps of more concern to parliament and His Majesty, King George. I fear the colonists are pressing ever more strongly for independence which simply repealing the Tea Act won't divert. We have lost good men there and it would seem to me to be time to grant independence and withdraw or be defeated in a battle we cannot possibly win with the troops we have there."

Henry grunted. "I would be careful to whom you express that opinion, sir. Twould smack of treachery to some ears."

"I'm obliged for your warning, sir but I speak as a soldier, not as a politician who has mismanaged the situation for many years with tax laws that have found little favour with the colonists. They say no taxation without representation and they wish to be free of our parliament and govern themselves. I put it up as a marker for the future."

"I would pass on your concerns to His Royal Highness with whatever diplomacy I may. He finds your grasp of affairs to be refreshing but may in this instance believe your analysis too much of a mouthful to swallow."

"Ain't that a fact," Chris said under his breath. He had a feeling that his opinion would not cut much ice with the upper echelons of British government and was relieved. It wouldn't be right for his involvement in another age to have cataclysmic consequences for the future. He resolved to have no further opinion on America and to let history unfold at its own pace. He would concentrate on events closer to home.

"Now, sir, why have I been summoned to Horse Guards without undue delay?"

"The duke wished to have your report most urgently," Henry said. "There are rumblings afoot and he needs be fully apprised of events before Lord Whitworth returns from Yarmouth. He believes speed is of the essence. He will call for you betimes.

"Now, sir. How fares sister Catherine?"

Chris couldn't hide a wry smile. "I believe she is well and prospering the last I saw her. Perhaps I could have been better acquainted with her character ere we were married."

Henry grinned in turn. "Dammit, sir, you could not see beyond the glow in your heart, that the spark in her eyes did portend a woman of unusual determination. She did run me ragged as a girl with her tomboy ways. That sweetness of nature that so becomes her and did beguile you is but one facet of her character. You did, sir, reap a sweet and bitter whirlwind in your romance. I did believe that Anthony Dean was not half man enough for her and so it did prove but you, sir, are of a different mettle. I hope you will serve her right."

Chris gave a slight bow. "That is my sincere intention."

There was a rap on the door and the footman came back with a note for Henry. He read it and grimaced. "Tis not to Horse Guards you are summoned but to Downing Street."

20

Downing Street. Built by property developer Lord Downing over a hundred years before was little like the Downing Street of Chris's day where most of the terrace on the south side had been demolished to make way for the Foreign and Commonwealth Office. There were no gates on the junction with Whitehall; those had been erected during the Irish troubles of the 1970s and 80s. Now a public footpath ran through to St James's Park beyond and pedestrians hustled their way past with barely a second glance at the First Lord of the Treasury's official residence.

Although the buildings looked well designed they had been built cheaply on shallow marshy foundations which would cause problems in latter years. Some of the buildings were privately occupied with one or two on the south side used by the War and Colonial Office but Number 10 was the seat of British government. In the terrace opposite, Chris noticed that one of the properties was unoccupied and looked a little forlorn. And further along was a public house, the Rose and Crown. That was a surprise, he had no idea there had ever been a pub in Downing Street.

He knocked on Number 10's door. He was admitted by a liveried footman, shown into a room on the ground floor and asked to wait.

It was a good thirty minutes later that a man came in. He appeared to be in his late thirties or early forties, wearing a dark frock coat and a careworn expression. Chris stood. He recognised the man who had been sitting at the Duke of York's window. He gestured at Chris to sit. "William Pitt, Colonel. I'm obliged for your time."

"First Lord of the Treasury, an honour, sir."

"Yes, yes, do sit, Lennox, I have not the time nor the taste for undue politeness."

"In that case, sir. What is it you want with me?"

"Good, to the point. I will not bore you with details, Lennox, but we are beset on many fronts, one of which is the Irish problem which seems to persist, despite my earnest efforts to defuse it. His Majesty is dead set against my proposals for Catholic emancipation and I struggle to get the bill through parliament. Therefore the Irish, in the guise of this secret league of United Irishmen, are continuing with their undeclared rebellion. You have come across their Grey Wolves in Denmark, have you not?"

"Yes, sir."

"I have read your despatches. You dealt with their threat most satisfactorily."

"Some eluded us, sir. They are still at large."

"And likely to cause further mischief, yes, yes, I did glean that from your reports. You are an interesting man, Lennox. His Royal Highness did inform me of your part in the formation of the Corps of Riflemen, your part in developing the training tasks for said riflemen and how you did give Bonaparte a bloody nose in Portugal. I have made enquiries of you, Lennox but cannot find a single soul who will admit to knowing you or your family apart from those with whom you have come into contact over the past year. A land called New Zealand, I am told is your home and loyal to the Crown but the Exchequer can find no record of taxes for such a place and there is no record of supply or trade."

"We are a small community, sir and well able to fend and provide for ourselves. We have more sheep than people, the land is fertile and we grow everything we need.

We have discovered native medicines and learned a different art of war which tenets I'm eager to pass on to the Crown's forces."

Pitt frowned. "That explains much but not all. But for now we will leave that subject and move on to the reason I have summoned you here. I wish you to report to me on a matter of great concern."

"Which is?"

"I do much admire your pithiness, Lennox, long may it continue. You will find me in turn more direct than the duke. It is this league of United Irishmen that much concerns me. There are rumours that they plan an attack on England. I wish you to discover its purpose and put a stop to it before it can gain ground."

"I've no idea where even to start such a task, sir."

"I appreciate that you would needs prefer to be at Shorncliffe with the Rifles but that I cannot allow. I have asked the duke to appoint General Moore to the training of the soldiery and you will pass that mantle to him. You will be quartered here in London and you will have dealing with Major Wadman who will apprise you of all the intelligence that we have."

"Henry Wadman?"

"Do not sound so surprised, sir. Major Wadman sees all that comes across every desk at Horse Guards and is a veritable mine of information."

"As you direct, sir. I now have a wife of a few weeks ..."

"So I am informed. And ...?"

"... I wish her to be with me whenever and wherever possible. If I am to take lodgings in London I would like her to share them with me."

"A natural inclination, although why a soldier would wish to be married is beyond me. Military service is arduous at the best of times with wives oft left to languish alone for many years."

Chris gave a tight smile. "If you had met the lady, sir, you would understand why. However, I raise the matter as I noticed a house opposite was unoccupied. Perhaps it would be a suitable place for me to rent for the foreseeable future."

"I will ask my secretary to look into the matter on your behalf, Lennox. Do what you must to put your affairs in order at Shorncliffe and be back here in seven days to begin your task. There is no time for delay much beyond that if the rumours to which we are privy are to be believed."

"I will need a staff, sir, and soldiers to call upon."

"You shall have them. I will write to Shorncliffe and have them allow you take the pick of your chosen men. They shall be billeted at Knightsbridge. The cost of that and of your duties, except for your personal usages will be borne at the Exchequer's expense."

"Thank you, sir."

"Do not thank me so readily, Colonel Lennox. There is always a price for such largesse and be certain the piper will be paid. Be assured also that there will be no laurels or promotions to be made from this. It is to be kept from public attention and no one will know of it outside of these walls and that of Horse Guards' inner sanctum. No credit will be allowed to your name for your successes and no requiem should you die.

"You have been chosen not solely for your military acumen but also as there will be no family here in Britain and few to mourn you. It is your lack of connection that makes you eminently qualified to work in secret. Your name will be struck from all past despatches and it shall be as if you never were."

21

Chris's brain was in turmoil as he left Number 10. There was so much to think about he didn't know where to start. He was being relieved of his command with his beloved Corps of Riflemen and was being tasked with setting up the country's first security service; that's what it amounted to. He was to be a spymaster and work in the shadows.

It was also a douche of cold water to know that his name counted for nothing in a country and time where birth and heritage opened more doors than worth and knowledge. It was something he would have to bear in mind in future. He had been favoured by the Duke of York and given an income twenty times that of a serving infantry lieutenant-colonel. That would engender a certain amount of jealousy in some quarters if the fact ever came out that his place was due solely to the largesse of a royal benefactor.

He grinned briefly at the thought. On the other hand, maybe it explained why his name did not feature in any history of the Corps of Riflemen in his own time. He had studied regimental history and knew that General Moore was admired for his training regime. That was somewhere to start, to get to Shorncliffe and brief the new training officer on how best to proceed with future engagements in mind. These were burned into his memory, all the battles of the future and the honours on the regiment's colours to be added in the next few years; Copenhagen, Monte Video, Rolica, Vimiera, Corunna, Busaco, Barrosa, Fuentes d'Onor, Ciudad Rodrigo, Badajoz, Salamanca, Vittoria, Pyrenees, Nivelle, Nive, Orthes, Toulouse, Peninsula and Waterloo. All still to come and all with their own peculiar variations.

Moore would need to continue the work that Chris had started and improve on it in the knowledge of the tactics that would be required and the skills the men needed to develop.

He turned back towards Horse Guards. He had left Henry's horse at the stables in Yarmouth and he had to arrange for a groom to collect it. He would also need to speak to Henry about his new assignment but that could wait until he returned from Shorncliffe.

Catherine would by now be back at Imber Court, that is if she had complied with his wishes on this occasion. He smiled again at the thought of his feisty young wife, so different from the demur lady he had first met. There had been clues; her ability to handle a carriage and four, her admission to being a tomboy in her childhood, her bravery when attacked by highwaymen. He should have known but Henry was right, he had fallen so totally and so quickly in love with her he had failed to read the signs. The idea of an early 19th century woman being so emancipated and independent hadn't occurred to him and he berated himself for his sexist views. He should have paid more attention to Jane Austen.

Not that he minded the change, he positively welcomed it. The idea of a subservient wife did not appeal. They were equals. It might be an unfashionable state in these times but to hell with that they were partners and Catherine was more than able to hold her own in any company. He was so proud of her.

Once he had settled on where to live he would send for her but in the meantime he needed to write to let her know that he was safely back in England and was working on finding them a place in London.

He reached Horse Guards, knocked on Henry's door and was called in.

Henry raised his eyebrows. "How went your time in Downing Street?"

"We have much to discuss but first I need pen and paper to write to Catherine, then the loan of another horse to get me to Shorncliffe as fast as its hooves can carry me."

Henry threw down his quill. "You will leave me to the mercies of London's pavements. You have one mount already and you wish to deprive me of the other?"

"Your first horse is stabled at Yarmouth and can be sent for. My need is urgent for the other mount."

"Then I have another thought. You will need mounts of your own. There is a brace of hunters, the property of an officer of the Life Guards who was killed in an unfortunate accident, for sale at Knightsbridge. You may purchase those at reasonable cost for horseflesh and stabling."

"In that case, pen and paper is all I require of you for now, brother. Please have the letter I'm about to write delivered to Imber at your earliest convenience."

Henry handed over the items with a grim look. "It seems to me that you are in the most unbecoming hurry, sir. I assume tis to do with your time at Downing Street."

Chris was scribbling hurriedly, the quill making scratching noises on the rough paper, but paused to look Henry in the eye. "You may think that, sir, and you would be correct. It is not something which I am at liberty to discuss right now. When I return we shall have time to ponder on it." He scratched a few more lines and sanded the paper before folding it, begging Henry's wax and sealing the letter with the gold sovereign he had mounted as his wedding ring with its image of St George slaying the dragon.

He left the letter with a perturbed Henry and hurried the short distance to Knightsbridge Barracks opposite Hyde Park. The buildings were relatively new, finished barely five years previously at the end of a frantic barrack building programme across England in the wake of the fear of a British revolution. Up until then troops were billeted in small towns or villages, usually alongside a pub, so that soldiers could mix with the populace and be part of the local way of life.

Chris wasn't sure whether Knightsbridge Barracks was part of the same hectic rush to internal security as it had taken over three years to complete and was probably built in the awareness of the improvement to discipline living in a barracks had on rough soldiery.

It was home to the King's Life Guards and the imposing three-storey building had stabling on the ground floor and barracks for the men above. The officers were quartered in a separate pedimented three-storey house and he made for this now, taking the raised steps leading to the front doors two at a time. A mess servant directed him to the officer's stables alongside the riding school where he approached a uniformed riding master who directed him in turn to the quartermaster's accommodation.

The two horses in question were superb geldings, their pedigree apparent to a knowledgeable eye. Chris was used to horses having ridden frequently in his training for the GB pentathlon team. He ran his hand over each animal in turn before nodding at the quartermaster. "How much?"

The man shrugged. "I have been asked to obtain the best price I may, Colonel. The young lieutenant's family are wealthy and in no need of recompense but do have an eye for the value of these animals. I am to ask for fifty pounds each, sir, to which you may add a further twenty pounds for their stabling per annum."

Chris pulled a face. Did officers barter in this day and age? "Make it a round one-hundred pounds to include a saddle and bridle and we have a deal, quartermaster."

The man rubbed his chin and gave a wry grin. "I have no doubt that will be acceptable, sir."

Chris grinned back. *He* had no doubt the man was making a few pounds of his own from the deal. In the man's cubbyhole of an office he wrote a promissory note on his account at Coutts, had a groom saddle one of the horses and rode out towards the south and Shorncliffe, on the road to a whole new and unforeseeable future.

22

Lieutenant-colonel Charles Stewart, the first commanding officer of the first battalion of the Corps of Riflemen, met Chris like a long-lost brother. They had fought together at the battle of Ferrol and he had been hit in the chest by a Spanish musket ball. He still showed signs of his injury in the way he carried himself but bore the pain with stoicism.

"Ha! Lennox, by all that's holy. Welcome back to Shorncliffe camp, my friend."

"Of necessity a short visit, Colonel Stewart, I have come to hand my position with the Rifles to General Moore as I have duties elsewhere."

"The devil you say, sir. You will be sorely missed within the corps."

"What of you, Stewart, how do you fare?"

"Tolerably, sir, tolerably. Your ministrations aboard the *Aquilon* on our return voyage did save me from worse privations, of that I am convinced. Your native medicines are a boon, sir. The surgeons could find no sign of infection on their examination of me at Portsmouth."

"You have been recalled to the corps, I see. You are fit to undertake your duties then."

Stewart made a dismissive gesture. "It is of no consequence. I would rather be soldiering than taking my seat in that bear pit of parliament which would have been my fate had not the call come to return to arms.

"You seem hale and hearty, sir. I do believe marriage becomes you."

Chris laughed. "So you have heard the good news."

"My congratulations, sir, you are a lucky dog. You could not have chosen a finer filly to ride. But be easy on the spur and crop. The little I know of the lady convinces me that she will not abide too strong a hand."

"As usual your reading of character cannot be faulted, Colonel. We are well matched."

Stewart nodded. "I would say so. Now, sir, to what do we owe the honour of your visit as you must be aware that General Moore has not yet taken his post."

"Firstly I needed to see you, my good friend, to enquire after your health. Secondly I am expecting that despatch from London that comes in your name that I wrote to you about and lastly to hand you these orders from Horse Guards and say goodbye to the Rifles that will not be leaving with me."

Stewart frowned. "You are taking soldiery from the corps?"

Chris nodded. "It's in the orders, sir. I am to relieve you of much of your training cadre who will be detached to barracks in Knightsbridge for the foreseeable future."

"And who is to bear the cost? Are they still to be on my roster."

"The Duke of Devonshire has that honour at present but the cost will now be borne by the Exchequer. I am sure the duke will be glad that the burden of £1500 per annum will be removed from his shoulders," Chris said.

Stewart gave a knowing smile. "I durst say he would not notice such a trifling amount, he would wager as much on a single turn of the cards. Now sir, this despatch you are so eager to receive which was addressed to me. I am much intrigued to hear of its content."

"It has arrived then?"

"Some days past. I have left it sealed awaiting your arrival. Is it something of which I should be made aware?"

Chris waved to some chairs, they may as well be comfortable as the explanation could take some time. He ran over the sequence of events at the Fleet Street inn and his suspicions that the two thugs were more than just footpads. Lloyd's letter might go someway in clearing up the mystery, if indeed there was one.

Stewart pursed his lips as he took in the story. "And this man Lloyd, he is to be trusted? The scandal sheets are prone to disloyalty bordering on downright insurrection and should be taxed beyond the means of the common populace lest they be infected by such. You are sure the fellow is sound."

"I believe so. He told me he worked for the *London Gazette* and seemed ink-stained enough to convince me of the truth of it. If anyone could discover the identities and motives of the two thugs, it would be a newspaperman."

"Now you confuse me, sir. Your terminology has turned to the unusual once again. What are thugs and newspaperman?"

Chris smiled an apology. I'm sorry, sir. They are terms I picked up in my travels. Thug is the short form of Thuggee. It is a man who is a member of a murderous cult of professional robbers and murderers in India infamous for assassination by strangulation."

Stewart ran a finger inside his tight collar and grimaced. "A terrible death to be sure."

Chris nodded. "Thugs have been preying on travellers for centuries and the British will need to control them as they are becoming an ever more serious problem. The name is used as a label for anyone who uses violence in a criminal act. Now the second term I picked up in the

Americas refers to an employee of a magazine or news sheet such as *The Times, The Morning Post* or, indeed, *The London Gazette.*"

"Your erudition continues to amaze, sir. I have the despatch in my quarters." Stewart raised a hand and instructed an orderly to fetch the letter. He was back within minutes and handed the folded paper to Stewart who handed it on to Chris.

Chris broke the seal and opened the paper. The writing was thin and spidery and took him a few seconds to decipher.

Stewart was growing impatient. "Well, sir?"

"Listen to this. I'll leave out the salutation as it runs to over a line.

'I wish to make you privy to the intelligence you requested as to the identities and manners of the two men who did so scandalously attack you at the inn on Fleet Street.

The first brute gave his name as Patrick Shaunessy, an Irish person who was known to the magistrate for common affray. The second gave his name as Timothy Donegan, again of Irish nationality. Both men have been convicted and sentenced most severely for their crime, sent firstly to the prison hulk at Woolwich and thence to transportation to the Australias.

I did make it my business to enquire most diligently as to their motives and one of their jailers, for the small recompense of one shilling, did elicit an answer from Donegan that the word is out in the Irish community to keep a watchful eye for any man wearing a uniform of green and to take such a person to a place near the new construction of docks in Wapping for the purpose of enquiring of where such other men may be found. On being pressed more assiduously by my confidante, Donegan did give up the tale that he had heard that the French would pay handsomely for such intelligence.

I trust, sir, that this news is of use to you. I remain etc.'

Chris put the letter down and looked at Stewart. "A story so obviously beaten from the man but still interesting, don't you think?"

"I cannot make hind nor tail of it, Lennox. Do you have any such inkling?"

"It seems to me that we green backs tweaked Bonaparte's nose so strongly in Portugal that he seeks news of us. That the Irish are involved has rather more sinister connotations than I care to imagine. Something is afoot, Stewart and you must ensure your piquet and sentries are kept alert. As for me, I will write General Moore some suggestions on training and tactics that he may find of use. After, with your permission, I will select my chosen men for their detached duties and issue orders for them to travel to Knightsbridge as soon as is possible. I must swiftly return to London myself. There is a storm brewing, I can feel it."

23

It had taken Chris longer than he thought to choose and organise his men. Some had been reluctant to leave Shorncliffe as their wives and children were living nearby and he had given them the option of volunteering for detached duties. Biggin of course was the first to volunteer along with another old comrade, Serjeant-major Pocock who had been with them in Portugal but not at Ferrol. He was now keen to make up for his previous absence. Between the three of them, they mustered another twenty-seven riflemen, most of whom were single and most of whom had fought with them in Portugal. Before he left Chris made sure that they were all kitted out in fresh uniforms. It would not do for the Corps of Riflemen to be seen in London in the threadbare clothing they normally wore.

The seven days were almost up as Chris rode back into Knightsbridge barracks. He was quartered in the officer's mess for the time being, which was an easy walk to Downing Street and to Horse Guards. He wrote notes to Henry Wadman and to the First Lord of the Treasury, William Pitt, informing them of his return. He then wrote to Catherine assuring her he was about to embark on finding them a house.

There was something else at the back of his mind but he put it aside for the time being as he wrote yet another note to Lloyd at the *London Gazette* and enclosed a guinea. One pound for the original sovereign he had promised plus another shilling to repay the amount spent on the prison guard. It seemed that Lloyd was not averse to a little chicanery when the need arose and he was worth keeping sweet. A useful ally in a strange new world of intrigue.

The next morning, at breakfast, he received notes from both Henry and Pitt. The first was requesting his attendance at Horse Guards that morning and the latter also requesting his presence at 10 Downing Street that same afternoon. He guessed that the timing of both wasn't unplanned and that Henry would brief him before his meeting with Pitt.

The days were turning cooler and wetter as the year passed into October and he covered his uniform with a riding cloak for his walk to Horse Guards. He wore his infantry sabre on his left hip and again carried his Glock 17 in the small of his back. His hand had almost completely returned to normal and he had no qualms over defending himself should the need arise. The Glock was an insurance policy but would beg too many questions if ever seen in use. He had used it at Ferrol when it had saved Biggin's life. He had sworn Biggin to secrecy with the yarn that the pistol was a secret new device with flaws that prevented its revelation. Whether Biggin had believed him was a moot point but the man was grateful for being spared a Spanish bayonet and had kept his word, never once mentioning it again.

Chris mulled this over as he strode towards Whitehall and it reminded him of his thought of the night before and a possibility of making his own fortune. He was still musing on the possibilities when he reached Henry's office but was quickly brought down to earth by the look on the other man's face.

"Come in, sir. Time is short and there is much to discuss. There is devilry afoot."

*

Grant had made the slow journey to Paris and the squalid house on the Rue de Rampart on the very edge of the city's mediaeval fortifications. He reached the solid oak door with its rusted hinges and knocked hard three times before pausing and knocking twice again. The door squealed open and a suspicious eye peered at him through the narrow crack.

"Oui, que veux-tu?" The voice was as unwelcoming as the eye.

Grant grunted and leaned his weight against the door. "Don't play games, it's me, Grant. I want to see Coileán Leech."

The door swung open on reluctant hinges. "Grant is it? You shoulda, said before yers hammered on the door."

Grant gave the man a withering look. "And announce my presence to the whole street. Get aside. Where's Coileán to be found?"

"At the back and he's not in the best o' tempers. He's heard that the British have stitched up a deal wi' the Danes and there be no money comin' from the French for the botched assassination. You'd best be havin' a care, James Grant."

Grant snorted and pushed his way along the stinking passage to the rear of the house. Weak sunlight was filtering through soot grimed windows and he could just make out a man sitting by a table piled with papers. He was smoking a long stemmed clay pipe but the upper part of his face and head was covered with a black mask and hood. Grant had never seen the whole of Coileán Leech's face and, he suspected, he never would.

Leech took a long draw and allowed smoke to trickle out of his nostrils. "What happened in Copenhagen?"

Grant kicked a stool to one side and sat on it. He was used to Leech's foul tempers. "We were surprised by British soldiers dressed in green. They mowed us down like a scythe on corn."

Leech's mouth showed a twitch of interest. "Green, you say. You are certain?"

"Aye, better than a dozen of 'em. Shootin' like I never did before see. Felled our boys quick as a wink. I was lucky to make it away meself. But what's this about a failed assassination? I saw the British plenipotentiary with a hole in his gut the size of a guinea."

Leech put his pipe down on the table where it smouldered. "The man somehow survived the shot. He was further able to browbeat the Danes into submission over the *Freya* incident. A whole year's work gone for nothing. The French and Russians will need to start all over again to get the Danes to agree to join their alliance.

"That is in the past and we must learn from it. Our French allies have expressed an interest in learning more of these green men. I have put word around in London to keep a vigilant eye open for any sighting of them. I have since received word that two of our people were recently tried for attacking an officer wearing a green tunic in Fleet Street but were bettered and arrested."

Grant showed his teeth. "I would dearly love to gain a measure of revenge on those green men for the hurt they did cause our Grey Wolves."

Leech nodded. "Then you shall be away to London to discover more of them." He shuffled some papers and pulled out two sealed packages. "Firstly you must advance our cause; do not let your thirst for vengeance cloud our real purpose. These are my plans for the future harassment of the British government. You must commit them to memory and destroy them, James, for it would not do for the contents to fall into the enemy's hands. Follow those orders closely and we shall have our own government of Ireland or the British will rue the day they ever stood against us."

24

Chris dropped his cloak in a corner and found a chair. The serious look on Henry's face prevented him from giving the normal polite greeting. "Fire away, sir. I'm listening."

Henry waved a hand over his desk. "Reports from Ireland, from Dublin in the main, that many Irishmen have taken passage to England in recent weeks. These are men, so our spies inform us, who are deeply entwined with this league of United Irishmen. They have taken packet boats and cattle boats from both north and south of Eire, many into Scotland, to Irvine in Ayrshire where the mayor of Wigtown has become so concerned he has called upon the Lord Advocate to demand papers of all of less than genteel appearance.

"Once ashore these men cannot be distinguished from the local populace as accents are so similar in that they can rarely be distinguished one from another."

"Then we have no idea of the numbers?"

Henry shook his head. "No sir we do not. Neither do we know whence they were travelling. There have been reports of itinerant weavers moving south through the towns of Yorkshire where they may be expected to seek employment but few staying to ply their trade."

Chis chewed his lip. He was desperately trying to remember his history and had a vague memory stirring. "What do you make of it, Henry?"

"There is much political unrest over Catholic emancipation as you are no doubt aware. His Majesty the King has set his heart against it and many in parliament are of the same mind. Mr Pitt may not get his Act through parliament and I fear that there will be another rebellion."

"And you believe they may be bringing their rebellion to these shores?" Chris said.

"I believe there are many in Ireland who would be so minded and I ponder why this surge in the passage of men."

"I'm certain that your instincts are sound, Henry. You are right to be concerned. Do you have any other relevant intelligence?"

"Dribs and drabs, sir. Nothing that I can put a finger upon. There is news of a large contingent of Irish labourers working on the dock construction at Wapping. There are others at Bristol and Dover but all may be perfectly innocent of wrongdoing."

"Wapping? That's interesting. My attention has been brought to Wapping Docks recently. Has any news of this nature also come from Portsmouth or Yarmouth?"

"Yes, as you mention it. The same vague reports of additional Irishmen seeking labour at those places. Why do you ask?"

"I'm not yet sure but something is stirring in my mind. Is this the reason I was summoned to Downing Street?"

Henry waved his hand across his paper-strewn desk again. "As you may see I have much to contend with. However, it is this Irish matter which is of the gravest concern. The First Lord of the Treasury, through the offices of His Royal Highness has bidden me to enlighten you on this intelligence before your audience this past noon. I do believe Mr Pitt is concerned that any inkling that the Irish will once again rise up may finally kill any hope he may have to pass the law with regard to Catholic emancipation.

There will be little sympathy amongst the honourable members of parliament for such a law should that occur."

"Then give me everything you have on the matter. I'll study it and try to deduce what can be gathered from it. With your leave, I'll set myself in the corner of your room for the time being. I'll need a study of my own but here will make do in the meantime."

Henry gave him a tight smile. "It must needs be of a temporary nature. The generals will not agree to having a green coat in their midst. I do hear some are critical of the Corps of Riflemen and of its tactics. Some also have heard of your secondment to Downing Street's employ and do wonder at the nature of it. Twould be best for you to obtain alternative accommodation."

Chris gave him a wide smile in return. "I fully intend to make myself less than at home here, sir. My duties are such that they should be best kept from the generals' notice. I hope to secure a lodging close by for Catherine and myself which will afford the privacy required."

"As is usual you have matters well in hand, sir. I shall leave you to your perusals as I have duties elsewhere." Henry picked up several documents, bowed and left.

Chris read through the notes Henry had given him. They were reports from docks, inns and lodging houses across the country and charted the sudden increase in the Irish working population. It intrigued Chris that the majority of the sightings and reports came from around the coast, particularly where the Royal Navy had its dockyards. Chatham and Dover in Kent, Portsmouth in Hampshire, Yarmouth on the Isle of Wight, and Plymouth in Devon. Bristol in Somerset was less of a naval base but was an important trading centre.

The docks at Wapping were only just under construction but twice it had featured. Once in the note from Lloyd and now in the documents in his hand. Wapping was where the Irish thugs had been prepared to take a kidnapped green back for questioning. Maybe it would be as good a place as any to start his quest for answers.

William Pitt received him at mid afternoon. "Well, sir, you have satisfied yourself as to the value of the intelligence to which Major Wadman made you privy?"

"Yes, sir. It was an interesting accumulation of news and it has given me a place to start my own enquiries."

Pitt nodded. "Very well, you must start immediately on your duties."

Chris picked up on something in Pitt's voice. "You have other information?"

"A report newly arrived from Paris of a man with a bruised visage visiting a known haunt of this league of United Irishmen in that city. He was last seen boarding a packet boat to Dover."

"Is there any idea what business he had in Paris?"

"None, Lennox. It is rumoured that the leader of the Grey Wolves has an abode there and is in the pay of the French but none has yet seen him or know his features. I believe this man is known by the name of Coileán Leech. It may be mere myth but perhaps we should take cognisance of it."

"You seem to have an impressive intelligence gathering organisation abroad, sir."

"Would that it was as impressive within these shores, Lennox. We seem unable to account for itinerant weavers and the like once they had landed. They seem to disappear as wisps of mist on a summer morn.

"Now to other business. My secretary has made enquiries on your behalf as to the renting of the house opposite. He has the details but I believe the cost will be one-hundred and twenty pounds per annum; a sum I think you perfectly able to stand."

"Thank you, sir. It falls within my present income."

"It is as well, Lennox, for you to be close by, as your duties will indeed be arduous. Report back to me as soon as you may once the mystery of these Irishmen has been resolved."

25

Pitt's secretary had indeed been busy on his behalf. Chris wrote a promissory note for a year's rent and received the keys to 19 Downing Street. He hurried across to the house and opened the big front door. Apart from the musty smell, evidence of a lack of occupation, the place was in good condition and partially furnished which was a relief. No doubt Catherine would wish to make her mark on the property but he was confident he could leave those decisions safely in her competent hands. He was sure she would be pleased with the house with its close proximity to St James's Park which would appeal to her country upbringing and also the appeal of London society. Not for the first time in his adventures to the past, Chris wondered if some outside force was guiding his destiny.

He had begged paper, quill and ink from the secretary and now sat at a bureau to write to Catherine with the details. He then wrote to Knightsbridge for Biggin and Pocock to attend him in Downing Street as soon as they arrived. He added a codicil that all the men should wear cloaks over their uniforms until further notice and that they should only leave the barracks in groups to drink at local inns until he had need of them. It would please the grizzled veterans of the Portuguese battles who would naturally wish to take in the sights and the taverns of London but, for the moment, the risk was too great for them to venture out alone.

Turning his attention to his own situation, he had one suit of civilian clothes kept packed and wrinkled in his Bergen. He would need more clothing and quickly. There was no such thing as off-the-peg and every item would have to be tailored.

He walked back to Horse Guards to ask Henry's advice on a good tailor and dropped off his letters with a runner. Henry wasn't in his office but he was spotted by an officer who buttonholed him

"Ah, Lennox, the man of green. His Royal Highness the Duke of York has expressed a wish to see you. I was about to send a runner to Knightsbridge but you have saved me the task. Come now, the duke is impatient to have converse."

The duke was seated in his window watching a regiment of foot guards drilling on the parade ground below. He waved Chris over. "See Lennox, how our finest soldiers drill, loading and reloading their muskets until each man could do it without thought. Volley fire, Lennox. That is the way of it."

"Forgive me, Your Royal Highness, but what is lacking is the ability to shoot straight. They practise reloading over and over but do not fire a single shot."

"Ah, you and your rifles, Lennox. It is but a passing fancy and surely cannot take hold within the army."

"I foresee a time when a light division, let alone a regiment, will be needed as skirmishers in future conflicts, sir and the officers will need to understand the tactics to be employed. The French are already training officers at a place called Saint-Cyr and the Americans at a place called West Point. Perhaps it would be wise to institute a military college of our own to train junior officers in the new tactics. Napoleon is also raising regiments of Voltigeurs to skirmish in front of their lines and we must be able to not only contain them but better them. The rifle will give us that advantage."

"The devil you say, sir. You appear to have a prodigious knowledge of these matters. My generals do not to agree with you on those points. However, we are pleased to hear of such an idea as a military college. There is an officer, Colonel John le Marchant, who has recently opened a training college for staff officers at High Wycombe and we shall promote the benefit of such a wider establishment to him but, we believe, the cost of such will not be to the liking of parliament."

"Both they and the generals will come around to it, eventually, although it may take some years and many battles before they see the rightness of it."

"By god, sir, you are an impudent fellow to have such views at such tender years. My generals have many years of experience in battle, why should we take your word over theirs?"

"I believe, sir that you have already concluded the rifle will be an extraordinary weapon to unleash on an enemy. As much of an advantage as the longbow at Crecy and Agincourt. Your wisdom on matters military is unrivalled and you clearly see the advantages of having men trained who can use the rifle to good effect."

The duke guffawed. "Stap me, Lennox, we do believe you are turning into a toady but we concede the point and it is well taken. We much admired your campaign in Portugal and the lessons thereof that can be gleaned from it. You have a soldier's head upon those young shoulders and we do confess we have a liking for those qualities. Now, sir, how are your qualities in regard to politics?"

"I confess, sir, that I'm not much of a politician. I tend to favour action over reaction."

The duke laughed out loud. "Pon my soul. We must remember that. However, Lennox, you must learn the ways of diplomacy if you are to progress. You will need persons of rank and privilege to speak for you. We warn you now that Mr Pitt has taken you as his lackey as you are bereft of such patronage. There is only so much we can give without appearing to show favouritism and that would not do."

"You have already done more than enough for me, sir."

"And it has been noted, Lennox. However your advancement was conditional on your continued progress with the Corps of Riflemen and as you have now been seconded to Downing Street we find it ever more difficult to persuade others in Horse Guards that your stipend is well spent."

Chris could see the way the conversation was going. "How, sir, could I convince them otherwise?"

"Continue to prove of value to us at Horse Guards. Perhaps if you would apprise us of Mr Pitt's intentions."

"You wish me to spy on the First Lord of the Treasury?"

"Come, sir. Spy? That is such a dreadful word that does not become you. No, we wish to be kept informed as to the nature of your secondment and how it progresses. Merely to ensure that Horse Guards may be ready to assist should the need arise."

"I have heard that His Majesty and Mr Pitt don't see eye to eye on the Irish question."

The duke suddenly turned less affable. "Be of care, sir. We do not take kindly to His Majesty's name being bandied in idle converse."

"My apologies, sir. I had no wish to appear to insult His Majesty, I was merely attempting, clumsily, to ascertain Horse Guard's intent."

The duke's voice dropped to a growl. "We were wrong about you, Lennox. Diplomacy is not foreign to you. We believe you have already divined our intent and we wish you to concur in it."

Chris gave a slow nod. He was caught between a rock and a hard place. He knew the piper was about to be paid for the duke's largesse and as much as it pained him, he could see no way out. He would have to play along and hope that somewhere along the line he wouldn't slip up. He could ill-afford to fall foul of the duke and he did not want to make an enemy of William Pitt. It was a game he would need to play very carefully.

He bowed to the duke. "Your instructions are noted, sir. Now, would you be so kind as to recommend a good tailor?"

26

The duke had returned to his earlier good humour as he assumed Chris had bowed to his wishes and recommended a tailor called Meyer on Cork Street in Mayfair, near to Savile Row. Meyers were known for their uniforms but also did a good line in gentlemen's attire, so the duke assured him.

He returned to Henry's room and called a runner to go to Knightsbridge and retrieve his kit from the officers' mess and deliver it to 19 Downing Street. He had decided to take up residence immediately and work from there without any distractions. He left a note for Henry and took the short walk to what he now regarded as home. The house sat, rather forlornly due to its outwardly neglected appearance, between number 18, occupied by the Colonial Office, and number 20 where the Tithe Commission resided. It was still privately owned although much of the rest of the street had been purchased by the government.

The implied threat from the duke that he could lose his income, weighed on his mind and he decided to put some plans in place in case of emergencies. Much of what he remembered about the commerce of the 19th century was centred around the second industrial revolution and the railways, both many years in the future and not something to give him an immediate return on investment. He could try gambling at Lloyds of London or on commodities but neither were safe bets given his sketchy knowledge. He knew that the electric battery had already been invented by the Italian, Volta, that steam engines were already in use in the first industrial revolution and factories were springing up around major cities in the north. Tea was heavily taxed and he was never going to invest in the Caribbean sugar trade as it involved so much slave labour. It was down to that which he really did know about, military history and firearms. He knew where he could place large bets on forthcoming battles and major political events that would give him a future income. He could patent the complete brass cartridge, the Martini and bolt actions for breech loading weapons, and the revolver and put the drawings into escrow. Finally he could buy up small pockets of land where he knew major developments would happen in future, thereby securing an income for years to come. It would be classed as insider trading in his own century but with Britain's aggressive laissez faire trading policy of the times, it was fair game.

First he had to outline a plan of action against the Grey Wolves, ready to put to Biggin and Pocock when they arrived. He had an idea in his head and firmed it up as he wrote. His knowledge of history again playing a big part in his decisions. History warned him where the Irish would strike and he had a good idea when. It was going to be a case of hitting first and hitting hard to take the sting out of the United Irishmen's plot.

Satisfied with his work he settled down to plan his own projects.

Biggin and Pocock arrived early the next morning, both wrapped, as instructed, in riding cloaks borrowed from the cavalry. It was raining and they shook the water from their shoulders in the large hallway before being shown into the drawing room.

Chris offered his hand to both men and they took it gladly; they were old comrades and had the measure of each other with mutual esteem.

"We have a task, Serjeant-majors," Chris began. "It is not an easy task and not one that can be trumpeted, nor one that will earn us fame or fortune. It falls once again to the Corps of Riflemen to break new ground.

"The First Lord of the Treasury has requested that we find and confront the league of United Irishmen in this country as it is believed they plan a coup of some kind. I have written out my orders." He handed the notes to Biggin.

"You may read them at a later time. How many Irish do we have in our cadre here at Knightsbridge?"

Pocock held up his hand. "Three, sir, a number that includes Corporal O'Dell, the man wounded by a sabre's cut in Portugal."

Chris nodded. "I know O'Dell. Who are the others?"

"Macmahon and O'Shaunessy, both with us on the Algarve and both sound men," Pocock added.

"I know them too. As you say, sound riflemen. I will need all three to put a scheme into operation. Have them report to me this afternoon. They must come here dressed in cloaks, as you have, Their green tunics must be kept hidden for now.

"You must also procure two heavy wagons and horses from the quartermaster at the barracks. I have included the requisition with your orders. Any dissent on the quartermaster's behalf should be referred to me. There should be none, but we must insist on having the wagons by tonight.

"Detach one of the younger riflemen to attend me here as a servant until I may employ others. His duties will require some ability to communicate adequately with senior officers to be able to pass messages and to be able to judge which action may be necessary at which time. In short, a man who can think for himself."

"I know of such a one," Biggin said. "A callow youth of seventeen years who has the nerve to speak back to the old hands. More than once I have offered him the back of my hand but he merely laughs. Impudence is ingrained in him but he is a fine shot for a Johnny Newcome and a good clean soldier who volunteered to be with us."

Chris grinned. "He sounds an ideal choice. Send him with the Irish soldiers. He is to bring his rifle hidden beneath his cloak but the others just two pistols apiece along with their sword bayonets."

The two old soldiers left grinning to each other at the thought of imminent action. Neither yet knew what was about to take place but both were anxious to get back into any sort of fight after so long on training duties.

Chris left shortly after them and made his way to Meyers. He was shown into the fitting room where a young man was lounging on a chair with one foot up on the only other. Chris gave him a look and he sat up and dropped his foot back to the floor.

Chris removed his cloak and the man sat up straighter.

"Green, sir? You must be with the Corps of Riflemen."

"Lieutenant-colonel Lennox, sir. You are correct in your assumption. I wear the green of the Corps."

"A most unbecoming colour, sir if I may be so bold as to express that opinion."

"Your opinion may be somewhat coloured by your own gaudy attire. The green is ideal for skirmishing as the Rifles need to fight from every rock, bush and scrap of cover. Red stands out like rouge on a harlot's face."

The young man laughed good-naturedly. "By god, colonel, I believe you have bested me there. I am never too assured that the fripperies of uniform perform any function other than to provide the wearer with ample opportunity to strut and preen."

"And provide perfect targets for the French muskets."

"Practicality is less of an ideal than looking the part, sir. I was once with the hussars who must die looking at their best or it is not worth the coin."

"I am no adherent of the overly ornate, decorated or finicky." Chris said. "I prefer dress, be it civilian or military, to be essentially plain and fit for function. The French mode of dress for gentlemen with decoration, frills and lace is now passé and I prefer a good English gentlemen's country style."

"By god, sir, I believe you are correct sir. I shall see to it that my next suits will be the plainer and the better for it."

One of the tailors came in and beckoned. "Your attire is ready, sir. Your servant may collect it at your leisure."

The man climbed to his feet and bowed to Chris. "My pleasure, Colonel Lennox. May we meet again in amiable circumstance."

Chris inclined his head in return. "And your name, sir?"

"Brummell, sir. George Brummell, late of the 10th Hussars."

27

Chris had other errands to run but made it back for a quick lunch at the Rose and Crown in Downing Street before his soldiers arrived. He found a gentleman waiting for him at his steps.

"Henry Addington, Colonel, Viscount Sidmouth, at your service."

Chris raised his eyebrows; he knew who Addington was and that he would take over from Pitt as First Lord of the Treasury in a few months time. Chris saluted. "To what do I owe the honour, my Lord Sidmouth?"

"May we retire inside? I wish to enquire of certain information."

Chris showed the man into the drawing room. "My apologies for the unkempt appearance of my house, my lord, I have been in residence just a day and my wife has not yet arrived."

"The First Lord of the Treasury has apprised me of your domestic situation, Colonel. There is no need to apologise. It is about the matter with which he has charged you that I come to enquire."

Chris indicated a chair. "Will you sit, my lord?"

"I thank you but there is little need as I shall not remain long."

"Very well, my lord. You may inform Mr Pitt that I have put arrangements in hand and shall be embarking on a course of action soon. My reports will be frequent and accurate so there is little need for a lord of such eminence as yourself to call to enquire."

"Ha! I see that I have hit upon a nerve. My apologies in turn, Colonel. My friend, the First Lord of the Treasury, has much to concern him of late and this matter weighs heavily on his mind."

"I can understand Mr Pitt's concern. You may assure him that I share it and will not allow grass to grow beneath my feet. Action is imminent, but as yet there is no knowing how successfully it shall be. Only time can be the arbiter of that intelligence."

Addington gave a tilt of his head in acknowledgement. "Then I daresay he shall be pleased to learn of your diligence and will pray for your success in whatever endeavour you embark upon."

"My thanks, my lord, to Mr Pitt and to yourself."

There was a clatter on the steps outside and Chris waved a hand. "It appears that my men have arrived. You will have to forgive me if my duty now takes precedence."

Chris showed Addington to the door and just before he opened it he said, "you will take it, my lord, when it's offered."

Addington looked puzzled. "Take what, Lennox?"

Chris smiled. "I'll remind you of this conversation should we meet again in a few months time."

Addington gave him an odd look then sidled past the four riflemen bunched on the steps. Chris left the door open for them to file in behind him.

"O'Dell, Macmahon, O'Shaunessy, you have been informed as to your duties this night?

"Aye, sir," O'Dell replied, "Serjeant-major Pocock did so inform us, if it please the colonel."

"Good." He turned to the fourth soldier. "What's your name, Rifleman?"

"It be Tom Dales, your worship."

"And you have been informed of your duties?"

"Aye, sir. To be a good servant and to pay attention to my betters and not to speak out of turn."

Chris stifled a chuckle. "That will do for now. Where do you hail from, Dales?"

"Lincolnshire, your worship, from the fair city of Lincoln itself."

"One home of the Magna Carta, besieged and taken by the roundheads in the civil war. I know of it, Dales."

Dales' face lit up. "You know of Lincoln, sir?"

"A little. Enough to know that its inhabitants are loyal to the crown. I shall expect much of you in days to come so ensure you are ready to perform your duties to the best of your ability."

Dales knuckled his forehead. "Aye, as you say, your worship."

"You must call me sir, Dales, as do all the riflemen." He turned to O'Dell and the others who had been watching the exchange. "Are you all prepared for danger?"

The rain had stopped but there was a chill in the air and a thin mist that rose off the stinking waters of the Thames at Wapping in the bleak shadow of the Tower of London. Most of the buildings around were in disrepair and most in darkness except for one where weak light from candles filtered through a sackcloth curtain nailed over the small aperture. There was glass in the window but it was ingrained with decades of filth which further dulled the lights within.

Two men staggered along the cobbles dragging another, his toes bouncing on the rough surface as they walked. They reached the wide double doors of the building, an old stable, no longer fit for that purpose but now home to a gang of Irish dock labourers. One of the men dropped his part of the load, the arm flopping onto the wet road. He banged on the door, three loud thumps.

The murmur of voices that had been heard inside died away. The man banged again, louder. A voice called. "Who is it that's out there and what d'ye be wantin'?"

"We heard youse, be wantin' news of soldiers wearin' the green."

"Tis the wrong place yers have."

"The word was Wappin' docks, so twas."

"Mebbe, you did hear that but tis not here you'll be wantin'."

"Where then should we be takin' this here green coat?"

"You have a green coat with yers?"

"Aye, that we do. He's sleepin' but he'll be akickin' off soon enough so he will."

"Well you'd best be bringin' him inside, don't yers think."

Two massive bolts scraped back and the doors swung open wide enough to admit them. The room was big with the former stalls filled with trestle tables and cooking utensils, smoke hung thick in the air. Straw was piled up in corners as makeshift beds. People gathered together to stare at the newcomers. Mostly men but with one or two women working over braziers. There was a loft at the back, reached by a ladder. It was in darkness but vague shapes could be seen seated around a rough table. Someone called from there.

"Get some light to them, let the dog see the rabbit."

An oil lamp was lit and held aloft above the three men in the doorway. Two, roughly dressed in soiled working clothes with heavy coats, dragged in the third. The light glowed on his green jacket.

"By all that's holy. A green coat to be sure," the voice called. Where'd you lads find him?"

The two men dropped their load on the rough floor. "Drinkin' at an Inn wi his mates. We got 'im when he went outside ta piss. What's the reward?"

28

James Grant stirred in the shadows of the loft. His face was still showing the bruise from his fractured cheek and it hurt him to eat. It was that which was uppermost in his mind as the hammering on the door began. The Grey Wolves around him reached for their weapons and looked to him for guidance. He waved a hand to calm them; they were all jittery as the time for action was approaching. He could see the head of the workmen's leader turned towards him and he nodded as three more loud thumps echoed through the building.

He listened as the verbal exchange went on and stiffened as the news of the captive seeped through. Finding the green men was of little consequence to him other than the need for revenge; for the time being he had bigger fish to fry but Leech had specifically requested news of them and it was not something he could easily ignore. He nodded his approval and a Grey Wolf beside him called down for the lamp to be lit. He strained his neck with everyone else as the light shone on the green jacket of the man supine on the filthy floor.

The call for a reward brought a grim smile to his lips. He stood and peered down. "You'll be pleased to leave here with your worthless skins on your backs if you've killed him. We need a live one."

One man touched his cap. "He be alive, your lordship. Twas only a little tap on the noggin I be givin' 'im."

The stable door was still partially open and light from the lamp spilled out onto the cobbles. A figure materialised in the light, pointed a finger and screamed. "Murder, tis murder, help, help."

"Get him!" Grant yelled, "Afore he can bring help."

The figure ran, followed by many of the men on the ground floor brandishing cudgels and knives. There were only two or three men left with the women and the two strangers with their captive. Grant led the Grey Wolves down the ladder and they spread out across the floor.

Grant pointed at the body. "Turn 'im over will yers, let's be getting' a good look at 'im."

One of the men grinned at him showing his tobacco stained teeth. "It's not a sight you'll be wanting to see." He pulled aside his coat and pulled a pistol from a pocket, his companion did the same as the captive rolled over and showed a pair of pistols of his own. Outside there was a fusillade of rifle fire that brought all the Grey Wolves' heads up.

"You're taken," Chris said from the floor. "Surrender or you will die."

Grant screamed and the Grey Wolves lurched forward. Four pistols exploded and four men dropped but the others were on to the Riflemen with swords and clubs.

Chris leapt to his feet and drew his sabre in time to parry a wild swing from a sword and punch the man in the face with the sabre's hilt. His two soldiers, both veterans of close quarter combat, pulled their sword bayonets and closed together on either side. They used their pistols as clubs and battered heads and stabbed limbs as they fought off the frenzied assault. Boots rattled on cobbles and a group of riflemen entered the fray led by Biggin who soon forced back the Irishmen until their line broke and they ran for the back of the stables.

"Keep after them," Chris yelled. "I want every man jack of them caught."

He dusted himself down and walked into the street. At either end a large wagon was pulled across the width of the road. The horses' hooves and iron wheel rims were bound with sackcloth to dull their noise and the canvas was rolled up on the sides where the riflemen had engaged the mob from the stable. Some bodies were strewn on the ground and others stood in a forlorn group with hawk faced riflemen keeping watch.

Pocock approached and saluted. "We have them in the main, sir. Some slipped the cordon but most were caught or shot."

Rifle fire sounded in the distance and Chris grimaced. "And some still run. Use the bugle and recall the men. It's too dark to search and I don't want them separated from each other and taken down."

Pocock hurried off and the bugle's clear notes sounded the recall. His men were skirmishers and they were good but in the black alleyways of London they were at a disadvantage. He called to Pocock. "Hold the survivors here until I'm back from the stable. I need to get a good look at those we have inside first."

Biggin had already pulled the dead Grey Wolves to one side and had a guard mounted on the survivors. Chris eyed the sullen group, some bleeding from wounds, one still unconscious. "Who is your leader?"

One man, holding an arm with a nasty cut looked up and spat. "Long gone, you bastard."

"Take this man outside and shoot him, Serjeant-major."

Biggin grinned. "Aye, sir. You two," he pointed at two riflemen, "you heard the officer, take him out and finish him."

"Twill be a pleasure," Macmahon said as he and O'Shaunessy pulled the man to his feet. His eyes went round with terror as he was pulled out screaming. A single shot sounded and the screaming stopped.

Chris eased a thumb around his belt in a nonchalant gesture. "Now I shall ask again. Who is your leader?"

There was no reply and each Grey Wolf glared at him defiantly as he looked each of them in the face. "Take this one next," he pointed to a man with a scar on his face that ran from his cheek to his jaw.

O'Dell, who had been the man in the doorway shouting murder, shoved his bayonet under the man's nose. "On yer feet, yer spalpeen or I'll give it to yers where yer sit."

The man spat. "Tis murder you be doin'."

"Summary execution of traitors," Chris said, "and I'll keep doing it until either I'm told what I wish to know or you are all dead."

The man looked shifty and glanced at his companions who would not meet his gaze. O'Dell jerked his bayonet up in an unmistakeable gesture.

"All right, keep your hair on. I'm in no rush to meet my end, so I'm not but I not be talkin' to youse or anyone else."

"Fair enough," Chris said. "Take him out."

The same two grinning riflemen pulled the man to his feet and marched the man outside. He went quietly at first but yelled "I die for Ireland," before a shot cracked out.

The three remaining conscious Grey Wolves shuffled and looked at one another.

"You can't be doin' this," one said.

"I *am* doing it," Chris replied. "And at the risk of repeating myself, I shall continue to do so until I have what I need. Are you to be next, sir?"

"The man is known to us as James Grant," a second man said.

"He be well away from here," the third said. "You'll not catch him, he be too fly for youse."

Chris looked from one to the other. "Away to where? Bristol, is it?"

From the look on their faces he knew he had struck a chord.

29

The dumbstruck looks grew even more comical as O'Dell marched the previous two Grey Wolves back into the stables at the point of a bayonet. Both were red in the face, bound and tightly gagged. Chris enjoyed the amazed disbelief for a few seconds. The old Hollywood cliché might not have worked in the 21st century but the ruse had the desired effect on these men.

"James Grant is the man with the discoloured face, I assume, the one who ran as soon as the fighting began and left you to fend for yourselves."

"Twas the plan," the first man said, "that he should make good his escape in such a happening as this and take with him his lieutenants to fight another day."

"Another day in Bristol, it would appear. You may thank your lucky stars that I'm not the murdering kind but your lives are still forfeit. It will be the hangman's noose for your treachery."

"We fight for Ireland and the right for Catholics to choose who governs us."

"Ireland will now be part of the union with England and Scotland which makes your actions treason. Whatever your excuses that is unforgiveable."

"We fight for Ireland. Your new laws will make little difference as good Irishmen are ever ground under the thumb of English tyranny," the second man said.

"And you bring your fight to our shores, do you?"

"To show that we cannot be treated with impunity," the third man added. *"And there is nought you may do to stave off the hour of our destiny."*

*

Grant and his three remaining lieutenants slid through the dark alleyways, heading north to a more populated area where they could more easily disappear.

He had recognised the man in green, the very same man who had led the ambush against them in Copenhagen. He remembered the tall figure who had advanced on the carriage as he lay in the dirt. The blow to his face had dazed him and made his eyes water but there was no mistaking the size and build of the man who carried a sabre as if born to carry one. He had barely glimpsed the face under the shako but it was one he would never forget. It was one and the same; he was certain of it.

Breathless from their flight the five men paused by the entrance of yet another alley to listen for any sound of pursuit. Grant had learned that much from his flight in Copenhagen. The night was still, apart from the sounds of raucous laughter from a nearby tavern where yellow light spilled from a partially open doorway.

Grant shuffled his feet. "Hear anything?"

"Only the noise of ale sliding down thirsty throats," one of the others growled.

"The alarum has yet to be given but I daresay these streets will be swarming with soldiery come the morn. We were took by surprise and I do wonder from whence the enemy received word of our hiding place."

"They knew of our quest for a green coat. Twas not wise for us to hide in so obvious a place as that where the Irish of London were bidden to take a captive."

Grant nodded in the dark. "Twas an error we shall not be repeatin'. I want each of you to fly to our Grey Wolves in Portsmouth, Yarmouth, Dover and Plymouth. Spread the word that we congregate at the farm near to Bristol where we shall put our plan in hand. Go quickly and be assembled one week hence.

There was a commotion outside the stables and Pocock poked his head around the door. "Beggin' your pardon, sir. Redcoats."

Chris nodded and spoke to Biggin. "Treat the prisoners' wounds, Serjeant-major and bind those that are capable of escape."

He didn't wait for a response but walked into the street where his regrouped riflemen were facing a company of red-coated soldiers. "Who is in command, here?" he called.

A young officer stepped forward with his sabre over one shoulder. "Lieutenant Yea, of the Seventh of Foot, sir, the Royal Fusiliers. Whom do I have the honour of addressing?"

"Ah, the Shiny Seventh. I am Lieutenant-colonel Lennox of the Corps of Riflemen, Lieutenant. Please stand your men down."

"We heard the musket fire from the London Tower close by, assumed miscreants at work and called out the guard."

"You were correct in one respect, Lieutenant. We do have miscreants in our charge and would be pleased to see them held at the Tower for the magistrates."

Yea bowed. "As you wish, sir, but of whom do you speak?"

"They are a band of renegade Irish whom we have been hunting for some days. We were led here and have made arrests in the King's name. Those behind us, at the wagon, are mostly men working at the dock construction. Others, those armed with knives and cudgels, will be handed to you for common affray. We will leave the dead for those who wish to claim them.

"Inside the building are dangerous men. Members of a secret society called the Grey Wolves. You must take especial care with them as they will try to escape at the earliest opportunity. They must be kept closely guarded as there is intrigue and danger afoot and they must not be allowed to add their weight or voices to the fight."

Chris returned to 19 Downing Street to write his report of the night's happenings for Pitt. He was met at the door by Dales who handed him a sealed letter and had a pot of hot tea waiting. Candles were lit in the drawing room and a fire was burning in the grate. The place was beginning to feel lived in again. Chris put the letter to his nose and smelled rosewater. It was from Catherine and he slit it open with a thumb. He took it to the nearest candles and read the neat script that informed him she would be arriving in Downing Street two days hence and he should be prepared to receive a wagon beforetimes.

Chris grinned. He wasn't surprised how much the letter reminded him he missed her. Dales offered him some tea. He smiled his thanks and took the teacup from Dales' hand. "How did you come by this, rifleman?"

Dales gave him a cheeky smile. "I did strike up a friendship with the kitchen maid at the Rose and Crown, sir. I did get the makings from her with the wood and coal for the fire."

"Top marks for scrounging, Dales. Tomorrow I'll show you how we take our tea where I'm from, with milk and sugar. We call it a brew."

Dales scratched his head. "With *milk*?"

My wife will be arriving to take up residence soon. I want you to find servants to clean the house from top to bottom and have it ready for the day after tomorrow. A wagon will also be arriving with a household in it I daresay. Be prepared to receive it."

"I shall do my best, sir, even though tis out of my experience."

"You'll cope." Chris grinned and waved him away. He had some thinking to do. The savage remark from the Grey Wolf disturbed him. History recorded that the United Irishmen had planned an attack on the docks in Bristol, that hadn't been a surprise but the way the man had said his piece with utter contempt and conviction worried him. Was he missing something?

30

Chris finished his report the next morning and dropped it into Number 10 on his way to Meyers to have a final fitting for the three suits he had ordered. It amused him that 'Beau' Brummell had been there and he had set the man's mind on future fashion trends. It would be some time before the dandy would rise to fame as the confidante of the Prince Regent and earn the title of 'Beau' but he felt sure the scene had been set by his remarks. It seemed to him that he was changing history into what would be accepted in his own time and not changing history into something he would not recognise when and if he returned. Time travel was a very complex thing and the feeling that it was pre-ordained comforted him.

He left Meyers and walked to Brooks's Club in St James's Street. Not being a member, he enquired at the door whether the Duke of Devonshire or Colonel Stewart were in residence and was relieved to hear that the duke was sitting in his normal seat by the fire.

He was shown in and William Cavendish, the fifth Duke of Devonshire, rose to meet him with a wide smile of welcome.

"Lennox, by god, sir. I am pleased to renew our acquaintance. How fare you?"

Chris bowed and returned the smile. "Well, your grace and I hope I find you so."

"Sit, sit, dear boy. Partake in a glass of port."

Chris held up his hand. "My thanks, sir, but it is a little early for me."

"Nonsense. Tis never too early for good port." He waved over a servant and ordered two glasses of the fortified wine. "Now, Lennox, I deduce you have a reason for seeking me out. More intelligence? I am greatly in your debt for introducing me to the gun maker, Ezekial Baker, and for relieving me of the burden of your £1,500 per annum for the victualing of your Corps of Riflemen. I trust you have more good news."

"There are some things that may be to your advantage if you are keen on a wager."

Cavendish beamed. "A wager, by god. That tis greatly to my liking. On what shall we wager?"

"I'm not a member of this club. I have a proposition that you will wager on my behalf."

"Indeed, sir. I could propose you for membership; none would blackball a nominee of mine. But perhaps I discern a deeper reasoning."

"Perhaps you do, your grace. I am now engaged on duties for First Lord of the Treasury Pitt. As such, I am privy to certain information not yet in the public domain. This information gives me the ability to make certain assumptions on future events. I hasten to add that these assumptions are not bound to occur and are mere possibilities. I would wish to wager on them coming to pass but my association with Mr Pitt may make it appear that these are less than assumptions and not worth the candle to wager on."

Cavendish leaned back in his chair with a calculating gleam in his eye. "You say that these assumptions are based on nothing but your reading of the runes?"

"That's correct, sir. They are merely my interpretation of that which might or might not occur in the coming months."

"And what are these assumptions, Lennox. I cannot agree to something about which I know nothing."

Chris pulled a paper from his pocket. "I have written down five occurrences that I consider to be possibilities."

Cavendish took the paper and held it to the light of the fire. His jaw dropped. "The very devil you say, sir. How come you by these assumptions?"

Chris knew he had some explaining to do and was prepared for it. "The first item, that First Lord of the Treasury Pitt would resign in the New Year, is based on his inability to persuade His Majesty over the issue of Catholic emancipation in Ireland. Having met Mr Pitt I have concluded he is a man of honour who will resign over the issue. Secondly, having also met his lordship, Viscount Sidmouth, I do believe him best placed to succeed Mr Pitt.

Cavendish snorted. "I also know Sidmouth and am assured he would not take such a position."

"Therein lies the wager, your grace."

"Yes, I see the way of it but you will be risking a heavy loss as many in Brooks's will be of a similar opinion to mine."

"I like the odds, sir."

"And will you be wagering more than your customary one-hundred guineas?"

"We will come to that. The third item wagers that the navy will attack Copenhagen in April of next year."

Another unlikely outcome, sir, as an accord was so recently reached."

"Perhaps, sir. The fourth item. You may know that Bonaparte left Egypt in something of bad odour and did abandon his army there. I wager that come March, before the hot weather sets in, the British will set about the French in Cairo."

Cavendish nodded. "A possibility. Now what of this final item. How could you think such a thing, sir?"

"The death of Tsar Paul of Russia? My reading of the politics of nations is such that I believe that the Tsar is becoming increasingly unpopular with his own people and has dug himself into an untenable position with the French. Knowing at first hand of their penchant for assassination it may be as likely an outcome as any."

"It is a monstrous assumption, there is no doubt of it. There is also little doubt that these wagers will appeal to the rakes of this establishment. Now sir, what is your proposal?"

"I'll wager two-hundred guineas on each assumption and will accept up to ten to oppose it at a cost of just two-hundred guineas each, or a maximum of two-thousand guineas from any one person. That will limit my indebtedness to two-thousand guineas for each wager. I have no wish to bankrupt myself or to cause hardship to any other man."

"Pah, sir. These are paltry sums but knowing of your wish not to make enemies over gambling I see it as an honourable proposal and I will carry the book on it. I may wager myself and I do believe there is a chance I can gain some modicum of satisfaction from besting you in this. I am still smarting over the spin of the coin that did cost me one-hundred and twenty guineas."

Chris grinned at the memory. "I did warn you then, sir that I would normally only bet on certainties. Coin spinning is a matter of physics. The head side weighs heavier than the tail and it would fall to the bottom eight times out of ten."

"These wagers then be more metaphysics and open to chance. I admire your spirit, Lennox but for the life of me, I cannot divine your true motive in this. However, one part of me wishes you success in your machinations and another part wishes otherwise if I am to take some of my own satisfaction from it. Now, sir, drink your port. Make a toast to your own success and I will drink to mine."

Chris raised his glass and made a silent wish that his meddling would not somehow change history over the next few months.

31

When he returned to Downing Street that afternoon, Chris found a large heavy wagon outside his house with two beefy men carrying furniture up the steps. Catherine's maid, Esther, met him at the door and dropped a deep curtsey.

"Hello, Esther. I wasn't expecting you today."

"Mrs Lennox did send me with the cart if it please you, sir, to prepare for her arrival on the morrow. I am to ensure that her wishes with regard to the household are met."

Chris grinned. "Then I shall leave you to it, Esther. Do you require any assistance?"

"No, sir, I thank you, but the boy that is here did have servants in hand with mop and bucket. Matthew too has been given leave by Sir George Wadman to be of assistance and he is within, guiding the labours."

"Thank you, Esther, you may go about your duties. I shall be in the withdrawing room."

"The boy, sir, does have letters for you. He asked that should I meet with you I should pass on the message."

"And where is Dales to be found?"

"He retired to the Rose and Crown, sir. Should I send for him there?"

"No, it's just a few paces. I'll find him."

Esther curtsied again. "As you wish, Colonel Lennox."

Dales was nowhere to be seen in the bar but an enquiry from the landlord discovered that he was in the kitchen. He was called out and stood beside Chris as he sat at a table.

"You have letters for me, Dales?"

"Indeed, sir, I do sir. One from across the road at Number 10 and another from a runner from Horse Guards."

Chris held out his hand and Dales fumbled in his pouch for the two sealed notes. "These 'ere letters, sir. I thought it unwise to leave them at the house with strangers inside."

Chris raised his eyebrows. "Do strangers steal other men's mail in Lincoln, Dales?"

"No, sir, indeed they do not, sir. The Serjeant-major did say that none should know of our work. I thought it best that these letters be kept on my person, sir. Did I do wrong, sir?"

Chris shook his head. "No, you were quite correct. You have a head on those shoulders, Dales. Can you read?"

The boy grinned. "I knows my alphabet, sir and my numbers up to one-hundred."

Chris smiled back. "That's a start. I'll arrange for you to have reading and writing lessons, Dales. It could prove useful in future."

"Thankee, sir but …"

"No buts. I'll pay for the lessons. I believe my soldiers should all learn the basics of literacy and numeracy. It is a point I shall make to General Moore and Colonel Stewart. I'm quite prepared to put my money into your education as I believe you will benefit from it. Now, close your mouth and hand me those notes."

Dales, whose mouth had dropped open at the thought of going back to school, closed it and sheepishly passed the notes to Chris.

"Take a seat at the next table while I read these," Chris ordered, "I may need to send a reply." He broke the seal on the note from Number 10 and read that Pitt wished to see him later that afternoon. The other note was from Henry who wanted to see him as soon as possible on a matter of urgency. Chris sighed, put any thought of a late lunch from his mind and stood. "Dales, run across to Number 10 with my compliments to say that I shall call upon the First Lord at four-o-clock this afternoon. Be sure to mind your manners. I am going to Horse Guards now. Inform my wife's maid, Esther, that I shall not be back for some while and she is to ensure that she, Matthew and yourself have food and drink for this evening and to stock the larder in readiness for Mrs Lennox's arrival."

Dales knuckled his forehead. "I do believe the maid did bring such things in the wagon, sir but I will pass on your wishes." He turned and ran out.

Chris followed at a more leisurely pace and walked to Horse Guards. Henry was in his room and gave Chris a grim wave of acknowledgement as he opened the door.

"Ha, sir. I have news."

"So I assumed. Bad news?"

"In truth I know not what to make of it."

Chris tossed his cloak over the back of a chair. "Perhaps I can help you decipher it."

"If anyone can tis you, Lennox," Henry said. "These despatches were sent overnight from our men watching the Irish at the ports. It appears there is something afoot." He handed Chris the notes and he quickly read them.

"Portsmouth, Yarmouth and Dover. Nothing yet from Plymouth?"

"No, nor from Bristol. Perhaps the riders are to horse as we speak, the distances are greater."

Chris nodded. "It appears that these Irish communities have received visitors recently and the men have been called to meetings, the word spread immediately amongst them. I would conclude that whatever the message it was an urgent one. It's a pity our men could not gain entry to these gatherings."

"Indeed, sir," Henry said. "But as to the gatherings, it appears that they did not disband afterwards and that the groups stayed ensconced together. What make you of it?"

"I suspect more will become apparent in the next day or so, but, if I were to hazard a guess, I would surmise that there is trouble brewing and it won't be long in the coming."

"Should we take action now, afore this trouble presents itself?"

"We can't jump the gun, Henry. There is no proof that there is anything untoward or amiss. Our suspicions are not enough to convince a magistrate of evil intent. We need to watch these groups carefully and be ready when they do reveal themselves in their true colours."

"Tis hard to stand idle by as men such as these do conspire against us."

"I agree but let's wait until we hear from either Plymouth or Bristol before we rush to judgement. If what I fear is correct, we should then have an indication of where to act should it come to it."

"What is it then that you fear, Lennox? Do you have some foreknowledge, some intelligence with regard to this that you may confide?"

Chris frowned. If his memory of history was correct he knew what was about to happen, a least what was planned to happen, but how to phrase it so that it did not appear that he already knew or that he was barking mad. "Since I first heard that the Irish were grouping around the docks and that their numbers were increased by men from Ireland, I have had the suspicion that they intend to attack a naval installation somewhere on the south coast.

Bonaparte fears the Royal Navy and it would be a coup for him should some of our first-raters be disabled without leaving port.

"That they are so spread leads me to believe their numbers are too small to have any hope of success should they attack every port, so I believe they will group together to attack just one with large numbers to ensure success. I do not yet know if I surmise correctly, or to which port they will go, which is the reason I ask you to await despatches from Plymouth and Bristol, for, if I am right, it will be one of them or the other."

"But Bristol is but a port for commerce. Why, if you are correct, should that be included?"

"Why indeed. An *important* port for commerce, an equally appetising target in the light of our trade embargo on France and one with a soft underbelly. There will be no marines to guard it."

32

Pitt kept Chris waiting his customary half hour. If anything he looked more careworn than before and Chris could see why the man was heading for an early death. The cares of government in these turbulent times weighed heavily on him. He had Chris's report in his hand.

"Ah, Lennox, my apologies for tardiness, there is much to concern me."

"No apology necessary, sir. I'm only too aware of your responsibilities."

"Indeed, sir? You are privy to the cares of government?"

"I have been made aware of the burden you carry as First Lord of the Treasury."

"A title as long as it is burdensome. I have not brought you here to discuss the affairs of state, however. This despatch of yours makes worrysome reading. I have since had report from the 7th of Foot on the prisoners at the Tower but it seems some others did make their escape last eve, before they were apprehended."

"The man known as James Grant and some associates did not stand to fight but made their escape. Our pursuit was curtailed as I deemed it too dangerous to have my riflemen at risk in the dark alleys."

"You have a care for your soldiery beyond that which is beneficial to the Crown, sir. Had they continued their pursuit we may now have this man Grant in custody."

"Or we may have several dead riflemen. I have been after this man Grant in Copenhagen, I know he is both slippery and dangerous and that his followers are fanatical enough to give their own lives to keep him from capture. It would have been a waste of good British lives to have continued the pursuit ... sir."

"These riflemen must be allowed to earn their shilling a day, tis that for which they are paid."

"Although I understand your concern, sir, I believe that a good officer should be allowed to judge when withdrawal is more beneficial than advance. I could see no benefit accruing to the Crown to have dead soldiers and still no captive. You must let me to be the judge of the correct tactics on these occasions."

Pitt gave Chris a hard look but then sighed and sat in an armchair. "As you wish, Lennox but are we now no further forward in this other than to have miscreants locked in the Tower at a magistrate's convenience?"

"I have just returned from Horse Guards where Major Wadman has received word of movement amongst the suspect groups of Irishmen at the ports. Almost all had visitors arrive, messages passed and groups formed that remain together. I would surmise that the men that escaped us made directly for these groups to pass instructions and they are making ready to strike. Their target is as yet unclear but I believe it will be either Bristol or Plymouth. I'm awaiting further news."

"And you are prepared for what may occur? It will lay heavy on your shoulders if a tragedy did arise that may have been prevented."

"If you would be so kind as to advise their Lordships at the Admiralty that I require a fast ship to be on standby in the Thames with sailing orders for the west country, I would be obliged."

"And when would you require such a vessel?"

"At once, sir, for I believe timing will be of the essence. Would you also authorise despatches sent to the Somerset

Militia in Bristol to have men to hand should they be needed."

Pitt stroked his chin. "I believe we have the 13th of Foot garrisoned there. I will do as you ask but these orders must pass through the hands of Horse Guards. I will have my secretary draft you a request but you must raise the subject yourself with them. Leave the Admiralty to my ministrations and I will ensure that a ship is at your command when tis required.

"Do not fail me in this, Lennox for tis a dangerous game that is being played."

Coileán Leech had moved to Calais. It took over a day for the report of the battle in Wapping to reach him there and he threw the letter down in a fit of temper. His plans were being thwarted. It was as if someone was reading his mind.

Twice Grant had allowed himself to be bested, twice by soldiers wearing green. It had been foolish of Grant to use Wapping to hide in. Somehow word had leaked out and the green coats had turned the tables. The word from Grant was that it was the same officer who had led the attacks both in Copenhagen and in London. He would make it his business to discover the man's name and visit upon him a suitable retribution for the loss of so many Grey Wolves.

That was for another time. Now he needed to concentrate on the plot in hand as its climax was nearing fruition. There was much still to be done and he needed to be in England himself to ensure his orders were diligently followed. Grant was proving a less than capable commander, he was making too many mistakes but he was still useful and would provide an adequate smokescreen for the true object of his machinations.

He pulled his mask across his face and called. His doorkeeper answered in his usual surly fashion and kicked open the door to Leech's room.

Leech eyed him without warmth. The man was half French and half Irish, trusted only because of the amount he was paid to keep loyal. "Arrange for my passage to Dover, Lefevre. I shall sail on the morning tide."

Lefevre spat on the floor. "Is that all?"

Leech tossed him a small cloth bag which jingled as it was caught. "There is the passage fare, enough for six men with some extra for your trouble. Have my five compatriots board separate packets for the crossing.

"And be careful you are not followed by spies. You must ensure you are not observed in this."

"Those clods? I should see them coming from the other side of La Manche. Six passages then is it to be? All for the morrow?"

"Spread over two days. I do not wish us to be associated with each other. We must arrive separately so that no suspicion is raised against us."

"I hears that anyone arriving from Calais is treated with suspicion. The British are naturally suspicious, it comes from living on a paltry island."

"My fellows are dressed as gentlemen as will I be and will give no cause for alarm. I did hear that genteel persons of substance arriving from Eire were not questioned or asked for papers. Tis a weakness of the British to assume that all gentlemen can be trusted."

33

Chris had walked straight back to Horse Guards after his interview with Pitt and kicked his heels waiting for further news. He knew time was of the essence but could not appear presumptive until the rider arrived from Plymouth, or, if he was wrong, from Bristol.

Pitt's final words worried him. Was there something that Pitt wasn't telling him? He racked his brains for a memory of the history lessons his teachers and his parents, both great history buffs, had drummed into him. There was nothing that came to mind other than the abortive attack by the United Irishmen on Bristol Docks.

It was a tumultuous period in history and there may have been something everyone had missed, or something that had been under-reported at the time. It was a niggle that made him feel vaguely uncomfortable.

He spent the time writing fresh orders for Biggin and Pocock to have the men ready to embark from below London Bridge at Wool Quay. The customs men wouldn't like it but they would have to live with it.

He had passed Pitt's request for help from the 13th of Foot to Henry who disappeared with it to return some minutes later with a grim nod. "Tis agreed. A rider will be despatched to the regiment's colonel. I have also taken it upon myself to inform His Royal Highness of the possible threat to Plymouth and yet another rider will be despatched to the captain of marines there."

Chris mentally kicked himself for not thinking of that. He had been so fixated on Bristol. "Thank you, Henry. That was an oversight on my part and I am in your debt."

"You have much to concern you."

"Even so, it was a mistake and I'm grateful for your thoughtfulness."

"It seems your mind is set upon Bristol."

"It seems to me to be the most likely place but without news to the contrary I cannot be sure. These United Irishmen could yet surprise me."

There was a rap on the door and a young cavalry lieutenant came in, saluted and handed Henry a sealed package.

"From Plymouth, sir." He stepped back, saluted again and left.

Henry broke the seal and read the letter. "Tis from our agent. The Irishmen have gathered and are preparing to leave the city. He insinuated himself into a gap in the roof and overheard instructions for them to make for Bristol. It seems your assumption was correct, Lennox."

Chris grabbed his cloak. "That's all I need to know. I shall be with my men at Wool Quay to await the arrival of our ship. We embark for Bristol on the next tide."

He rushed back to Downing Street and called for Dales. The boy came rubbing his mouth. "We are leaving forthwith. I see you've eaten supper."

"Aye, sir, right well."

"Take your kit and your rifle and report to the stables at Knightsbridge Barracks. You know where that is?"

Dales nodded as Chris scribbled a note. "This is an order to have both my horses made ready and saddled within the hour. Can you ride?"

"No, sir, I cannot."

"Very well I'll order a groom to take my second horse and you will ride behind him. He is to return the animals to the stables once we no longer have need of them. Quickly now, Dales. You will instruct the groom to return here for me and we will all ride to Wool Quay. Do you understand my instructions?"

"Yes indeed, sir. I am to roust a groom to saddle your horses to ride here to collect you, thence to Wool Quay where he may return the animals to Knightsbridge."

"Exactly. Now go to your duties and be back as quickly as you are able. Before you do call Esther and Matthew to me."

The boy rushed off and Chris quickly penned another note for Catherine. He was sealing it as the two servants entered. "Esther, Matthew. I must leave Downing Street forthwith. Here is a note for Mrs Lennox. Please give her my sincere apologies for not being here to welcome her to her new home. I have explained matters briefly in the letter and she will know that it is my duty that takes me away from her side as nothing else could.

"Esther, I haven't eaten today. Please bring me a cold collage."

Esther hurried away and Chris turned to Matthew. "I have ordered three suits from Meyers, would you be so kind as to collect them tomorrow. The bill is already paid so there is no need to worry on that score."

Matthew bowed. "When should we expect your return, sir?"

"That I don't yet know, Matthew. Possibly a week, possibly longer. Ensure that Mrs Lennox is comfortable. I am depending on you and Esther in this matter. How long a leave of absence did Sir George allow you?"

"Until Mrs Lennox is settled, sir."

"Good, I'll write to Sir George and inform him that your stay will be longer than anticipated. I'll leave the letter on my bureau for you to post tomorrow."

Esther returned with a large plate of cold meats and doorsteps of bread and butter accompanied by a tankard of cider. No one drank water, it was too filthy, and ale for men or cider for the gentry, was generally taken in large quantities. His soldiers were allowed several pints of ale a day but they were hardened to it and rarely showed signs of drunkenness.

He dismissed the pair and ate slowly as he revolved the day's happenings in his mind. The next few days would be crucial if he was to save Pitt's face and the docks at Bristol from a devastating attack.

He finished his meal and found his Bergen tucked away in a corner of the master bedroom. Esther had made the bed and hung flowers from the bedposts. Autumn flowers that were already withering but their scent hung in the still air. Coming from a time when flowers and vegetables were available all year round it still startled him that winter brought on shortages of such things that he had always taken for granted.

He dressed in his combat suit and Kevlar vest. The heavy ceramic plate that fitted over the chest and could withstand high velocity bullets wasn't needed in this day and age and he packed it away. Rather like the marine who had stood in for Lord Whitworth, he might end up with a cracked rib but it was a small price to pay.

He checked his Glock 17 and gave it a quick clean. He had two full magazines, each holding sixteen rounds and two partially empty from his combat in Portugal and Ferrol. It still confused him that his medicines and non-metallic objects reconstituted themselves but anything metallic did not. Once used it was the last of them and he would need to husband his supplies carefully. He took rounds from one partially empty magazine to completely fill the other which left him with several loose 9mm rounds which he put into a pocket in his combat jacket. He could not wear his thigh holster so pushed the pistol into his belt beneath the Kevlar vest.

He had just finished a letter to Sir George Wadman, thanking him for his generosity and explaining why Matthew was needed for a while longer and another note to Pitt outlining the situation and the course of action he was about to take when a clatter of hooves in the street announced the arrival of his two horses. He left the notes on his bureau, shouldered his Bergen and walked into the street. Dales was perched on the rear of one horse behind a uniformed cavalryman who held the reins of the second horse. Dales looked far from comfortable and held his arms around the cavalryman's waist in a limpet-like grip. Chris grinned in the dark. Torches burned in brackets outside several of the buildings but darkness ruled over the best part of London. He took a deep breath as he swung a leg over his saddle and wondered what the next few days would bring.

34

It came as no surprise that the ship being rowed out of the early morning mist was *HMS Aquilon*. It seemed to Chris that their fates were inextricably entwined.

They had spent the night on the dock wrapped in their cloaks with just the calls of the sentries falling muffled by the fog drifting off the Thames. Biggin had roused the men and they were chewing a cold breakfast and listening to the dip of oars as the longboat dragged the ship through slack water. Soon the tide would be on the turn and the *Aquilon* would use it to float downstream towards the sea. There was no wind as yet and the tide and the longboat were the only two forms of propulsion available.

The frigate made fast and Chris led his detachment aboard, saluting the quarterdeck as they filed past. Some of the men had seen service as marines and others had fought aboard the *Aquilon* against a French fourth-rater which had been captured. The bounty from that had seen them each given a week's pay and they held the *Aquilon,* its captain and crew in high regard because of it. Some exchanged greetings with tars they recognised and were soon settled below decks out of the morning chill.

There was no sign of Cunningham and Chris was saluted by the ship's first lieutenant.

"Welcome aboard, Colonel Lennox. I am Lieutenant Hawkins and the ship is at your disposal."

Chris looked around. "Where is Captain Cunningham?"

"He sends his regrets. He was called ashore last night to Greenwich and will be rendezvousing with the ship as we pass that place this morn."

"Very well, lieutenant. You may cast off."

Hawkins grimaced. "Little wind and this damned fog will make navigation slow work. We will drift as we may on the tide and hope these conditions will keep river shipping in its berths."

Chris nodded. "I understand you would not choose to sail in this murk but needs must when the devil drives. We must make as much time as we can and head for Bristol."

The longboat pulled the ship's bow away from the dock and the tide caught it to turn it downriver. It was hard work for the oarsmen to pull the heavy ship until the stern was clear of the stonework and pointing in the required direction. Now they could relax as the ship gathered speed and they kept pace with an occasional dip of the oars on the barked order of the cox'n seated at the tiller in the stern. His was not an easy job as he had to gauge the speed of the ship behind him to avoid being rammed from the rear and, with a powder monkey staring into the mist ahead, had to warn of obstacles or other ships in their path.

Chris paced the deck, anxiously peering up towards the sky for any sign that the fog was thinning. The sun was up but still low in the sky to the east, its light painting a rosy glow but not penetrating. At that time of year there was not enough strength in its rays to lift the fog quickly with smoke from breakfast fires from the hovels along the riverbank adding to the problem.

The lieutenant came up to Chris's elbow. He too was anxious but for another reason. He did not want the ship to run aground or be involved in a collision whilst he was in command as that would surely ruin his promotion prospects for years to come. He put a brave face on it and tried to sound casual. "We have jury rigged ship's anchors to be dropped off the stern should we need to reduce way.

Dropping the bow anchor would cause the ship to swing on the cable with calamitous results."

"The marine version of brakes. I hope it won't be necessary to drop them."

"Amen to that, Colonel. As the tide ebbs the speed of the water beneath our keel will increase and we shall drift with it. Sea anchors will be of little use as they will float at the speed of the tide. We are on spring tides and the race will be the quicker for it."

Chris was no sailor but he knew that spring tides rose higher and dropped lower than neap tides and therefore the volume of water draining out of the Thames would be greater. He was beginning to regret asking for a ship.

"Ahoy the deck" The shout came from the longboat. "Ship on larboard beam."

The bow lookout repeated the warning and there was also a shout from the crow's nest where the lookout could now see mastheads poking through the top layer of fog.

The lieutenant turned and screamed at the helmsman, "Hard-a-starboard, throw out the starboard drag anchor, look lively now. Bosun hands to the larboard side and prepare to fend off."

Sailors scurried around the deck to a chorus of "aye aye," sirs. Chris could see nothing ahead except a bank of yellow fog.

"Where away now?" the lieutenant yelled. The cox'n in the longboat knew his business and his crew were pulling the bow to starboard, swinging the ship on the drag anchor but the tide was ripping now and the anchor wasn't biting enough to do more than help to alter the ship's course a degree.

"One point off the larboard beam," the call came from the crow's nest.

"Still we shall collide," the lieutenant hissed. "Officers to your posts. Get all hands up from below. Your greenbacks also, Colonel, the ship may be holed."

Sailors and soldiers boiled up from the companionways. Biggin and Pocock came out and stared at Chris in a mute request for orders. He cast his eyes around the deck looking for inspiration. There were various spars and rigging from the pinnace and longboat lashed to the deck. He pointed at them. "Cut the spars away and use them to fend off. Six men on each and join the tars on the larboard side."

Chris could now see a black shape looming through the fog, an ugly East Indiaman anchored in the main channel awaiting the fog to lift. The watch on board, lax up until now, had seen the frigate bearing down on them and were shouting warnings.

The *Aquilon* was moving at a fast walking pace and weighed over six-hundred tonnes unladen. She was heading for a fully laden merchantman of over nine-hundred tonnes. Irresistible force and immovable object came into Chris's mind as the huge hull loomed blacker and larger.

The long boat's crew were pulling hard on the oars and the ship's bow swung a fraction more to starboard, enough to prevent a bow on collision, the bowsprite passed by the hull, one of the cross trees caught the merchantman's rigging and snapped with the crack of a musket. The *Aquilon's* left bow was dragged towards the merchantman's hull and hit with a dull thud and cracking of timbers. The sailors at the bow used long poles to fend off but these snapped under the weight with splinters flying.

Chris joined his men on a spar and urged them forward to the point where the hulls were beginning to swing together. The bosun was using his rope's end on the tars screaming at them to push harder. The riflemen needed no urging and pushed their frailer spars and masts against the merchantman's hull. One spar shattered and a man screamed as splinters pierced his arm. Chris roared encouragement and the ship's junior officers joined in. Virtually the entire crew manned the poles and as the ship recoiled from the first collision their combined efforts pushed the hulls apart. There was a scraping and twanging as the two hulls slid past each other and rigging snagged and freed itself. Pulleys dropped from the rigging onto sailors beneath but the two ships now had clear water between them and the *Aquilon* was gliding past.

The lieutenant had had enough. As the merchantman disappeared into the murk astern he ordered the second drag anchor to be thrown out and the ship came slowly to a halt.

"My apologies, sir," he said to Chris, "but I believe it too hazardous to continue this passage until this damned fog lifts."

Chris gave him a rueful grin. "I'm inclined to agree, Lieutenant, but I do believe the fog is thinning already. Check your ship for damage and continue as you see fit. I have an injured man to tend and I see two of your tars have been struck by falling rigging. I have some knowledge of wounds and shall assist your ship's doctor. Be aware, though, that we can't delay for long, there is too much at stake."

35

The ship had got off lightly with just two bow timbers sprung and the crosstree on the bowsprit broken. The crew made the repairs in a couple of hours and completed the task in autumn sunshine as the fog finally lifted. A layer of paint was splashed onto the damaged bow by a seaman suspended in a bosun's chair and as he was hauled aboard the lieutenant gave the order to raise the stern anchors.

A slight breeze had also sprung up, further dismissing the last vestiges of mist and giving the ship steering way as her topsails were unfurled.

As they reached Greenwich Cunningham's jolly boat rowed out to meet them and they hove to.

He was piped aboard and his seaman's eye took in the missing masts and spars from the deck and the new brightly clean rigging and crosstree. He raised his eyes to the lieutenant. "An eventful passage I assume, Mr Hawkins."

Hawkins blushed. "Indeed, Captain. Most eventful."

"I shall enjoy reading your log, sir. Now, tarry no longer we have passage to make."

"Aye, aye, sir." Hawkins knuckled his hat and turned to issue a stream of orders. Cunningham turned to Chris with a welcoming smile. "I trust you were not unduly perturbed, sir. Welcome aboard my ship once again."

"Thank you, Captain. It was an experience but your first officer did his duty in most excellent fashion and brought us safely through the fog."

"Not entirely unscathed, I perceive, but the ship is still afloat and in good order so I shall count it as a task well done." He lowered his voice. "Not that I shall let Hawkins off so lightly. Now come to my cabin, Lennox, we have much to discuss in private."

Cunningham made himself comfortable and poured a glass of Madeira for them both. He reached into a pocket of his sea cape and tossed a package onto his table. "From their Lordships at the Admiralty, my orders to be of service to you and your greenbacks. This is becoming a common event, sir."

Chris sipped his drink and looked at Cunningham over the glass's rim. "I for one am grateful for your assistance, Captain. A trustworthy friend in time of need."

"Our history together is short but eventful, Colonel and I believe the trust is mutual. Now what of this current escapade?"

"It's this league of United Irishmen. I have deduced that they will be making an attack on the docks at Bristol and I need to have my men in place to thwart the plan. Hence the urgency to reach Bristol with all possible speed."

"Do you realise that Bristol is a most difficult port? The docks are unattainable at low tide with barely a runnel of water passing through. We are on spring tides which makes matters more difficult as the water will be at its lowest ebb in St Augustine's Reach on the Frome. We may only enter on the flood. Should we arrive at the wrong state of tide we should be obliged to anchor off-shore until such times as there is enough water beneath the keel to make passage. Many a fine ship has run aground in those docks."

"We are in your hands, Captain. If the need arises we shall take the longboat ashore in relays but it needs to be done at night. I've no wish to alert the Grey Wolves to our presence."

"Grey Wolves?"

"Yes, the name that the United Irishmen have given their military wing. The men who plan to bring rebellion to our shores with whatever destruction and loss of life that entails. Dangerous men, Captain."

"And ripe for the noose. Mere hanging be too good for the blackguards."

Chris had to smile despite the seriousness of the conversation. "Drawing and quartering is not such a fashion now, sir."

"Indeed not but still an apt and allowable punishment for high treason and to put the five parts of each man on display in Dublin and across the whole of Ireland lest any should feel the need to follow their footsteps into rebelling against the Crown."

"As was done with William Wallace in Scotland but I seem to recall that did little to quell the Scots' rebellious nature."

"You are correct, sir." Cunningham sighed. "Not until the act of Union and King James ascended the throne of England. I shudder to think of an Irishman on the English throne especially a papist. Mr Pitt's Act of Union with Ireland and his emancipation of Catholics would make such a thing possible should his Majesty the King not have set his face so steadfastly against it."

"I understand His Majesty's decision as he is head of the Church of England but I do foresee centuries of strife and wickedness resulting from it."

"Pah, sir, you are too defeatist. We shall have them scuppered ere long, mark my words. With men such as yourself against them they cannot prevail."

Chris grimaced, he knew differently. "This will be one battle in a very long war. I can feel it in my bones."

*

James Grant reined his horse to a stop and looked around at the group of men he had just reached. There were twelve of them, the Grey Wolves from Portsmouth who had walked up from the south coast port over the past three days. They eyed him with some suspicion until he hailed them and gave the word they were expecting.

He looked them over. Despite the travails of the walk, eighty miles in three days, they all looked fit and hard, their faces taut with fire in their eyes. They knew their momentous task was imminent and could already taste the victory and the spoils. Amongst their number and in the other groups were seasoned sailors. They were to destroy and loot and steal two ships loaded with booty to sail to a cove off Rosslare where the ships would be unloaded, their names planed off the mainmasts and new names chiselled. The ships would then be sold and the money shared between all who fought at Bristol. Grant thought is was little wonder they were so eager.

Grant sought out the leader, a big man with a pock-marked face, a squint and a heavy cudgel in his belt. "You have a legend should you be challenged?"

"Aye, that we have. We be a crew in search of a ship. Honest hands with a need to work the merchantmen."

Grant nodded. The story would pass muster should they be hailed by yokels but may not bear examination by the militia. "You should split your men into smaller groups that do not beg suspicion. Yonder are the small villages of Thickwood, Ford and Slaughterford. Divide your men betwixt each and arrange to rendezvous at a place called Dykes Farm outside Pucklechurch in two day's time where you will meet with men from Plymouth. From there tis but eight miles march to Bristol Docks.

"I ride now to intercept the men from Yarmouth, one day away, and Dover who are yet two days behind. You must keep from discovery until we are all gathered at Dykes Farm lest notice be brought upon yourselves. And betwixt times, hide yon cudgel lest ye be taken for footpads."

The man gave a slow nod. "Twill be done, sir. I can sees the sense of it, so I can."

"Once we have taken Bristol we shall drink to our success but until that comes to pass ensure your boyos stay away from drunkenness. News of drunken Irish will spread like the plague through these villages and may beg enquiry."

"There be nought to worry on that score, sir, we be sober enough 'til the time does come for us to make merry dancing in the blood of the English."

36

The voyage from the Thames past North Foreland on the Essex coast, south past Deal, Dover and Dungeness and then west along the south coast had been accomplished in a day and a night but now the wind had dropped and it was slow progress from Eastbourne to Worthing. Chris paced the deck like a caged lion, checking his hidden Breitling wristwatch as the minutes and the landscape crawled by.

To ease the boredom he had his riflemen exercising on deck, drilling them incessantly on reloading and firing at debris floating in the Channel. Some took pot shots at passing gulls but with his 21st century sensibilities over nature conservation, he put a stop to that. The men did not understand his reasons, frowning over the order but complied with good grace. Whatever Chris wanted he got. He was a god in the men's eyes; a thought that sat heavily on his mind. Some of these trusting men would die from his commands as others had in past battles. Each death was engraved on his heart. In these days of massed ranks and mass slaughter, losing a couple of riflemen was not worth consideration by the red-coated officers and generals at Horse Guards but he felt each death as a personal failure. He had done his best to protect his men by devising the iron faced weskits that had saved lives but even that small mercy was frowned upon by the hierarchy where honour took precedence over prudence and soldier's lives were worth less than a shilling a day to dependents. The weskits would be discarded once his time with the Corps was over and their use lost in the mists of unreported history.

He watched his riflemen drill with a sense of growing paternalism. They were products of their age but had taken to his alien training methods with skill and good humour. He was proud of every one of them. He vowed to do what he could with his time in the past to ease the burdens on soldiers but he knew it would be an uphill fight. He had obtained a promise from Colonels Coote Manningham and Charles Stewart that flogging would only be used in extremis. He believed those two men would honour their pledge but that others in future command of the Corps would not. He fervently hoped that by setting his example of firm discipline without corporal punishment it would gain in popularity but there was a mountain of petty-minded vindictiveness to overcome from within all ranks of the army that used the lash to make an example as well as to dole out punishment.

He was brooding and he knew it. The ship was barely making walking pace and he had the awful feeling they would arrive too late for the Irishmen's party. By Cunningham's calculation there were still two-hundred miles to cover from Worthing to Truro, then they had to round Land's End and beat northeast up the Bristol Channel to the mouth of the River Avon. Still three to four days sailing unless the wind picked up.

As if he could read his mind, Cunningham called him to the poop deck.

The captain sniffed the air and glanced at the topsails. "The glass is dropping, Lennox. We shall have a blow come eventide that will see us better than eight knots. You should not fret so at our progress."

"You read my mood well, Captain. I'm champing at the bit that we will be too late to help Bristol fend off the Irishmen."

"The wind is from the southwest. We will be sailing before it once round Land's End and should reach a good twelve knots with the rising tide."

Grant had collected his lieutenants and rode ahead of the main bodies of Irishmen to the farm where a supporter had stockpiled weapons, powder and ball. They swung down from their horses as they were greeted by the man who had ridden from Plymouth and had brought the Plymouth group with him. Theirs had been the shortest journey and they together with the Bristol men had set up camp in the barnyard with braziers glowing and meat cooking on spits. It was growing both cool and dark and the light and the warmth were welcome.

Grant handed the reins to a man and pushed his palms towards a fire.

The other man said, "warm yourself whilst ye can, James. We have game on the spits for your supper."

"Have your preparations been completed?"

The man barked a laugh. "Not one for the small talk are yers? Aye, all the muskets have been cleaned and oiled, the cutlasses sharpened, the powder made into cartridges and the ball counted into pouches. We have enough muskets powder and ball for sixty men."

Grant rubbed his hands in the heat. "That's good. We will have a dozen men arrive on the morrow, a further ten and five on the next day and another dozen yet a day later. With your ten from Plymouth and those ten from Bristol already here that makes nine and fifty. We will make a brave showing and none durst stand against us.

"Now, what of the arrangement at yonder docks?"

The other man grinned, his stained teeth catching the firelight. "There are but four watchmen. Two sleep off the night with gin for comfort to keep the cold at bay. One is but a mere boy who tends the watch fires. But one man sets to his duties as he should. We have two of the Bristol boyos keeping watch and will warn of any change in circumstance but twould seem each night is fashioned as I have said."

Grant nodded his satisfaction and his shoulders dropped as he relaxed his muscles. "Then we go three nights hence, when the tobacco ships have docked and been relieved of their cargoes. We will need torches to fire the warehouses; twill be a pretty stink that Bristol will awaken to on that morn. Men may take whatever they may carry and burn that which they cannot. Any man, woman or child that comes 'gainst us may be cut down where they stand. No quarter given and our Grey Wolves should expect none in return. With God's good grace and good luck we should have our way and be gone before any militia gets wind of it."

The other man grinned again. "Twas a good scheme to fall upon Bristol. There be no soldiery or marines to stand against us, merely four hapless watchmen."

Pitt was worried. In one hand he held the letter from Lennox and in the other a recently received despatch from Calais. The riflemen were en voyage to Bristol, his Praetorian Guard sailing further from London by the hour.

He read the despatch again. Six men had taken ship from Calais over two days. Men dressed as gentlemen and therefore unlikely to be challenged by the customs at Dover. One of these six was the man known as Coileán Leech, the traitor in the pay of the French. He had no description, according to his informant Leech kept his face covered from all who had dealings with him. The other five had not been seen by the informant and no description was forthcoming there.

Pitt sank into a chair and crumpled the paper in his fist. What was the meaning of it? Why had Leech chosen this time to leave his lair in Paris?

Wild rumours abounded in the febrile atmosphere of the French capital. There was much talk of intrigue and of Bonaparte's intentions towards England and indeed towards the so-called Northern Alliance with Russia and Denmark. No one could divine the little Corsican's mind and in that atmosphere rumours flourished. It was these rumours that caused Pitt the most worry. If just some be true then Britain had best be on its guard. He sighed and called his secretary to take note and despatch it to the spy in Calais. Monsieur LeFevre would be best placed back in Paris and he should make haste to return there. That was where the game was now afoot. The French-Irishman had no qualms over playing both sides, as long as the money was forthcoming and he was a keen ear to the ground. Pitt did not trust him but found him useful. No doubt LeFevre would be equally adept at betraying the English should the pay be worth the candle.

Pitt also dictated a letter to Lennox in Bristol and had it despatched by courier via the good offices of the 13th of Foot. His suspicions were such that he could not voice them to Horse Guards on pain of being thought a fool, or worse, unhinged, so vague was the notion, but Lennox had the reputation of having keen insight and may view the matter more seriously than the generals. The thought made his stomach flutter and he wholeheartedly hoped his suspicions were unfounded.

37

Grant snapped shut his telescope and grunted. It was as he had expected. Two watchmen were hunched over a brazier, a bottle of gin on the ground between them. A boy was tending the fire, a youth of around sixteen years, he estimated. Of the other watchman all that could be seen was a swinging lantern as the man made his rounds checking on warehouse doors along Princes Street.

His men were growling and shuffling behind him, eager to be on the move. The two lookouts had earmarked the closest two ships to be taken, both brigantines manageable for his few sailors.

Weak moonlight glinted off the water in St Augustine's Reach and the temperature had dropped with the clear skies. He grinned. It was no wonder the two drunkard watchmen crowded the brazier on nights such as this.

"We are ready, James," one of his lieutenants hissed in his ear. Now that the time had come, he felt more at ease with the thought of victory and the blow to British commerce, the tobacco trade and the revenue to the Crown. It was but a small bite from a large cherry and there would be others to follow; possibly the port of Liverpool which was growing in west coast importance to rival Bristol.

Dimly, there was no reason to distrust them, but some doubts troubled his mind over the French insistence on attacking a centre of commerce. There were other juicier targets that would make the British government take note of the United Irishmen's cause. Then again, he was merely a foot soldier following the orders of Coileán Leech. Now there was someone who had his finger deep in the pie and he was not about to question the man's motives; he was as faithful an Irishman as could be found.

A nearby church clock struck the midnight hour, its chimes hanging heavy in the cold air and Grant squared his shoulders. "Now then me boyos, for Ireland and the Pope."

The men roared and waved their muskets before breaking into a lumbering run towards the dockside and the watchmen seated there. The boy poking the brazier dropped his stick and reached behind a barrel. The two sots shook off their cloaks, stood and turned to face the galloping horde. They were limned in the glow of the fire and Grant could see them raise their hands. There were three flashes, three sharp cracks and three Irishmen fell.

The charge faltered for a second then a roar of vengeance went up. Some raised their muskets and shot a ragged volley at the three watchmen who quickly retreated around a corner.

"After them," Grant screamed. "Avenge our fallen."

The men screamed their war cries and raced for the dockside. Grant held back his lieutenants. "Let the mob loose. We must break the doors and set our fires. Let them have their revenge, we shall be more cool headed in this. Who carries the torches?"

"I, James," one said and thrust forward four pitch soaked staves with rag tied at the ends.

"Set fire from the brazier and we shall begin this night's work in earnest."

Dales had a cool head in a crisis. He heard the Irishmen's screams, murmured to the two riflemen around the brazier and leaned to pick up his rifle from where he had lodged it behind a barrel. The two riflemen, Stokes and

Branscombe stood and shrugged off the heavy coats which had hidden their rifles from view. They turned together and all three aimed and fired into the charging mob. Three men fell and a ragged volley of musketry replied but no ball came close.

"We best be away now, lads," Stokes said from the side of his mouth, "afore they be upon us." They ran around the corner and through the lines of a company of the 13th whose ranks blocked the quayside. Soldiers let the riflemen through then closed back shoulder to shoulder as if they had never been parted. The three riflemen continued to run further along the quay where they doubled back to join their fellow greenbacks.

The mob followed the disappearing riflemen around the corner of the warehouse in full cry. The leaders looked up from the cobbles to see the red line stretched out in front of them in the moonlight. Some stopped dead in their tracks and were knocked down by others coming from behind. They were the lucky ones as the soldiers shouldered their muskets and fired a disciplined volley. Many Irishmen went down and two of the soldiers as return fire sparkled in the night. The soldiers, bayonets fixed, advanced at a slow march through the powder smoke with muskets at the hip.

It was the smoke and their grey cloaks that allowed some cover and the survivors, thirty in all, began a ragged withdrawal firing the occasional shot as they went before turning to run. There was no time to reload the muskets and some were dropped in the dash for safety. The more cool-headed amongst them, some who had served in the French army after deserting the British, kept their weapons.

Grant watched open-mouthed as the ragged retreat passed by the end of Princes Street. Two of the pitch soaked torches had been lit and he handed these to two of his men but he cast the others aside. "Run to the tobacco warehouses, break the doors and throw in the torches. These torches will act as if they are beacons to the redcoats so we must be swift in our actions. One man to break the doors, the other to raise the fires. I and one other will rally our Grey Wolves to secure a brigantine for our escape."

They split into three groups, those with the torches turning to run further down Princes Street and Grant with his companion slipping furtively along a narrow alley between two warehouses. On the quay, the second rank of soldiers passed through the first and fired another volley at the retreating Irishmen. This one was far less effective as the Irish had split up into small groups and were using the cover of barrels and stacks of cargo from which to fire an occasional return. Grant materialised amongst them and began to organise a stronger resistance, rallying the old soldiers and sailors and building a rough barricade from which to fight behind. It worked as the advancing soldiers were ordered to halt.

Grant had chosen his ship and sent four men onto it to secure any of the crew who were still aboard. He did not want them killed as they would be needed to help sail the ship and would be pressed into service.

The powder smoke was clearing and moonlight was gleaming on bayonets. Grant wondered why the advance had stopped. There were one-hundred soldiers to his thirty and they would surely be overrun. Those who still held muskets had reloaded and there would be a toll of lives amongst the redcoats but that did not usually stop the British. They had halted just out of effective musket range and the red ranks parted to allow an officer through. He had a sabre in his right hand sloped on his shoulder. His bicorn hat and plume with single gold epaulette and single white crossbelt marked his rank. He raised his sabre and called.

"We have you surrounded sir. Our second company, of this minute, are sealing off egress and you shall not escape. Surrender your weapons or it may be the worse for you."

Grant stood to his full height to reply. "What could be worse than dyin' for somethin' we believe in? I'll tell you that which is worse, sir. It is bein' hanged by the British in some rat-infested prison, that is what is worse, sir. You will needs to take us by force for we will not surrender."

Grant was buying time. Time for his two fire-raising teams to do their work and time to get the ship ready to sail. The odds were massively against them but he still held on to the hope they might yet escape in the confusion once the spectre of fire was raised.

38

Chris nodded to the three young riflemen as they re-joined the main group. He was pleased with their work and the nod signalled it. They stood, invisible in the shadows as they watched the two glowing torches bob towards them, one on either side of the wide street that ran between rows of warehouses. The tobacco warehouses were halfway along, marked by the strong aroma that issued from the vents in the walls which allowed air to circulate to keep the leaf dry.

Chris waited until the bobbing lights came to a halt and they could hear the sound of cracking timbers. He raised his voice. "Stand in the King's name."

The noise of splintering wood stopped. Chris could make out four faces turned towards the sound of his voice, caught in the flickering torch light. A pistol was fired and a ball pinged of the cobbles yards away. The cracking of timber began again.

"Last chance," Chris yelled, "put down your weapons and stand away from the buildings."

A second pistol was fired and a wide door was dragged open, a torch arced back. Four sharp cracks echoed from the floor above and the torches were dropped. Chris had positioned his sharpshooters in the loading bays where they had an uninterrupted view along the street. Biggin led a group of riflemen forward to check on the fallen men. He picked one of the dropped torches from the cobbles and waved it.

Two of the Irish were dead and the other two mortally wounded, black pools of wet blood staining their cloaks. The heavy calibre rifle balls took few prisoners.

Chris cocked his head and listened as the sounds of battle faded from the quay area.

"I'll need to go to see how the 13th is faring. Make these two prisoners as comfortable as you can, Serjeant-major."

"Both gut shot, they will not see the night out, beggin' your pardon, sir."

"No reason for them to pass their last time on earth face down on cobbles. They may be traitors but they deserve to be treated as human beings."

Biggin knuckled his forehead. "Twill be as you say, sir, but, beggin' your pardon, the likes o' them do not deserve such kindness as you offer."

"I daresay not but you will show them the milk of kindness and they may yet wonder at the mercy of man before they meet the mercy of their god. I believe we should show some consideration to the defeated no matter how much we detest their cause. And Biggin … no looting, let them be buried with their possessions intact."

"The gravediggers will have it should we not," Biggin grumbled.

"Never let it be said that my riflemen are thieves, not while I command them. The gravediggers will have their own consciences to contemplate."

Chris left Biggin to wonder at the perverseness of his officer and made his way to the Quay where the 13th were drawn up. He found the captain commanding the company.

"What is the position, sir?"

The captain saluted. "Ah, Colonel Lennox. We have the blackguards contained and are awaiting further orders from General Ainslie as to whether we are to force the issue for the damage it might further cause to the dock."

Chris glanced along the quay to where the Grey Wolves were stacking barrels and crates to improve their fortifications. "I fear your hesitation will cause further loss of life amongst your men. The Irishmen are preparing for a siege. Those defences will be costly to break down."

"We may bring up the cannon to breach the wall."

Chris grinned. "Sledgehammer and walnut springs to mind." He grinned again at the puzzled look on the other man's face. "Even more damage will occur if you use heavy ball on this quay."

"You have an alternative solution, sir?"

"Leave it with me."

Grant had his scope on the two officers and recognised the man in green. He snapped the scope shut with an angry grunt. The green men again.

There had been no fire raised and his hopes of escaping were growing less. He wondered at the fate of his four lieutenants. He also wondered why the redcoats had not stormed his position. He knew the military mind and that their overriding urge would be to attack regardless of losses. It was to his good. The sailing master with him had returned to say the brigantine was his to command, the crewmen aboard had been taken with hardly a fight, cowed by the swords and cudgels with which they were threatened.

Grant's barricades now stretched from the walls of a warehouse to the quayside both front and back of their position. Redcoats could be seen further south along the quay and the officer had not been lying about them being surrounded. Their only avenue of escape was the brigantine. Slowly, two by two, he sent men to slink aboard the ship where the sailors were making ready to cast off.

He felt luck was with him as the sky was now clouding over and the wind was rising with the onset of dawn. The moon would soon be covered and in the near full darkness they could make away under sail.

He left four men with muskets guarding the barricades. The redcoats had lit torches and they could be seen in the flickering light. Any advance by them would be noticed instantly. The Grey Wolves were in darkness and their small number hidden by the barricades. Grant would call them in at the last minute as the ship cast off.

Sailors were running on the decks and scaling the rear main mast. It was gaff rigged but had topgallants that needed to be unfurled to give the ship way. The foresails too were needed to turn the ship away from the quayside. Many whispered orders were given and the four pressed seamen each had a guard with a sword to ensure they kept silent as they worked. Grant winced as a sail flapped in a sudden gust and a block squeaked as a line run through it. He hoped the soldiers were too far away to hear the sounds.

He sent a man ashore to bring back two more men, leaving just two, one facing north and one south ready to give an alarm. He pulled the senior sailor to him and whispered, "how do we fare?"

"Five minutes more, the man whispered back. You can call the boyos in from the quay and they may take station at the bow and stern. A few more minutes and we shall be away. Once we have the gaff sail up no one will catch us, tis a fast ship beneath us."

Grant gave a nod, although the man could not see it. "We are in your hands, captain. It seems as though God and the saints also smile upon us this night." He caught a passing man by the arm and had the last two sentries brought aboard. "We are ready, captain. At your pleasure."

"Aye, aye, Mr Grant" He turned and hissed orders. "Bring the boarding ladder in. Cast off forrard, ease the spring aft."

Grant's smile faded as no motion could be felt beneath his feet. "Why do we not move, captain?"

The sailor rushed to the side and dropped a belaying pin into the water. It hit with a dull splat of wet mud. He turned his head to where he knew Grant was standing. "We have missed the tide, Mr Grant. We are aground."

39

The riflemen forced an entry at the rear of the warehouse outside of which Grant had built his barricades. Chris led the men to the second floor, sending Pocock and six sharpshooters to the top floor. Each floor had a loading platform overlooking the quay with a block and tackle assembly for lifting cargo to the individual levels.

They picked ropes from the bundles lying around and made these fast to pillars, leaving the ropes coiled on the loading platform. The doors were eased open. Well used and greased they opened without a sound.

It was pitch black below but Chris fancied he could detect movement. As his eyes adjusted better to the gloom he realised that men were boarding the ship tied opposite. He pulled out his own telescope and the light collecting properties of the big object lens made picking up movement a little easier. He passed the scope to O'Dell who was kneeling beside him. "What do you make of it, corporal?"

O'Dell peered through the optic for several seconds. "Tis my notion that they be takin' to the water, sir."

"Mine too. What else do you see?"

"What I don't see, beggin' your pardon, Colonel, is water. The tars be sayin' the tide runs out here, risin' and fallin' by thirty feet on the springs. They be stuck fast until the turnin' o' the tide."

"That's why the freeboard appears to be so low. One could almost step over the rail onto the deck from the quay."

"Tis a wonder and their bad fortune they did not notice its settling. Look, sir, two more men have left the barricades I do swear."

"That may be the last of them. While it is so dark have the men lower themselves down the ropes onto the quay and wait against the warehouse wall. Do it without a sound. The rifles may be lowered down to them on cords. Four men at a time. Send Dales to Serjeant-major Pocock to inform him of the plan. His men are to give covering fire as we assault the ship at first light."

Grant was fuming. It was little wonder the redcoats had not attacked. They would be waiting for day. His Irish captain had told him it would be a good six hours before enough water was under the keel to float the vessel into the main channel. By that time the sun would be up and the ship a perfect target. He placed men with muskets at the bow and stern to watch for any movement from the soldiers and to give defence and warning against any attack. The thick timbers of the ship would give ample protection from musket fire but he did not have enough men to repel a determined assault. It would be weight of numbers and not give a damn for their losses that would carry the day for the redcoats.

He could hope for fog but the stiff breeze held no promise of that. Halyards were rattling against masts along the quay in a constant tattoo that beat upon his nerves as much as the constant crowing of a cock in the barnyard at Dykes Farm before he had dispatched it with a cut of his sword. That nerviness he had put down to the prospect of action but this was now mere grinding on his nerves as he could not see a way out of his impasse.

He found the Irish seaman he had designated as captain. "What does this brig carry in its holds, captain?"

"The holds are empty, sir. The ship awaits a cargo of slate and timber to be loaded."

"Is there any gunpowder aboard?"

There be a stern chase four pound gun in the captain's cabin. No doubt used to warn off privateers. There are two kegs of powder and some round shot with it."

Have the gun loaded with nails and brought to the deck. It may yet prove its worth. Bring me what is left of the powder. If we cannot hold the ship, we shall ensure the soldiery do not take it clean. Have the longboat and jolly boat lowered into the mud. They shall float long afore this brig does and may offer us a route of escape."

"Aye, aye, sir," The captain said and hurried off. Grant could hear approval of the plan in the man's voice. Perhaps God was still on his side; the idea that had popped into his head an intercession from the saints and the presence of the gun the work of the angels.

The cannon was trundled on to the deck. There was a keg of nails in the ship carpenter's berth and these were rammed down the barrel with wadding. Home-made grape shot that would decimate an attack. Grant had the gun placed centrally on the deck where it could be swivelled to face in any direction. It could be used only the once as the recoil would send it flying across the deck but it may be enough to gain them time to clamber into the boats alongside the hull. The two things he had no control over were time and tide. He hoped his faith in God's mercy would see that fall to his good.

He took the two kegs of gunpowder in to the large hold and placed them against the ships side which was held taut against the quay by the mooring lines. This he hoped would send the explosion outward and upward, again catching any attacking troops in its blast and holing the ship beyond any repair other than a dry dock. Perhaps fire would take hold in the tar-soaked timbers and finish the job. He ran a trail of powder to the base of the ladder and put tinder and flint on the lowest rung in preparation.

Chris and Dales were the last two to lower themselves down the ropes onto the quay. The riflemen had rolled barrels into place and crouched behind them, hidden both from view and from musket fire should they be detected. It was small touches like this that made the Corps of Riflemen so different from regiments of the line; the ability to think and act for themselves without orders from the chain of command.

They hunkered down and waited for the light to improve. Above the keening of the wind and the rattling of rigging they could hear movement on the ship's deck, low voices and the rumble of heavy equipment.

"They be up to no good," O'Dell whispered.

Chris grimaced. He had the same thought. "A volunteer to go forward to discover what they are about."

"I'll go, sir," Dales said. "I have the least service of the riflemen and should be no loss to the fight."

"There I disagree but very well Dales. Black your face with soot, then crawl on your stomach along the line of the barricade until you are close enough to hear more of what is happening. Take no risks. The value of sending you there would be lost if you are unable to return."

"I shall be careful, sir. I have done my share of partridging."

"These partridges will shoot as well as any gamekeeper. Leave your rifle with O'Dell, it will be too much of an encumbrance, but take your bayonet."

The boy slid away and within seconds was lost in the darkness. He crawled on his stomach until he was close enough to the ship's rail that he could rise to his knees without being seen. He found a place where the rigging stays were clustered together and raised his head. He could barely make out the shapes on the deck but something squat and black was surrounded by movement and the dull chink of metal on metal. It was a few seconds before his brain registered the importance of what he saw. They were loading a cannon and it was pointed straight at the riflemen's position.

In his excitement he raised his head higher and peered around the stays. The movement attracted the attention of a passing Grey Wolf and he lashed out with a cudgel.

Pain exploded in Dales' head and he fell to the quay.

The Grey Wolf swore a loud oath.

"What be that?" the Irish captain hissed.

"A rat, I be thinkin'. Biggest, fattest rat I did ever see."

"You keep your mind on the task and never be mindin' the rats aboard this brig. There be bigger and nastier rats in red coats to be worryin' over."

40

A cacophony of herring gull calls heralded the first pink streak of dawn in the eastern sky. Chris stirred and stretch cramped limbs. Black was slowly turning to grey as the light strengthened. He checked his flintlock Dragon pistol and put it on half-cock. All around his riflemen were doing the same with their weapons with the quiet clicks of bayonet lugs as these were attached to the barrels of the rifles.

The fact that Dales had not returned worried him but there had been no alarm raised so the boy had not been discovered. The problem of his disappearance was for another time. Now he had an attack to carry out. He pushed the pistol into his belt and took Dale's rifle from O'Dell's hand. "Ready men. On my command. Stand by."

He hoped that surprise would be complete but he knew nothing was ever guaranteed in war. "Go!"

They rose as one and ran towards the ship which appeared to be abandoned. One man fell and his rifle discharged with a loud crack. Heads appeared over the ship's bulwarks with cries of surprise. Two men leapt for the cannon, a smouldering fuse in hand. The riflemen closed the distance as the fuse hovered over the cannon's touch hole.

A volley of rifle fire crackled from above and both men manning the cannon fell, punched backwards by heavy rifle balls.

The riflemen screamed their battle cries as they hurdled the rail and got in amongst the Irish. Men at the bow and stern swung around and fired randomly at the green wall of men. Chris fired his rifle and hit his target. He dropped the weapon and drew his sabre, slashing at a Grey Wolf who loomed up at him. The man fought briefly but was no match for Chris's skill and dropped wounded.

Battles raged all around as weapons flared and men fell. O'Dell led a party onto the poop deck and engaged the men there in hand-to-hand fighting. Branscombe did the same at the bow but was felled by a ball in the head and his attack faltered. The Irishmen were reloading their muskets ready for a further volley, one that might disrupt the entire attack and negate any gains made. Pocock had seen the danger and directed his riflemen to engage the Grey Wolves at the bow. The rifle fire was devastatingly accurate and five men were hit giving a clear field for those on the ship to press home their advantage.

Men were screaming and the deck was slippery with blood. Chris emptied his Dragon into one man and fended off another with his sabre. His Kevlar vest had a jagged rip in it and an ear had been nicked by a sword blade, he had blood running down his face but he did not feel it. Two men were climbing over the port rail. Chris spotted them and charged forward. One turned and fired his pistol point blank into Chris's chest. It took the wind out of him but the Kevlar stopped the bullet. He lashed out with his sabre, caught the man across the wrist and the hand fell to the deck still clutching the pistol as he fell overboard crashing into the longboat beneath. The second man jumped down into the boat which was barely floating but took his weight.

Other men were already in it and were unshipping the oars. Chris looked around and called two riflemen to help him. Together they rolled the unfired cannon through the gap where the gangplank was usually placed and it dropped into the longboat beneath snapping the hull and keel like matchwood and tossing the occupants into the shallow muddy water.

A sailor rushed forward and Chris turned his sabre at the guard but the man stopped and held up his hands. "Mercy, sir, I be a merchant seaman and a crewman aboard this brig. They have taken gunpowder below, I did see it with my own eyes."

"Where?"

"The main hold, sir."

Chris looked around, his riflemen now had control with just a flicker of resistance still at the bow but O'Dell was ordering more men to the fight and it would not last much longer. Along the Quay the lines of redcoats were marching forward, drums rattling. The Dorsetshires were on the march, late but heading into unknown danger.

Chris made for the hold ladder. He rattled down the steps. A flint sparked and tinder caught as Chris jumped onto the man's back and they collapsed in a heap.

The man lashed sideways with his fist and caught Chris on the temple. He pulled himself clear and blew on the tinder to turn the spark into a tiny flame that lit up his face.

Chris shook his head to clear his sight and glanced up in time to see the purple mark on the man's cheek. "Grant!"

The man spun. "You! The green man. You shall thwart me no more." Grant dropped the tinder into the powder trail.

Chris kicked out at him and caught him on the knee. Grant staggered but lurched back and fell on Chris with a knife clutched in his hand. He stabbed downwards but the knife could not penetrate the tough Kevlar.

Chris grabbed his wrist with one hand and elbowed him in the face with his other arm. He had lost his grip on his sabre and it was somewhere in the dark out of reach.

The smell of burning gunpowder filled the hold as the powder trail fizzed slowly across the deck in little spurts as it crossed joins in the planks.

Chris tossed Grant off and scrabbled on his back across the deck to make a break in the powder trail with his shoulders.

Grant roared his anger and leapt on Chris again, his knife plunging at his throat. Chris twisted aside and the knife buried its point in the wooden deck and Grant lost his grip on it. They rolled together, each trying to gain an advantage. Grant seized Chris's throat with both hands, his thumbs pressing against the windpipe attempting to crush it and bring an end to the fight.

Chris pushed both his hands through Grant's arms and pulled outwards, breaking Grant's grip. He used one hand to hold Grant away and smashed the other palm under his chin in a classic chin jab that knocked him over against the ladder.

Chris rolled onto his knees and felt around for his sabre. He found the hilt and raised it. A click stopped him dead.

There was now enough light seeping down the gangway to see the pistol in Grant's hand and the awful smile of victory on his face.

"You are bested, sir. You have lost this day."

"Chris stood upright and dropped the sabre to his side. "I think not, Grant. Your Grey Wolves are dead or captured. Bristol is saved from your depredations and you will not escape from this ship. You may shoot me but you will not have won this battle."

"There are more ways than one to win a battle, sir. While your eyes have been turned toward Bristol there is another more deadly plot afoot of which you have no notion and will blight England far worse than savaging its commerce."

"Give up the pistol, Grant. The 13th of Foot is at the quayside. There is no hope for you other than to turn King's evidence which may save your life."

"Hah! Do you have such low opinion of me, sir that I would sell my soul to save my worthless life. I assure you I have no intention other than of dying for my cause and taking as many red and green coats with me as I may. And you, sir will join me in my victory but I will be on my way to heaven and you to a burning hell."

He swung the pistol towards the gunpowder barrels and Chris swung his sabre.

The pistol exploded.

41

Chris dropped to his knees and let out a deep breath. Grant was still twitching and gurgling as the blood gushed out of his severed throat. He gave a final convulsive jerk and lay still as his final breath whistled out of his severed windpipe.

Chris rose to his feet and inspected the beam where the powder barrels were stacked. The lead ball was buried in the timber not half an inch above them. He let out another deep breath as a voice called down from above. It was Biggin. He had arrived with the Dorsetshires and was enquiring after his health.

Chris didn't reply but pulled himself up the ladder. He was coated with blood, both his own and Grant's which had sprayed out from the severed carotid artery.

Biggin took a pace back and gawped. "Are you wounded, sir?"

Chris shook his head. "No Serjeant-major. I don't think so."

You are blooded, sir, beggin' your pardon. You are gashed to the head."

Chris put his hand up and felt the wetness. The top of his ear was missing a thin slice and he hadn't noticed it. "It's nothing."

"My apologies for being so tardy that I did miss the fight, sir. The redcoats would not let me pass their cordon for fear it may provoke a skirmish."

"How did we fare. Have we lost many dead?"

"Three dead, sir, and three sorely wounded. The iron weskits did save many from worse."

"Have you seen Dales?"

"Aye, that I have. He were sitting on the quayside nursing a sore head but otherwise unhurt. There is an officer of the Dorsetshires who requires converse with you, Colonel."

"I'll meet him when I've dealt with the wounded. Have my haversack brought to me." "The officer did say the matter was mightily pressing, sir, beggin' your pardon."

"Then have him brought aboard. I will speak with him while I'm working."

"As you wish, sir," Biggin said and turned away.

"One moment. Who were the dead men?"

"Corporal Picton, sir, Rifleman Branscombe and Rifleman Leadwell."

"Did they have family?"

Picton was wed, sir, with three sprats. Branscombe had a woman but Leadwell was unattached."

"Thank you, Serjeant-major. Where are the wounded?"

"Attended in the captain's cabin, sir. They are making use of the wardroom table." Biggin turned away again then had an afterthought. "How would you wish to deal with them others, sir?"

Chris gave him a puzzled look. "What others?"

"Them, sir," Biggin pointed over the side.

Chris walked to the rail and peered over. Three men were stuck up to their waists in thick mud with the shattered remains of the longboat around them. The tide was rising rapidly and was already up to their armpits. One saw Chris and Biggin looking down and waved. "Have mercy, sirs, lest we drown," he yelled.

"It's drowning or hangin' for you," Biggin called. "You makes your choice."

The other two stared up round eyed with terror. "Do not let us drown sir, we have not made our peace nor confessed our sins to a priest. We would die without the blessing of God."

"It's no more than you deserve," Biggin called back and looked sideways at Chris.

"Throw them lines, Serjeant-major. Pull them out and hand them to the 13th. The Dorsetshires shall have the honour of their capture. Now away to your tasks but first bring me my knapsack. Those three have a few minutes before the water reaches their necks and I have my men to attend."

Biggin scurried away yelling orders at the top of his parade ground voice. In just a few minutes his Bergen was carried up by a rifleman soon followed by an officer in a very finely tailored uniform. He followed Chris into the captain's day cabin and held a lace handkerchief to his nose as the smell hit him. "Colonel Lennox, if you please?"

Chris turned. "To whom do I have the honour?"

"General George Ainslie, sir, at your service. Colonel in Chief of the Dorsetshires."

Chris gave a curt bow. "I have urgent business, General. How can I be of assistance?"

"Tis I who can be of assistance to you, sir. This despatch did arrive from the First Lord of the Treasury last eve. I do declare I believe it to be of the most urgent nature." He handed Chris Pitt's letter."

"I thank you, sir, but first I must attend to my wounded."

"You, sir? You must let my surgeon attend them."

"My thanks. I will perform the triage and call your surgeon when I have ascertained the extent of the injuries and how best they may be treated."

Ainslie frowned. "Are you a man of medicine also, Lennox?"

"I have some small skill. Now, sir, if we are done ... "

"I will have my surgeon attend at your pleasure. But if I may turn your attention to the despatch at your earliest convenience ..."

"Of course. At which time does the post coach leave for London and from where?"

"The post, sir?" Why at four hours past midday from the Full Moon Inn in North Street."

"Then I have until then. Good day, General."

Chris stuffed the letter into a pocket and went to check on the wounded. One had a head injury that required stitches, one with an arm dangling useless in his bloodied sleeve and another with a leg injury where the muscle had been torn away by a ball.

The head and leg injuries were minor compared to the arm and Chris was sure the man would lose it. He dosed him with morphine and left him for the surgeon to do his worst. Head injuries were usually bad news but it seemed that this one had been lucky a sword had scalped the man but missed the skull. Luck, Chris thought was a relative thing. He gave doses of morphine to the other two and coated their wounds in Baneocin powder to help prevent the real killer of infection and left them to the tender mercies of the surgeon.

He wiped his face and cut ear with cognac from the captain's decanter which stung and made him wince, powdered the wound and wrapped a clean bandage around his head. He thought he either looked rakish or stupid but did not much mind which.

He walked on to the open deck in time to see three mud-caked men hauled dripping from the water and dragged away by jeering redcoats. The decks had been cleared of bodies and the four captive sailors were, cleaning the decks of the scars of battle. Chris sat on a hatch cover and broke the seal on Pitt's letter. He read the words and wondered whether those, and Grant's last boast, were connected. He had an awful feeling in the pit of his stomach.

Dales walked up and stood to attention beside him. "Beggin' your pardon, sir. I did fail you, sir."

"Then you must make amends. Go into the town and book two places on the four-o-clock post coach to London for you and me. There is trouble brewing back in London and I must return forthwith."

42

The Bristol to London Post Coach had been the forerunner of the postal service making the journey in sixteen hours that had previously taken stage coaches thirty-six. It had convinced Pitt to extend the service to other cities.

The overnight journey was not easy. The black and red coach rarely stopped, except to change horses, with the mail often being tossed out or snatched from of the hands of post workers as they passed. Toll gates were opened at the sound of the post horn with fines levied if they were left shut. The roads were poor and Chris was thrown from side to side, hanging on to a leather strap to avoid being thrown onto other passengers. He wondered how well Dales was faring on the box next to the driver.

He had changed out of his blood-covered combat suit and Kevlar vest and into his green dress uniform beneath a riding cloak. He had designed the uniform himself and was gratified that the other officers of the Corps had adopted it. One or two of the new officers were wearing red sashes which added a dash of colour that would otherwise be missing. Biggin had taken his combat suit and would give it to the washerwomen at Knightsbridge to be laundered.

The discomfort of the journey precluded sleep and it gave him time to think. His brain was slow, he had not slept since leaving the *Aquilon* thirty-six hours earlier, rowed ashore in longboats, meeting with the 13th, giving them their instructions and setting the trap for the Grey Wolves under the noses of the two Irish scouts. They, no doubt, had perished or had been captured with the rest. It seemed that the Grey Wolves were no more and would no longer trouble the kingdom.

The letter from Pitt had voiced qualms about that. It appeared that the man known as Coileán Leech had recently taken ship with five others to Dover. Pitt did not know what that might augur but was concerned it would not benefit the British government or Crown. Hence the urgent recall. Pitt wanted him back where he perceived the danger to be both deadly and imminent.

With fatigue creeping up on him, Chris could not work out how six Irishmen could cause such concern. The Grey Wolves had numbered more than sixty and had been dealt with. A tenth of their number should not cause too many problems. Then the memory of Guy Fawkes and the gunpowder plot surfaced. There had been few conspirators in that but still able to stack gunpowder unhindered beneath Parliament. They were aided by slack security, Fawkes being challenged twice by guards and got away with it, but it was still an object lesson in how a few dedicated fanatics could achieve their aims. Another stark reminder was the terrorist atrocities of 9/11 and 7/7 and the thought jarred him.

The coach lumbered to a halt for a change of horses and he climbed out to stretch his legs and check on Dales. The teenager was asleep. He had tied himself to the handrails and had nodded off despite the chill wind and crunching ride. Chris envied him this youthful ability as lead weights were dragging down his own eyelids without the blessed relief of slumber.

They arrived at High Holborn at nine in the morning. Dales was awake but not his usual self as the blow on the head was still troubling him with a large lump inside a bruise and a sharp headache. Chris checked his pupils. There was no sign of concussion. The lad had a thick skull.

They walked quickly along Kingsway, around the Aldwych and along the Strand to Whitehall. Chris eyed the properties along the south side of the Strand and filed the observations for future reference. They reached 19 Downing Street and were met at the door by Matthew. His eyes widened at the sight of Chris's bandaged head and the egg-shaped lump on Dales's forehead. He took their cloaks but forbore to comment.

"Where is Mrs Lennox, Matthew?"

"At her breakfast, sir. With Miss Amelia, sir."

Both women rose as he entered the dining room. Catherine gave a small squeal and threw herself at him. He caught her and buried his face in her hair. She pulled back a pace and stared at him.

"You are injured, sir."

"He gave her a tired smile. "It's just a scratch. It will heal in no time."

Dales had come in behind him and stood just inside the door looking awkward. Catherine gave him one of her looks.

"Who might you be, young sir?"

Chris laughed. "Don't be afraid of Mrs Lennox, Dales. Her bite is far worse than her bark but she seldom bites friends."

Catherine raised a delicately arched and querying eyebrow.

"This is my batman, my servant from the Corps. His name is Dales and he has been of great service to me in your absence. You may thank him for the cleanliness of the house as he did arrange it."

Chris turned to Amelia. "Dear sister. It is a pleasure to see you again. I hope Catherine has made you comfortable."

Amelia curtsied. "Indeed, sir, most comfortable. We have been entertained by a visit to Drury Lane with Matthew for company. Mr Shakespeare is indeed well famed for his penmanship. Twas Romeo and Juliet which did touch our hearts so."

Dales was leaning against the doorpost with his eyelids drooping.

"I do believe Dales is unwell, Colonel,"Amelia said. "Perhaps you could see your way to dismissing him until he is recovered."

Chris nodded. "Thank you, Amelia, for your concern. In all the excitement of seeing my dear wife and yourself again I was forgetting my duty." He turned to Dales. "You may stand down, Rifleman. I shan't need you until tomorrow. Get some rest while you may."

"My duty is by your side, sir."

"You may rest assured that Mrs Lennox will not allow any harm to come to me in your absence. Now go, boy. That's an order."

Dales stood to attention and knuckled his bruised forehead. "As you wish, sir."

Catherine dragged Chris to the table once Dales had left. "Have you breakfasted, my dear?"

"No madam, not yet. I have urgent business with the First Lord of the Treasury in Number 10 across the street. I must attend to it."

Catherine gave him a stern look. "You will eat first else you will fall on your seat and that may do your dignity no good. We have eggs and meats with oat porage and honey. Esther has purchased some tea and we will have it freshened. Now sit, sir, afore I resolve to be more stern with you."

"I will convey the request to Esther," Amelia said, curtsied and left them alone.

Chris took Catherine's hand. "I've missed you."

"And I you but it seems you find yourself in the most dreadful scrapes when away from my side. How came you by this injury?"

Chris let go of her hand long enough to pile eggs and ham onto a plate. "It's not something that will trouble the pages of the scandal sheets but it was in the service of King and country. I should not be telling you this but I know you will keep the confidence. The Irish have brought their rebellion to England and we have been engaged in putting it down. Mr Pitt will not want this to be common knowledge as he dreads the news may encourage a similar rising to the French Revolution amongst the English. I cannot see it happening but there are many covert Republicans amongst the people and I'm sure he has no wish to excite them further.

"Now to more mundane things, how do you like your new home?"

"I like it very well, sir. In the heart of town with the greenery of the park a mere stone's throw. But you should not attempt to change the subject and I wish to know the happenstance of your acquaintance with Mr Pitt."

43

Chris sent Matthew across to Number 10 with word of his return before he launched into an explanation of his current association with the First Lord of the Treasury. He seemed to recall that the easier to get his tongue around title of Prime Minister wasn't used until the early 1900s.

Catherine listened with her head to one side as he narrated the story, warts and all, including the Duke of York's veiled threat to have his stipend from the privy purse removed should he fail to keep him informed of Pitt's intentions. He had resolved that there would be no secrets in their marriage and whatever happened they would face it together.

Catherine's eyes widened when he explained his wagers at Brooks Club and the amount of money that he could lose and also of his plans to buy up several plots of land as future investments around the city with his winnings.

The biggest secret of all, that he was from the future and that the wagers were dead certainties, was one he was bound to keep. For one, she would think him insane and for another she might think him less than a gentleman for taking money under such pretences.

She kept her silence as he reeled out his gambling confession but gripped his hand in tacit support. He had other subjects to broach.

"Darling, Catherine. I know you are aware exactly how much I love you. However, I must warn you that my new duties may cause me to be away from your side far more than even service with the Corps of Riflemen. I want you to know that every second we are alone together is so very precious to me and every second I am away from you or in company where I cannot show my true affection is painful, although sometimes it may seem to me that we are the only two people in a crowded room. Our time alone together is so sweet that I never want it to end, that is the truth of it. You must forgive me my absences and know that I will return as soon as I may from wherever my duties take me.

"There is another thing. Mr Pitt has ordered that my activities must remain confidential. I will confide in you as I value your opinion and your counsel but no one else, not even Amelia or your father, must know of them."

Catherine squeezed his hand. "I shall of course keep your confidences. You have told me so much, I scarce know where to start or what to think. I do know that you are my dearest husband and whatever your destiny shall be I shall bear it with you with an open heart. The thought of your frequent absences does pain me to my soul but I shall bear them with fortitude knowing that you may return to me. I know not what these duties may be or where hither they may take you but when I cannot be with you in body my heart will be with you in spirit. All I ask is that you take such care of your life as is possible. Your St Kevlar may one day be forced to look another way when danger threatens."

Chris pulled her to him and kissed her. "You must forgive me, Catherine. My eyes droop as I've had no sleep for nearly two days. I must rest until I hear back from Mr Pitt."

"Then I shall lie with you until that time for the room is cool and should like to warm our bed for you."

"The mere touch of your hand warms me but I fear I will not be good for much else until I have slept."

"Then we must hasten the hour. Come, sir."

Pitt called Chris across later that afternoon and received his verbal report in silence. A despatch rider from General Ainslie had taken a written report of the battle, and of the 13th of Foot's part in it, to Horse Guards. Henry had sent it on to Downing Street and Pitt raised this now.

"General Ainslie makes little reference to the part the Corps of Riflemen played in this, Lennox. I have heard your account and like two pieces of a puzzle I may join them together."

Chris gave him a wry smile. "General Ainslie is a good commander promoting his troops' part in this. Indeed but for them the outcome may have been different. As it is there was little damage to property and no citizen of Bristol was harmed. I would count it a successful action altogether."

"You say the assault on this brigantine was made by the Corps?"

"Yes, sir. We lost three dead and three wounded. I must write to their families and dependents with the sad news."

"And you did say that the man Grant was dispatched fully."

Chris nodded. "By my own sabre, sir, before he could explode the ship."

"And no mention of this did seep out?"

"The 13th believe the Grey Wolves to be Irish pirates. There may be some amongst the ranks of the Dorsetshires who will speak of it to whomever may wish to listen but the news is of not such great import that it would cause anything other than a footnote in history."

"In contrast to your taste in uniform, you have a colourful turn of phrase, Lennox but I am beholden to you. It is one thing to be unburdened of the Grey Wolves but yet another to be assailed with doubts over the true nature of their sally into Bristol. What is it that the man Grant did say before his just end?"

"If I recall correctly, he said *'while your eyes have been turned toward Bristol there is another more deadly plot afoot of which you have no notion and will blight England far worse than savaging its commerce'.*"

Pitt grimaced. "What make you of it?"

"The man was about to die and thought I was about to die with him. I don't believe he was making an idle boast. There is something else afoot that we don't yet know of."

Pitt pulled another wry face. "That opinion echoes my own and I believe that the Irishman Leech be at the bottom of it. The despatches from France tell me little of him only that he was in the pay of the Directorate, a body now defunct as Bonaparte has declared himself First Consul and thrown them out of their lairs," Pitt's grave features broke into a small smile, "some through the windows I did hear. However, the Directorate's machinations do continue after they are gone and Leech is master of one of those. His face is kept covered from those who serve him and his features are unknown. He lurks somewhere in England. You must find him with his five 'gentlemen' and curtail whatever plot he is decided upon afore it may come to fruition."

Chris scratched his head. "Is there any clue to his whereabouts? Somewhere I might start the search?"

"That I leave to you, sir. The matter is most urgent and you must begin your task immediately. I believe there is little time to dally."

44

Back at his bureau Chris penned letters to the families of his three dead riflemen and included promissory notes for £50 for each. The government would allow them a pension of nine pence a day but most would live in penury on so little. The wounded men also would receive a small cash sum. Two would be able to return to the Corps in time but the one with the shattered arm would be invalided out. He gave this man a letter of introduction to Colonel Stewart with the hope that once recovered the man would be taken on as a quartermaster's assistant. It was the least he could do for such brave men.

That sad duty done he turned his attention to the job that Pitt had given him. As a stranger to both London and to the times, with, as Pitt had pointed out, no contacts he could call upon, he was forced into a course of action that he would rather have avoided.

He wrote a letter to Lloyd of the *London Gazette* with a request that they should meet at the Rose and Crown in Downing Street.

He called in Matthew and arranged to have the letters delivered. He knew that Lloyd would receive his the same night and he would expect a reply in the morning at the latest.

He put the quill down with a sigh and flexed his fingers. His hand was working perfectly now but still cramped up with long use. Writing was harder work than pressing a few keys on a laptop. The thought brought him back to his situation with a start. As on his previous journey to the past he did not need to shave, his hair did not grow and neither did his nails. It was as if he was still living in the

21st century in stasis as time passed by at a seemingly normal rate in 1800. He once again wished he knew more about the theory of relativity which might explain the conundrum.

Catherine materialised at his elbow. He had not heard her come in and guessed she had walked on tip-toe to surprise him. "We must talk about the household, dearest. Esther is coping manfully with the duties of cook but cannot continue in that position for long. Matthew must yet say adieu and return to Imber. We must decide on staff. A cook, a coachman, a footman and a valet for you."

"Dales will serve me on that score for now. Could I ask you to interview the household servants and decide for yourself whom you wish to employ. You are a considerable judge of character, after all you did see through me, and I have every trust in your ability to choose wisely."

"George, you do flatter me too much. I will abide by your wishes in this as I perceive you have other weightier things to address. You may leave these appointments in my hands but do not thereafter complain that my choices are ill-considered."

Chris put his hands on either side of her narrow waist. "As if I would. You are the epitome of good sense and I would never question it."

"You have inky fingers, George Lennox and I durst you to mark my gown."

Chris took his hands away and grinned. Catherine gave him a radiant smile back and clasped her hands behind his neck. "See, this is so much more to your advantage, sir. You may now kiss me."

Chris did, enthusiastically but eventually came up for air. "Mrs Lennox, I do believe you are turning into the worst kind of vamp ..."

"Indeed, sir?"

"... and I wholeheartedly approve as long as it is me that you tease and no other."

"You do mock me, sir and you may find that to your disadvantage betimes. Now I must away to the kitchen to discover what it is that Amelia and Esther have decided upon for your supper. It if were me I should say a bowl of gruel should suffice for your ill-manners."

She left with a teasing wave and a knowing smile. He wondered what he had done to deserve the love of such a woman and how he would cope with her loss.

Leech was in London, at the home of a completely innocent friend who knew nothing of his part in the league of United Irishmen nor of his nefarious dealings.

It was an ideal situation for him, hidden in plain sight in the home of an honest man, a wealthy Irish lord with a summer home under the white flag of County Kildare just west of Dublin and as loyal, as any Irish Catholic could be, to the Crown.

Leech secretly despised the man but was pleased to find him of use. He was introduced to the lord's set of English aristocracy and ingratiated himself, agreeing with their often naïve political views and playing the backwoods noble to the full. His own title gave him entrée to their soirées and a place at their tables.

He affected an air of amiable idiocy peppered with a little witty repartee that amused his hosts but gave him an air of harmless eccentricity that drew little attention and little comment from the haughty London elite.

He prevailed upon his host to provide him with the billiard room to invite a group of writers with whom he was acquainted and who were in need of a place to regularly meet. The man readily agreed but said he did not wish anything to do with such creatures as he had little interest in written works or such as plays put on for lascivious edification.

Leech had hidden a smile. The man's antipathy towards the arts was well known and would keep him out of the billiard room whilst United Irishmen's business was being discussed. That he was willing to indulge Leech's apparent interest in such things went to prove his weakness in Leech's mind.

The thoughts passed through his head as his five men settled down. These were the only five of the United Irishmen who knew his true identity and he trusted each of them with his good name and his life. They in their turn were dedicated to the cause and to him and would die for either.

He looked each man in the face one by one and liked what he saw. The determination, the resolve, the strength and the courage that he required was present in all of them. They did not yet know what was in store but he knew they would not flinch from their task once it was asked of them.

He coughed to clear his throat and a frisson of anticipation rippled around the group. This was the moment they had been awaiting.

"Gentlemen," Leech said in as solemn a tone as he was capable of voicing. "The time approaches when we shall strike a deadly blow for Ireland. The task may stick in your craw but I believe none of you will shirk it. If any among you has a doubt as to where his duty lies he may leave now and no one will think the worse of him. If you elect to stay you will be bound by an oath of honour that you will pursue your task with every ounce of your strength until success or death is attained. If you cannot do this you may leave now." He paused and again looked from face to face. Each man looked him in the eye and he was satisfied.

"Very well. From this point on you are all sworn to secrecy." He took a leather bound bible from the table. "Each man must place his right hand on the good book and swear his oath that only death will prevent him from achieving his task."

One by one the five men did as they were asked and settled back into their chairs.

Leech had a smile on his face. Not one of triumph but one of quiet satisfaction that at last his plot was in hand. "Gentlemen, your task will be to assassinate the King of England."

45

Regicide! Of all the forms of homicide, killing a king was the most heinous in the eyes of the law. It was high treason punishable by the most awful of deaths. Never in their wildest imagination would such an act have occurred to the five men and Leech knew, despite their protestations of loyalty and the oath they had taken, that the notion would be anathema and they would need to be further persuaded.

"King George is ruler of Britain and soon, with the Act of Union, of Ireland, but he has set his face against our emancipation. With Pitt's Act of Union which passes into law this coming January, we lose our own parliament and the right of self-governance. If the king in his intransigence were removed it would open the path to control our own destiny once more."

The eldest of the five, a man in his fortieth year, gave a nervous cough. "Surely, Coileán, retribution would be a terrible thing. Our families executed and our businesses forfeit. The English would not rest until each root and branch of our existence would be torn up and destroyed."

"The English will not know where truly to place blame. Each of you will have false papers. Should you die or be taken in the act they will throw the English off the scent. You will all speak in French with each other for the benefit of prying ears. We have been taking money from the French as it suited our purposes and they have supported our cause and will be readily accepted as blameworthy of such an act. They in their turn believe we will be spying for them but we have always intended we be working towards our own ends. Still your concerns. The French will bear the blame for this act. I shall ensure it.

"Remember Wolfe Tone, remember Vinegar Hill and the battles of the rebellion where so many good Irishmen did perish, some your kith and kin. This is just retribution"

"The king is well guarded," another man said. "How shall we get near to him?"

"He is not as well guarded as you may think. His household brigades are in the main ceremonial. He travels often from his house in Kew to the queen's house in the Mall with but a handful of pikemen and cavalrymen for company. There are loyal Irishmen amongst their number who are willing to divulge the duties they are bound to perform on each day and we shall be well informed of the king's progress."

"And how shall this deed be accomplished," the first man asked.

Leech gave a thin smile. "With guile and with determination. You have all been well-tutored in the arts of warfare. Your skills will be tested but I have little doubt that you will succeed in your task and will live to see a new day dawn for Ireland."

Chris had Lloyd's reply directed to Horse Guards. A runner brought it over at breakfast time with an agreement to meet at the Rose and Crown later that morning.

It had been a far from restful night as he and Catherine had a lot of catching up to do. He yawned over his breakfast plate.

Amelia gave him an amused look. "Do we keep you from your slumber, sir?"

"My apologies, dear sister. I haven't yet recovered from my exertions ..."

"I do believe you have exerted yourself mightily, dear George," Catherine said.

Chris coughed. "… in the service of the king."

"If but every soldier was so diligent in his service as you appear to be, sir, His Majesty would have no cause for complaint." Catherine shot Chris a secret smile. "No one is more ardent in his service than Colonel Lennox and you should not gainsay it, Amelia. A man so robust in his duties should bear nothing but admiration."

"Then let it be so," Amelia said. "I am agog with admiration, can you not divine it?"

Chris laughed. "To be so admired by not one but two of the most beautiful ladies in the whole of the kingdom is surely more than a simple soldier deserves. Now ladies you must forgive my poor manners for appearing bored in such pleasant company and for my absence as I have business to conduct."

"Bored, sir?" Catherine said. "Must you now claim indifference to such ravishing creatures as we?"

"Fie, sir," Amelia added, "I do believe I must feel insulted."

"Then put your mind at rest, dear Amelia, as I meant no such slight. Have it that I am so comfortable in your company that I can be myself and not put on airs.

"I really must leave you but you have brightened my morning with your wit, albeit at my expense."

He left them to it, grinning at the seemingly innocent but racy undertones of Catherine's remarks. It was another side of Catherine that he was seeing and it endeared him more to her. She could take his gentle leg-pulling and return it in spades when he least expected it. She had warned him.

He walked the few yards to the inn and waited by the log fire for Lloyd to arrive with a glass of port by his hand. He could not get used to the habit of drinking this early in the day and the wine remained untasted.

Lloyd sauntered in on time and ordered a drink at the bar before joining Chris at his table. He waited as the landlord brought the ale, running a curious eye over Chris's new civilian suit and scabbed ear before speaking. "Colonel Stewart, sir. To what do I owe this further pleasure?"

Chris was playing with fire if he was to keep Pitt's demand for secrecy. Talking to the press was as dangerous in 1800 as it was in the 2000s. He didn't beat around the bush and came to the point straight away. "I need your help, Mr Lloyd, and there is nothing in it for your publication. Anything I tell you must be on the understanding of strict confidentiality."

"And why should I agree to that, sir? Tis my livelihood to winkle out tales to inform, amuse and otherwise add to the fount of knowledge of our readership. I would be foolhardy to agree to such terms. Especially as tis you who requires *my* assistance."

"Very well, Mr Lloyd, it appears I have wasted your time. Good day, sir."

Lloyd took a pull on his ale and gave a grudging nod. "Let us not be hasty, sir. Is there no crumbs in the loaf that could be scattered?"

"No sir, not in this but should you agree I have other crumbs that will make your reputation in future times."

Lloyd put down his glass, a spark of interest in his eyes. "I am intrigued, sir, as to what that may be."

"News of a general nature given to you before other news sheets come to learn of it."

"How will *you* come by this intelligence?"

"Suffice it to say that I have my sources and you will be the first, in fact the only, scribe to be informed when such things come early to my notice. Did I not treat you fairly over our previous business?"

Lloyd gave him a shrewd look. "Indeed, sir. However, I am still awaiting an account of what may have transpired from it. May I ask what it is that you require of me now?"

"Firstly your word that anything arising from our following conversation will be completely confidential. Be aware, Mr Lloyd, that any undertaking on your part will not be treated lightly. If you renege on the deal I shall ensure your career will be a short one."

Lloyd gave him a tight grin. "Ah, the carrot and the stick. I see I am in the presence of a master. Very well, sir. You have my word and I shall not go back on it."

"You have your contacts, Mr Lloyd, of that I am sure, your eyes and ears around London and it is those I have need of. I want to trace six gentlemen who came off the Calais to Dover ferries over the past days. Any new arrivals in any part of London, be it in the slums or the best salons. Anyone who has raised an eyebrow, or who does stand out as unusual in any way. I need to know which lodgings they are using and whether they gather together and, if so, at which place. Your eyes and ears must not be seen and you will report any sighting of these men only to me, care of a Colonel Lennox at Horse Guards."

Lloyd grimaced. "Tis a gigantic task that you do set me. Is there a description of these *gentlemen*?"

"Unfortunately not. All I know is that there are six and that they came from France on separate ferries over a period of two days. Where they went from there is a matter of conjecture but, from past experience, I would hazard a guess that it would be London.

"The only other snippet I might venture is that these men may all be Irish but there is no way to be sure of that, and they may also be dressed in the French fashion as they may have spent some time there."

Lloyd gave a knowing smirk. "Ah, Irish. Do I deduce a connection with our previous business in that you were assailed by Irish footpads?"

"The matter is connected yet unconnected, Sherlock."

"My name is Charles, sir, should you be so bold."

"Forgive my slip of the tongue, Mr Lloyd, you did remind me of another man called Sherlock Holmes with your words. This is to go no further but the footpads were tasked with taking a soldier in green to be questioned on behalf of the French. Bonaparte's soldiery were given such a bloody nose in Portugal this past year and he wishes to know more of the Corps of Riflemen. The six gentlemen are concerned with an entirely different matter of which I have yet no firm notion only that they may pose a grave danger of disturbance to the peace of the land."

46

Chris went straight from the inn to Horse Guards to find Henry Wadman. He explained Pitt's worries and outlined the task Pitt had given to him.

Henry cleared papers from a corner of his table and offered Chris paper and a quill. "Sit and write it down, sir, that it may so inform His Royal Highness. Do you know what lies beneath Mr Pitt's concerns?"

"Only that it's to do with this league of United Irishmen and a man known as Coileán Leech."

"The United Irishmen were outlawed some years past. They were a band of desperate Irish rebels both Protestant and Catholic who wished Ireland ruled, not by the British but their own kind. If memory serves, they numbered but thirty-two, some executed for their part in the rebellion of 1798. Has the spectre raised its treacherous head once more?"

"In the name of their martyred leader, Wolfe Tone. They call themselves the Grey Wolves in his memory."

"Those who were defeated at Bristol."

"All but those whom Mr Pitt fears are now abroad in this country to make mischief. I myself am greatly worried by this."

"There is to be a vote in the House of Commons on the Act of Union with Ireland. Their Lordships in the other place have suggested amendments to the Act, on His Majesty's behalf, that the Act does not offer emancipation to the Catholics. Do you believe this may be some form of demonstration against this amendment in order to embarrass the King's majesty?"

"It may well be that you have put your finger on it, Henry. But what form this demonstration may take eludes me."

"You have taken steps?"

"As far as I'm able with the information I have to hand. I cannot go into details but the search for some knowledge of the whereabouts of these Grey Wolves is proceeding."

"I wish you well of it, sir. It seems that Mr Pitt has a high opinion of your abilities, giving such an onerous task with so little knowledge to guide you."

"I hope that I can meet his expectations."

Chris sat and began to write his report then had a thought. "Any news of the riflemen arriving back from Bristol?"

"They were taken back aboard the *Aquilon* and, as the winds are set fair, are due at the Wool Quay tomorrow eve."

Chris gave a satisfied nod. "Please keep me informed of any delay. I wish to be there to meet them."

Henry gave his tired smile. "As you wish, sir. Your energy is unbounded; oh that I were of your tender years."

Chris frowned. "You can't be that much older than me, Henry. What are you, thirty-six?"

"Five and thirty, sir. I believe I can give you ten years to the good."

"It seems to me you are working too hard, sir. You must join Catherine, Amelia and myself for supper tonight. The change will do you good."

"I should be delighted but as you see," he waved a hand over the papers on his desk, "I have much with which to concern myself."

"You will concern yourself into an early grave, my friend. You must come, I insist. Catherine and Amelia will be distraught should you not."

"Then I shall not disappoint my beloved sisters, nor you, sir. I will accept your invitation with the greatest of pleasure."

"Do you wish to bring a companion?"

"There is one such, if I may be so bold, who may not find the occasion too imminent."

"Bring whomever you wish. They will be more than welcome. Any friend of my brother is a friend of mine."

"You are too kind, sir."

Henry and his companion arrived after dark and were shown into the hall by Matthew who took their hats and cloaks. He showed them into the drawing room where Chris and the two sisters were seated. Candles were burning from chandeliers and in sconces around the walls but the light was still dim. It wasn't until the two visitors had fully entered the room that Chris started in surprise at a glimpse of the second man. He rose to his feet.

Amelia gave a small squeal of pleasure and rushed to take both Henry's hands in hers.

"Brother dearest, I am so delighted to see you I might swoon."

Henry gave her a fond smile and pulled her gently to one side. "You are forgetting yourself in your delight, child. The master and mistress of the house are to take precedence. You must await your turn."

Amelia blushed but returned his smile. She turned to Chris and Catherine and curtsied. "I do beg your pardon. I was so overcome to see my dear brother I did forget my place."

Chris smiled and took her hand. "You are forgiven. Major Wadman, would you be so kind as to make the introductions."

"As you wish, sir." He turned to his companion. "I have the pleasure to present Lieutenant-colonel George Lennox, his wife, my sister Mrs Catherine Lennox and my youngest sister Miss Amelia Wadman. I do believe you have made the acquaintance of Colonel Lennox, Colonel Wellesley."

"Indeed, briefly, but not your charming sisters. I am overwhelmed. I had that Mrs Lennox was of exceeding beauty but that is understating the actuality. And to have another sister her equal. You are indeed most fortunate in your siblings, sir, and Colonel Lennox is to be most envied in his choice of bride."

Catherine curtsied. "You are too kind, Colonel Wellesley, you do us too much honour."

"Indeed, madam, I do not. Tis plain to me that it would be difficult to find yours and Miss Wadman's equal in beauty in the whole of London."

"That is most gallant of you, sir. Come now sit and take some Madeira.

Matthew who had followed them into the room poured the drinks and passed them round. "Dinner will be announced at seven of the clock, madam," he said to Catherine. "The new cook has prepared goose and a haunch of beef."

Catherine nodded. "Then it will serve as a test as to whether I have chosen well."

Chris buttonholed Wellesley as Henry was monopolised by his sisters. "You are in London long, sir?"

Wellesley shook his head. "I take ship to India this coming week. I have already dallied overlong. There is much work to do on the sub continent. The maharajahs are testing our strength and I am needed there."

"I daresay you will make a brave fist of it, sir. Did I hear there was talk of a knighthood?"

"Premature gossip. I am indebted to his Royal Highness for his kindness in consulting my opinion but that honour has yet to be earned."

"But earn it you will, Colonel, of that I am sure."

"You have a reputation for calling the odds right, sir, but I am bound to say that it would be devilish conceited of me to agree with your opinion."

"As you are leaving soon, is there not more urgent business you could be employed upon other than joining us for dinner, as pleasant as is your presence with us?"

"My god but you are as forthright with your views as I have been led to believe, Lennox and you may unerringly pin the tail to this donkey.

"I have come to seek your views on Bonaparte's intentions. I hear you have travelled widely and have much to tell. As a soldier and student of warfare I would be greatly obliged for the benefit of your experience."

Chris nodded. "I can reveal something of what I have learned but it will be of little use in India. However, it may stand you in good stead at some future time. Be warned though, Colonel, you may not like what you will hear, nor agree with my assessments. There may come a time when you look back on this night and wish you had been more accepting of a particular point of view."

Wellesley laughed. "I do not doubt that, Lennox, for you appear to be a man of particular certainties but, as far as I can ascertain, no crystal ball."

47

The following morning Chris reflected on his conversation with the future Duke of Wellington. He had been careful not to be too specific and knew that much of what he had revealed about Bonaparte would be forgotten or ignored by Wellesley. He hoped that enough would stick to give the man his advantage when facing Bonaparte's forces in the Peninsular campaign but more importantly at the Battle of Waterloo still fifteen years in the future. He doubted that his ideas on the enforcement of discipline amongst the troops would take root for many years to come. Flogging was entrenched in the military psyche as a means of maintaining order and Wellesley had openly laughed at his suggestion that it should be curtailed in all but extreme cases.

He had been more amenable to further use of the rifle for his skirmishers but did not see it replacing the musket and volley fire as a major tactic although Chris had pointed out the monumental losses that were often incurred when packed ranks were faced by artillery.

The evening had ended amicably with them both agreeing to disagree and Wellesley had left with a thoughtful expression. Henry had stayed another hour over another glass of cognac and Chris replayed the conversation in his mind.

"You oft surprise me, brother with your grasp of both politics and matters military. I do believe you gave the good colonel much to ponder on," Henry said.

Chris hunched his shoulders and let them drop. "I know my views are unfashionable but I'm sure they will eventually find fertile ground. Much of the problem lies within the fact that I am a Johnny-come-lately with no family ties to speak of. I know I'm not taken seriously amongst the hierarchy at Horse Guards and I wonder whether the colonel was sent to test the water and ascertain whether I am merely a dreamer or whether my knowledge is sound."

Henry gave him a tight grin. "You are altogether far too cognisant. Since your secondment to Downing Street there have been whispers that perhaps your success in Portugal was a flash in the pan and it would be unwise for His Royal Highness to regard you too highly. Some feathers have been ruffled and I thought it opportune to invite Wellesley, a man held in esteem for his service in India, to have converse with you and to make his judgement on your character."

"Do you think that a wise decision in hindsight?"

"Ah, George, I do believe you may hold your own in any company. Tonight I am proud to call you brother-in-law. I do believe that Wellesley was impressed enough to give a good report to the generals which will no doubt enhance your standing, along with the news of your success against the Grey Wolves at Bristol, despite the attempt of the 13th of Foot to hog the glory."

"Can I detect a codicil coming?"

"You must still be ware. There are siren voices amongst the old guard who do not hold with new-fangled tactics and such weapons as rifles. Tread with care and temper your espousal of such things."

"Even though I know I'm right?"

"Especially as you think you are right. It is still conjecture, George and you must avoid appearing too forward in your views. As it is I have the unenviable task to inform you that as you are no longer attached to the Corps of Riflemen you will revert to your substantive rank of captain and your stipend will be reduced accordingly to half pay."

Chris threw down his quill as the memory jolted him. The duke had not entirely abandoned his faith in him and had allowed him a still significant sum of two-thousand-five-hundred guineas per annum. That was far more than any captain could expect but had made it more imperative that he found ways to increase his income on his own account.

Catherine came in and noticed his frown as he reworked figures on income and expenditure. "What is it that concerns you so, dearest. I have not seen so stern a visage since first we met."

Chris told her the story. She sat on his knee and folded her arms around his neck. "Have I not already informed you that I am able to live well within our means and our cloth shall be cut accordingly. We shall do without an upstairs maid and a fine carriage. Your man Dales did inform me that you own two geldings and they shall do for our needs. If you could but purchase a side-saddle for my use, we shall make the best of it. There is stabling at the rear of this house and Dales may act as groom. I shall write to papa to ask his permission for Matthew to stay longer so there will be no need to engage a footman. There, you see, already we have saved six-hundred pounds on the carriage and stabling alone and a further ninety pounds on wages."

"I thought I married you for love. Now I know that it was also for your intelligence. You are not just a pretty face, are you?"

"Pretty, sir? You do insult me. Did you not hear Colonel Wellesley opine that I am amongst the most beautiful in London?"

"He was wrong."

Catherine's eyes widened. "*Indeed*?"

"You are *the* most beautiful woman in the whole of the kingdom."

She tapped his shoulder with her fan. "I am not so sure I approve of your teasing, sir, although I may admit to opening myself up to ridicule."

"You were merely fishing for compliments."

"And you did take the bait, dear George, like a pike on a minnow."

"I'm more of a stickleback," Chris said with a grin. "Impossible to swallow."

They were interrupted when Matthew came in behind a delicate cough. He had a note on a salver.

"A runner brought this from Horse Guards, sir."

"Thank you, Matthew. Bring it over."

Catherine slipped off his knee and kissed him on the cheek. "I have business with the cook over last night's supper. The beef was a little overdone."

Matthew bowed as she went out and Chris could see he was red in the face. "I meant no disrespect, sir but if you would forgive me speaking freely."

Chris nodded. "Please continue."

"I did not wish to intrude on so private a moment and do apologise for it."

"Don't be embarrassed on our account, Matthew. We do not hide our affection for each other and I hope that the servants will share in the joy of it. I hope this will be a happy household and that you will remain part of it. Mrs Lennox will be writing to Sir George to ask for his permission to allow you to stay longer."

"I am truly grateful that Mrs Lennox is so entirely happy with my service. I have known her since she was but a small girl and have a good deal of affection for her.

However I do have another affection of my own that does trouble me."

"Would that affection be called Mary?"

Matthew bowed. "Indeed, sir. We were but recently betrothed and with Sir George's permission will wed in the Spring. I do miss her company and but for that matter would be honoured to stay in your service for as long as I am needed."

"I'll ask Mrs Lennox to also write to Sir George on that score. He may have little need of her services at Imber as Miss Wadman is with us here. I hope he will be amenable to the idea."

"It would greatly ease my mind, sir."

"Leave it with me, Matthew. Now wait while I read this note. A reply may be needed." He broke the seal with his thumb and opened the single sheet of paper. It was from Lloyd and he had news.

48

It was several nights later that Chris stood with Lloyd outside a coffee house in Covent Garden. A daytime market place, Covent Garden turned into a den of vice after dark which had forced the aristocracy to move out and their place taken by opportunists who opened gambling dens and whore houses alongside the politically active coffee houses.

The street, opposite the Royal Opera House, was alive with the rich and dissolute of the capital. Chris kept his sabre concealed beneath his cloak and a Dragon pistol in his pocket but still felt unaccountably unsafe. Lloyd was also nervous, a fact given away by his fidgeting and fingering a sword cane.

"Tis a devilish place to be once the sun has set," he said. "A footpad or whore on every corner with easy pockets to pick. Tis little wonder your gentleman does choose this place to lodge."

Chris gave him a sideways look. "How certain are you that this is one of those men?"

"Not at all certain, sir, given the lack of real description, but that he is recently arrived, speaks little, oft in French, and wears clothes better suited to the streets of Paris than of London. He meets with another similarly attired in yonder coffee house each evening and they oft travel together to a house in Kensington, the home of a distinguished lord."

"Who is?" Chris prompted.

"Lord Cavan of Kildara, so I am informed. An Irish lord but a loyal kingsman."

"Or so the story goes," Chris muttered.

Lloyd pulled him further back into the shadows. "Observe, they now leave together and head west to Piccadilly and thence to Kensington. Shall we follow them?"

Chris gave him a grim smile. "There is no need. I have my riflemen in attendance. They have been instructed not to follow too closely and to relieve each other of the task at regular intervals so that those two are unaware they are observed. We will take a carriage to Knightsbridge to be there ahead of them to see what transpires." He had Pitt's carriage waiting in the Strand and hurried there, brushing aside the overtures of overconfident prostitutes who populated the alleys. Dales was seated next to the driver on the box and stepped down to open the door.

"Where to, Colonel?"

Chris looked around to see that Lloyd was still some way behind. He lowered his voice. "Kensington, but it's captain now, Dales."

Dales took the hint and eyed Lloyd's approach over Chris's shoulder and said equally quietly, "you shall always be my colonel, sir. Kensington it is then, sir. I shall so inform the coachman."

"Mr Lloyd has the address. We need to find a place to conceal the coach and await some visitors."

They found a dark patch under some trees where they could watch the front of the terraced house. A smart coach with a crest on the door pulled up outside and an elegantly dressed couple came out and stepped into it.

Chris took a surreptitious look at the glowing hands of his Breitling. It was nearing eight-o-clock and the night was getting cold.

Lloyd shuffled in his seat and wrapped his cloak tighter around him. "I do swear they are dallying this night. I would expect their appearance ere this time."

Chris saw the flash of a lamp deeper in the trees. "They're here now. There's a signal from my riflemen."

"Not afore time. This frost is biting my bones."

"Then spare a thought for my riflemen who don't have the comfort of a coach roof over their heads, nor leather seats to recline on."

"You are a strange fellow, Colonel, to have such thought for your subordinates. I have not met your like before."

"Nor will you again, Mr Lloyd. I fear I am a man born before my time."

"Then I daresay, should your views become general, the *London Gazette* will remark upon it."

Chris pointed. "There are our two gentlemen who have two companions with them. Perhaps that would explain their tardiness."

Light spilled from the house as the front door opened and four figures slunk inside.

"It seems they were expected," Chris said.

"But the lord of the house has left," Lloyd mused. "Tis strange indeed that this meeting should take place in his absence."

There was a rustle outside the carriage and Dales poked his blond head in. "Serjeant-major Biggin wishes further orders, sir."

"Are all the riflemen present?"

"The serjeant-major says to tell you all two dozen bar one."

"Very well. Ask the serjeant-major to have Serjeant-major Pocock and ten men report to me here and position the others behind the house to ensure no man can escape from there. You will act as runner between us. He is to take no further action until I order it."

Dales disappeared and Lloyd leaned over to Chris. "What is your plan, sir? Are we to sit here much longer?"

"You write about a soldier's life, now you'll experience it. Ninety-seven percent boredom, two percent action and one percent fear. We will wait until Lord Cavan returns. I must have all the wolves in one lair and it may be the noble lord who leads the pack."

"Look! There is yet another man going up to the door."

"That is five with Cavan making the sixth. Now we wait."

It was nine-thirty before there was any further movement as the big front door swung open and two men left. Chris frowned. Cavan had not returned and these men were leaving. A few minutes later the door opened again and another man came out, pulled his cloak tightly to his chin and walked rapidly away. A further ten minutes passed when the door opened for the last time and the last of the five left.

Candles were burning and the glow shone through the fanlight above the door. A sign that the servants had not yet retired.

"Still we wait," Lloyd grumbled.

"Don't you find it odd that these men did not await Lord Cavan's return?"

"I am not a gipsy with her tarot cards to be able to divine such things. Perhaps it was merely a card school or a society. Mayhap we have the wrong men."

"Then why would they leave separately, like thieves in the night?

"Of that I have no notion. Now may we return? My bed is calling me."

"A short while longer, until the candles are snuffed and I'm sure the house has retired."

Twenty minutes later the night silence was broken by the clop of hooves and the rumble of iron-shod wheels. Cavan's carriage rolled up to the front door which was opened immediately and a boy came out with a flaming torch held high. Chris could see Cavan and his wife clearly as they entered the house. Something wasn't right and he knew he would have to get inside the house to find out what it was.

49

"Stay here, Mr Lloyd."

Chris climbed out of the carriage and ordered Dales to bring Pocock and his men to him.

Lloyd leaned out of the carriage window. "What do you plan to do, sir?"

Chris glanced up at his barely visible blur of a face. "Work on the two percent."

With a rustle of movement dark shapes materialised. "Light torches, Serjeant-major. We are about to go fishing."

Flint sparked and two pitch-soaked torches flared. They threw deep shadows and lit up expectant faces. Chris glanced around him and nodded. "We are to call on the house and take possession of it.

"Dales, inform Serjeant-major Biggin to be on guard at the rear." He turned to his eleven soldiers. "We do not know what we may expect as a welcome. The servants may be armed and prepared to defend the house at any cost. We must be ready for that but do not harm them unless there is no alternative. Whenever possible use the flat of your blades and the butts of your rifles should there be any resistance. Come with me."

Candlelight was still flickering through the fanlight as Chris hammered on the door. "Open in the name of the king." He did not know whether he had the authority but it might elicit a non-belligerent response. Unless they were all involved in whatever plot was afoot.

The door swung open on the face of a frightened footman with a five-branch candelabra in his hand. Chris pushed him back against the wall. "Where is Lord Cavan?

The man's eyes were round with fear and he stuttered. "In the withdrawing room with milady and Lord Edenderry of Tullamore."

Chris turned to Pocock. "Secure the house and bring everyone, including servants to the withdrawing room. Two men with me now."

He pushed the footman ahead and followed him into the room where Cavan was standing with his back to the fire and a frown on his face. His wife was sitting on a chaise longue with another man who leapt to his feet as Chris entered.

"Stand still," Chris snapped and waved his Dragon.

Cavan had turned red in the face and spluttered. "What is the meaning of this? How dare you invade my house. By whose authority is my privacy denied?"

Chris heard the words but he was watching the other man closely. He had his hand in his pocket and he was quivering with suppressed fury. His face was long and blue-chinned and his eyes burned in the firelight.

"Remove your hand from you pocket, if you please Lord Edenderry, or I should be obliged to shoot you. Slowly, lest I mistake your intention."

Cavan's jaw was working and his eyes bulged. "Well, sir? I demand an answer."

Chris threw him a grin. "All in good time, my lord. If you would kindly be seated. You, Lord Edenderry, please remain standing while my soldier takes your pistol from your pocket. I would not wish there to be an unfortunate accident."

Edenderry's mouth twisted into a sneer. "You had best give good reason for this outrage, sir, or it shall be the worse for you."

Dales prodded him with his rifle. "Hands-up milord." He pulled out a long barrelled pistol from Edenderry's pocket and handed it to Chris who examined it.

"Ah a French manufacture, and rifled, poor form in a duel in this country, sir. Now you may be seated."

There was a muted commotion in the hall and several servants were ushered in, some in nightwear. They were made to sit with their backs to a wall with a rifleman standing guard over them. Two men were brought in, both fully dressed in household regalia. Both were unamused and resisted the rifles prodding them until one of the riflemen cocked his weapon and glared. Both men sat apart from the lesser servants with ill grace.

Chris nodded at Pocock. "Is that all of them?"

"Aye, sir, all accounted for. Head cook and bottle washer and all."

"Very good, Sergeant-major. Have the piquet at the rear of the house reduced to two men and bring the others inside to search the place from attic to basement."

Pocock scratched his head. "For what may we be searchin', sir?"

"Anything out of the ordinary. Papers, maps, an unusually large number of weapons or large amounts of powder. You'll know it when you find it. Leave Dales and two others with me here. You take the top two floors and Biggin the bottom two. Report back immediately should anything be found."

Cavan was growing ever more agitated as Chris's whispered conversation happened. Now he stood. "Well, sir! Am I to have your answer?"

"We have reason to believe there may be treason afoot and our enquiries have directed us to this house, sir."

"Preposterous poppycock, sir. How dare you suggest that I would be privy to treason."

"A group of men visited this place tonight. For what reason?"

Edenderry looked more relaxed but his eyes flickered. "They visit me, sir, a group of writers. We meet regularly to discuss each of their works. It is merely a harmless diversion."

Chris picked up Edenderry's pistol. "Do these writers become so angry that you need a pistol to defend yourself?"

"I was abroad on the streets earlier this eve and merely did forget to remove it from my pocket. There is no mystery there, sir."

"On whose authority do you question my guest, sir?" Cavan bawled.

"No authority but my suspicions, Lord Cavan. If you have done no wrong you have nothing to fear. I shall apologise for the inconvenience and leave you in peace. However I do strongly suspect that there is more to Lord Edenderry's story than he is willing to tell."

"How dare you, sir, impugn my friend, a guest in my house. This is outrageous."

"So is treason, sir and you should be ware lest you incriminate yourself by association. How long has Lord Edenderry been residing here?"

"But a few days. He is visiting from his estates in Ireland."

"Not from France, then?"

"From the west, not the east, sir," Edenderry said.

"With a French pistol in your pocket and French fashion on your back?"

"Is it against the law, sir?"

"No but it gives me pause for thought. Do you have names for your five fellow authors?"

"I do. They travelled from Dublin. Took ship with me and dispersed to their lodging around town but I do not know to where. Twas agreed with Lord Cavan that we could meet here in his billiard room to discuss our works."

"Let Lord Cavan's servant find you quill, paper and ink. I would be most obliged if you would list the names for me."

Cavan nodded and one of the uniformed flunkeys climbed to his feet. He was escorted out by a rifleman and passed Pocock on his way in.

Chris raised a quizzical eyebrow but Pocock shook his head, came close and whispered. "Nothing in the attic or upper rooms, sir. Nothing to match your needs."

"Stay here, Serjeant-major. The valet is bringing writing material for Lord Edenderry let him pass it over. I'll be but a few minutes. Don't be cowed by their lordships and ignore any threats they may make. They must remain here until I return."

He went to the billiard room. One candle was burning and he used it to light others until the room was bright enough for what he needed.

There was a long bench against one wall where the players sat between each turn at the table. Above it was a row of books on wooden shelving. On the opposite wall stood a large bookcase with writing bureau built into it cleverly designed to fold back into the woodwork when play was taking place. It was now opened out with sheets of paper laid on it. He picked up the top sheet and held it against the light to check for any indentations. It was an old trick but it didn't work. The paper was thick and it would have needed the hard pressure of a ballpoint to have marked it at all. He pulled out the drawers and checked inside. If this was where the Grey Wolves met there was an outside chance they had left a clue … somewhere.

50

It was another Hollywood cliché, Chris thought, that the hero stumbles on a vital clue that everyone else had missed but none of his soldiers really had a clue what to look for and wouldn't know a piece of evidence if it slapped them in the face; so in the end it would be down to him and the instincts that had served him so well. Instinct or divine guidance? That too was a matter of conjecture.

It was in that context that he just knew that Edenderry was bent and probably was the alter ego of Coileán Leech himself. He had that wild look about him and eyes that were as dead as a week old corpse. And he gave off that aura he had read about; the man radiated danger as tangible as the heat from a log fire.

The only other items on the bureau were a leather bound bible, about the size of modern foolscap paper and two inches thick and a quill. The leather was tooled with a family coat of arms on the front with a Latin inscription. '*Cave morsus anguis.*' Chris pursed his lips. He had no idea what it meant but the coat of arms had a snake entwined around a Celtic cross as part of the design. He thought it odd as there were no snakes in Ireland, except, occasionally, the odd human one. They were all driven into the sea by St Patrick, according to legend, as one had tried to bite him. It was an interesting conundrum.

He opened the book and flipped through the pages. It was all in Latin. No King James Bible for these lads, Chris thought. As he turned over the next page a loose sheet slipped out. He picked it up and held it to the light. It was covered in a spidery scrawl of Latin words but had a small diagram of radiating lines etched at the bottom.

He used the quill pen to quickly make a copy and pushed the paper back between the same pages of Leviticus. He placed everything exactly as he found it, snuffed the candles and went back to the drawing room.

Biggin met him at the door. "We have found nothing of matter, sir. No weapons other than those that a house may safely keep, some fowling pieces and a blunderbuss. Powder only enough for a week's hunting."

It was nothing that Chris hadn't expected. He entered the room and bowed. "My apologies, my lords and my lady. We have concluded our business and have found nothing of note and may only conclude that our information was false. Please accept my sincere condolences for this upset and rest assured we will do all in our power to uncover the culprit who did so maliciously slander you."

Cavan was on his feet, puce in the face. "Be that as it may, sir but from whom do I seek restitution for this unforgiveable intrusion."

Chris bowed again. "I am Captain George Lennox, sir. Should you require satisfaction you may enquire of me at 10 Downing Street."

"Ah, Downing Street, eh?"

"Yes my lord. I am commanded in this by the First Lord of the Treasury and do not carry out these actions lightly. You may apply to him for restitution should you feel so inclined."

Cavan coughed. "I will think upon it. What say you, Edenderry?"

Edenderry gave a tight-lipped smile. "I say you should let the matter lie and accept the captain's apology. It would gain you little to pursue it, with the First Lord, I fear."

"Chris bowed again. "Wise counsel, my lord."

"But that is not to say I will not pursue it with you, sir, at some future time. You have insulted my honour and when the time is right I will seek satisfaction."

"At your convenience, my lord. Shall I allow you the use of your rifled pistol as is the French custom."

"The choice of weapon will be yours, Captain. In the meantime I do have a request should you be so kind as to grant it."

"If it is in my power to grant and it's a reasonable request then by all means."

"Would you open your cloak?"

Chris smiled. He folded the riding cloak over one shoulder. "Are you satisfied, sir?"

"Tis as I supposed, you wear the green."

"I am detached from the Corps of Riflemen but I am proud to wear their colour. Do you have issue with that also?"

Edenderry had a cold look on his face. Given time, sir. Given time."

Lloyd was out of the carriage, striding back and forth. He rushed forward as Chris came out of the house. "What news, sir? I have kicked my heels in this damned cold night awaiting your pleasure."

"Do you have any Latin, Mr Lloyd?"

"No, sir, I do not. Do you think me a priest or, worse, a lawyer?"

"I need someone who can translate Latin. Do you have anyone we may call on?"

"At this hour?"

"Why not?"

"There is a schoolmaster of my acquaintance who teaches Latin at Westminster School. He is oft to bed at a late hour."

"We'll call on him. Direct the coachman." Chris turned to Biggin. "I want this house watched night and day, front and back. No one is to arrive or leave without my knowledge. And it should be done without the household or neighbours becoming aware of it. You know what is required."

Biggin nodded in the dark and knuckled his forehead. "Aye, sir. What do you wish with this list of names?"

"I doubt they will be of much use, I suspect the information is false."

Lloyd grabbed at Chris's sleeve. "What is afoot?"

"Nothing yet, Mr Lloyd. We are now embarking on the ninety-seven percent phase. I may know more once we have consulted your schoolmaster."

Westminster School was in Dean's Yard behind the Abbey and on the way back to Whitehall. It was a short journey and Lloyd was pounding on the schoolmaster's door in less than twenty minutes. Chris was expecting a Mr Chips but it was a young man, his wig askew, who threw open the door with a cane in one hand and a candlestick in the other. His surprise at seeing Lloyd took the wind out of his sails and he lowered the cane.

"Ah Mr Lloyd. I did think it was the upper fifth at their tricks again, absconding from their dormitory to bang on my door and run like vagabonds."

"Mr Petrie, I have with me a gentleman who requires your assistance."

Petrie blinked in surprise. "Well come in do. To what should I owe the honour?"

"I have some Latin I wish translated, sir, if you be so kind."

"You have none, sir?"

"This is Colonel Stewart of the Corps of Riflemen," Lloyd said.

"A soldier, oh, that would explain much. Where is this Latin screed, sir?"

Chris gave him his copy and he held it to the light.

"Before you begin on that work Mr Petrie. Could you translate a motto, 'Cave morsus anguis'?"

Petrie looked up from the paper. "That is simple. It is beware the bite of the snake." He turned his attention back to the written words. "Hmm! This leaves something to be desired in both grammar and lucidity. It appears to be a chess instruction."

"*Chess?*" Both Chris and Lloyd said together.

"Yes, let me see. *'Secundo movet rex reginae. Equites septuaginta homines immolare gambit forte requirat. Densis castles parte regis. Ludere animos'.*

""Secondly move the king to the queen. Horsemen with theatrical gambit may require sacrifice. Locking castles of King. Take the courage to play."

"That doesn't make an awful lot of sense," Chris said.

Petrie gave him a sharp look. "Neither does your vernacular, sir. Now let me ponder this. It may be allusion. Horsemen may be knights and they may make a sacrificial gambit which would cloak the player's true intention but should be played with courage."

"A feint?" Chris suggested.

"Quite so. Locking castles of king? That may be a reference to the rook and the king played together."

"And the reference to the queen?"

"That is strange. The king is alongside the queen unless the queen moves away which is opposite to what is suggested here. Here the king goes to the defence of the queen which appears to be in contradiction of the rules of the game. And why secondly? What is firstly?"

"What do you make of the diagram?"

"Oh, that is simply a map. It is a diagram of the roads here and the Mall which leads to the Queen's Buckingham House."

"Could your translation be incorrect? Is that secondly or merely second?"

"Possibly sir, why is that significant?"

"The second is tomorrow. We don't have much time."

51

As soon as he arrived back in Downing Street Chris sent Dales to Knightsbridge to await the return of the Riflemen not on stake out. No one was going to get much sleep this night.

Catherine was waiting for him in their bedroom, his clean combat suit laid out on the covers with a small cloth bag sitting on top of it.

"A man did bring this from Knightsbridge earlier this eve."

Chris gave her a smile although his mind was concerned with other things and he did not catch the question in her voice. "Yes, the washerwomen have laundered it."

"Is it to your satisfaction, sir?"

He gave the suit a quick glance. "It appears to be."

"They have repaired the tears in the breast. I see there are three now."

Chris paid more attention. "Rather there than in me, don't you think?"

"And your ear is healing quickly."

Chris took both her hands in his. "We've already had this conversation. Soldiering is a dangerous business but I know how to protect myself."

"So you say, sir. The holes of two balls and a cut from a sword all to the chest suggest otherwise."

"That I am alive and well should speak for itself."

"In the pouch on the bed, they did find some strange items in your suit pocket."

Chris picked up the linen bag and could feel the outline of the 9mm bullets he had taken from the Glock's magazines and forgotten. He gave her a strained smile. He could lie but decided not to. "These are cartridges that could change the shape of warfare if adopted. I brought them with me from where I came."

"This country you call New Zealand?"

"A place far from here."

"Will you take me there?"

"If time allows. Why all these questions, Catherine?"

"I had Matthew unpack your knapsack." She turned to pick up some items on a tray from a side table behind her. "These too are most strange." She had his toothbrush, multi-bladed razor, Silva compass, trauma kit, personal role radio and binoculars on the tray. She picked up the compass and peered through the transparent plastic with its printed markings. "Most strange indeed, sir. This is glasslike yet it does not break."

"That's because it's made of a material called plastic. It will snap if you try hard enough to break it."

"And these?" She picked up the binoculars.

"They are a viewing device, similar to a telescope but to use with both eyes at once."

"And this, sir?" She touched the PRR with its attached microphone.

"That's another invention that doesn't yet work. Now, Catherine, I have been patient with your questions but I have an urgent matter to attend to. If you wish to make a point can you please come to it quickly."

"There is this miniature." She took out a colour photograph. "It is so lifelike and of two people who are dressed most strangely. The artist has great skill, I marvel at the fineness of the workmanship."

Chris sighed. "Those are my parents and that is the style of dress where we live."

"I can see the resemblance to your papa. He is as handsome as are you. Your mama too has great presence. Do they both still live?"

"I hope so. They were alive when I left."

"You never speak of them."

"When there is time I will tell you all about my family but now is not that time."

"I do believe you are an enigma, George Lennox. A soldier, an inventor, a man of medicine …"

"A husband and a lover. That is all that's important. Given time you will learn more of me as I am learning more of you as each day passes. One year ago we were strangers now we are married. There is much we have to discover about each other which will make our time together even more delightful than it already is."

"I cannot help but think you are keeping secrets from me."

"My past is another country. What is not a secret is my love for you. You can trust in that."

She walked to him, put her arms around his waist and laid her head against his chest. "That I never doubt, dearest George. You are quite correct, time will reveal all and I shall be patient in my thirst to know you better."

He bent and kissed the top of her head, then lifted her chin and kissed her lips very gently. Rest now, sweetheart. I have much to do tonight as tomorrow may prove to be a momentous day."

Leech watched from the window of his bedroom to see any sign of movement at the back of the house. He was sure he was being watched but could not discern any shape or any form of movement in the darkness.

He was growing concerned. He needed to be away well before daybreak as the house slumbered and there was no one to give the alarm. He had no intention of returning here, no intention of giving polite thanks or regrets as tomorrow would change the world.

He heard the long case clock in the hall chime eleven. The house servants would now be asleep as they had an early start to their labours, most being up before dawn to light fires and candles ready for the day.

It was a risk but one he had to take. If there was a guard outside he would take care not to rouse him. He collected his bag and slung it across his back to leave both hands free. He pushed a pistol into his pocket; the one Lennox had returned to him, loaded, primed and on half cock. A sharp bladed scian he pushed into his belt, entwining the scabbard in the leather so that the blade could slip easily from it.

He hung a grey cloak from his shoulders over his load and between his legs before making a slit in the hem and tying the ends around his neck. The whole effect was to give him a hunchback appearance which he completed by shoving a disreputable felt tricorn on his head. He used soot from the fire to blacken his face and then made sure his hands could reach the knife and the pistol easily.

It was pointless to use the doors so he made his way to the scullery and forced open a window which faced onto the carriage house and stables. It was coal dark outside and he made no noise as he climbed onto the cobbles in sackcloth covered boots. He edged forward slowly with his back to the carriage doors. One creaked and he froze, listening. A horse quietly snuffled and a hoof stamped inside the stables. The horse blew again, a sign it was restless and he would need to take more care. The carriage gates were kept locked but there was a smaller semi-hidden postern gate set into the wall and he knew that the key was kept in a box next to it. He had remarked to the carriage driver on how stiff the hinges were on a previous day and the man had obligingly oiled them and the lock so that the key turned easily and silently and the door swung open at a touch. He eased through and sidled along the wall feeling his way in the pitch dark. His toe stubbed against a stone and it rattled away across the cobbled path.

"Who goes there?" The voice was not loud but it was strong and authoritative. Leech heard the hammer of a weapon click back. Ten yards away a carriage lamp was uncovered and its meagre light shone towards him. He closed one eye to protect his night vision and held up a hand to shield the other eye and cover his face.

He put a quaver in his voice. "Who is it that's asking? If you be footpads I have nothing worth your while to steal."

"We are on the King's business. Identify yourself."

"My name is Silas. I am but a poor costermonger. I lost my way in this dark night and happened upon this wall to guide me along to the Gore where I have lodgings."

The rifleman was in two minds whether to summon the rest of the piquet but decided the hunchback looked harmless enough and did not want to rouse his serjeant-major unnecessarily. He softened his tone. "You are lost all right. You needs to turn back on yourself and retrace your steps."

"Would you be so kind as to light my way for a few paces, it is so devilish black here." Leech heard the rifle put back on half cock and a soft grunt as the rifleman bent to pick up the lamp.

"Just a few yards mind, old man. I have my duty to consider."

Leech waited for the man to pass him carrying the lamp low so that it illuminated the cobbles. He pulled the scian from its scabbard, put a hand over the soldier's mouth and sank the blade into his neck. He held the man tightly as he kicked out his life. The rifle and lamp clattered to the ground and he was fearful that the noise would be heard. He dropped the still twitching body, picked up the lamp and walked quickly away. One less green coat was one less to bother him and he had more deadly work in mind.

52

An hour later the relief sentry found the rifleman's body by tripping over it on his search for the missing man. He called for Serjeant-major Pocock who lit another lamp and came with the piquet.

Pocock's jaw tightened and he shone the weak beam around until he saw the niche where the postern was sited and found the gate ajar. "Flown the coop and killed my man. He shall pay for his treachery with his life if I but come within ten paces of him." He turned back to the dead soldier. "Two men stay with our comrade. Wrap him in his cloak and stand guard over him. I will send a cart to carry him back to Knightsbridge. The rest come with me to Downing Street. We must convey this to Colonel Lennox as soon as we may. There is a monster loose on our streets."

It was past one in the morning when Pocock hammered on Chris's door. He was still writing despatches and ordering his thoughts for the coming day.

Dales had been napping by the remains of the fire but jerked awake and opened the big front door to admit Pocock with his news.

Chris's face hardened. "It's as I suspected, Lord Edenderry is neck deep in this. That he has shown his hand now can only mean that he is to put his plan into action today.

"I have written to Mr Pitt and await his instructions. I need orders to rouse the Household Guards. Did you notice, are the lights still burning at Number 10?"

"I did, sir, and they are, sir," Pocock said.

"I must go across and wait until I have an answer. Send a man to Knightsbridge and have Serjeant-major Biggin prepare the men to report to me here at first light. They are to bring rifles with bayonets and pistols and wear the iron weskits. I fear they will need them."

He left Pocock and hurried across to Number 10 where he was admitted by a sleepy-eyed servant. He was shown into Pitt's office where he was seated at his desk reading.

"Have you received my message, sir?" Chris asked.

"Abrupt and to the point yet again, Lennox. Yes, I have received your note but what credence to put upon it eludes me. Are you intimating that a peer of the realm is about to commit regicide. I find that incredible hard to believe."

"You have the information, sir. What else could it mean?"

"A chess gambit and a cypher which you say is a map but scarce looks like nothing of which I am conscious. A bid to murder our sovereign king, you say."

"It is code, sir. The Latin has been translated and points to this day."

"Lennox. I cannot possibly convey this to the king on such flimsy evidence. Where is your proof, man? How should I alarm His Majesty with mere conjecture?"

"Not just conjecture, Mr Pitt, hard fact. One of the riflemen I left to guard Lord Edenderry has been murdered and left in an alley behind the house where Edenderry was living. The postern gate was ajar and it is obvious that the killer came from within the house. He would not have shown his hand but for the fact that his plan is imminent. Why else would he take such a risk?"

"Ah, that explains much. You are overwrought, Lennox and will calm yourself. The man could have been murdered by a footpad or other ne'er-do-well. We shall have an officer call at the house after daybreak to ascertain whether Lord Edenderry is still in residence or not, which of itself is no proof that he did commit such a heinous crime."

"That will be too late, sir. I need an order for the Household Garrison to be roused."

Pitt sat back in his chair and studied Chris's face for a few seconds, then he sighed and nodded. "I see that you do truly believe what you do say, Lennox. However, I cannot convince others of this without further evidence. You have proved yourself an able tactician and I daresay that the people and merchants of Bristol owe you a vote of thanks but I would be a laughing stock were I to rouse the entire garrison and put His Majesty to alarm merely on your intuition.

"I will give you an order to take whatever action you deem fit with your chosen men. You will ensure that the populace of London are not inconvenienced and nothing of your suspicions should be made common knowledge lest it incite others to also think of such treachery. Should this, as I suspect, come to nothing, no harm will be done except to your reputation in my eyes," Pitt said.

"And should something come of it ...?"

"Then you had best be well placed to prevent harm befalling His Majesty, Lennox. I shall hold you fully responsible."

Pitt scribbled a note and put the First Lord of the Treasury's seal on it. "That is a warrant allowing you to make arrests. If you must use it, use it wisely or you shall bear the consequences on your own shoulders. Begone, now. I have much work to do."

Chris was angry but he could also see Pitt's point of view. The man was a politician and the evidence was flimsy but why take a chance? The French had guillotined their own royals without so much as a by-your-leave and he knew that the Russian Tsar was due to be assassinated. Revolution was in the air and it wasn't beyond the bounds of reason that a group of dissidents would seek to murder the king. Chris was sure that Pitt could see the possibility but he was hedging his bets and keeping his fingerprints off it should it rebound on him. He had hoped for more support from Pitt but he would have to seek it elsewhere. There was no time to send a message to Stewart at Shorncliffe but perhaps Henry could help him drum up some support. He checked his Breitling. Gone two-o-clock and Henry would be sleeping at his club.

He hurried back to his house where Pocock was waiting for further orders. "Stay here and await Biggin's arrival. Get some rest while you can. I'm going to St James's Street and will return before dawn." He pulled on his cloak and left to turn into St James's Park through it, across the Mall, through Marlborough Street and into St James's. He banged on the door of the club and was admitted by a suspicious night watchman.

"I have to speak with Major Wadman. It is a matter of the utmost urgency. Have him called down to Captain Lennox."

"He be asleep, sir I durst not wake him or it may be the worst for me."

"It will certainly be the worst for you if you don't. I am on the king's business."

"I shall have to ..."

"What part of utmost urgency don't you understand? Rouse him now or lose your position."

The watchman gave him an aggrieved look but shuffled off. Within five minutes a bleary-eyed Henry in dressing gown and night cap appeared.

"Good god, Lennox, what is the meaning of this?"

Chris took him by the elbow and led him into the salon where they sat in leather chairs. "I need your help and your advice. I believe there is to be an attempt on the king's life later today. Mr Pitt has refused to accept the case I set before him as insufficient and all I have is twenty or so riflemen to defend the king from the Grey Wolves should he need it. Henry, I may be wrong but I do not believe I am. What on earth can I do?"

Henry's frown deepened. "There is little I can do for the hour is late. His Royal Highness the Duke of York is at Windsor and cannot be disturbed at this hour. The generals at Horse Guards in all likelihood will take the same stance as Mr Pitt. The thought is inconceivable and they will not believe it.

"I do think you may be correct in your assumptions. Regicide is not a new crime for this nation; we did behead King Charles, murder Richard the Second and kill Richard the Third on Bosworth Field. What is one more monarch to add to the monstrous tally?

"I shall dress and accompany you in your endeavours."

"Accompany me to where? I have no notion where the king will be today except it appears to be somewhere in the area of the Mall."

"His Majesty has the habit of visiting Queen Charlotte at Buckingham House on the first week of the month. That is where he shall be journeying with a small group of pikemen and Household Cavalrymen as escort. Buckingham House is very lightly guarded by the foot guards."

"A soft target," Chris said. "Then that is where we shall have to be."

53

Buckingham House, later famously known as Buckingham Palace, and currently known as the Queen's House, was not the place Chris knew. It lacked the high walls and fences at the front of the house which was reached by a graveled drive through the central gate and arch into a quadrangle. There was no monument to Queen Victoria and no roundabout just an open aspect along the sandy surface of the Mall which was churned up by a myriad horses and lacked the imposing façade of Admiralty Arch at the Strand end.

St James's Park ran along one side with an open area on the other where Clarence House would eventually be built. Chris positioned half his riflemen along the Mall with their cloaks covering their uniforms and weapons. He had no idea where the attack would come or when but the wide open spaces of the park would provide ample opportunity for a swift attack and he hoped the riflemen's presence would act as a deterrent.

He and Henry called in at the house but were met with blank stares by the guard commander who would not allow the riflemen entry without an express order from his colonel. He said his ten guardsmen were perfectly able to perform any duty asked of them.

Chris left his soldiers in a small copse to one side of the house and pulled a wry face at Henry. "Somewhat of an impasse."

"Indeed, sir. I cannot see how else we may affect an entry without revealing our true intentions to the wooden headed guardsman."

"If you can't go through it, go around it," Chris said and called Dales to him. "Take a look around the house, Dales. You seem more than able to find kitchen entrances, find one into this place."

Dales knuckled his forehead and grinned. "Aye, Colonel. Give me leave of a quarter hour."

"No more than that. Time is not on our side."

The boy handed his rifle to a corporal and loped off around the side wing of the house. It was still pre-dawn, the light was dim and there were few people around to notice. He was back within the fifteen minutes with a smile of success on his face. "I have gained entry, sir. There is a garden gate that did not withstand attention from my bayonet. There is stabling beyond it and the kitchen entrance. There are candles lit and servants afoot within."

"Well done, Dales. Now go back and make the acquaintance of a pretty scullery maid to allow us entry."

Dales saluted and spun on his heel.

"This is prodigious risky, Lennox," Henry said. "We may be mistaken for ruffians."

"We have no alternative. Once inside, without an alarm raised by the guards and the servants convinced of our bona fides we can assess the situation and take whatever steps we can to prepare ourselves. We may end up with egg on our faces, Henry. If you wish to leave, to ensure your reputation remains unsullied, I shall think no less of you."

Henry grunted. "I have come this far, sir and I will not abandon you. If you could send your boy to Horse Guards to excuse my absence I will remain by your side throughout this day for good or ill."

Chris gripped his shoulder. "If you are sure ..."

Henry gave him a grim nod. "Brothers, sir, by marriage and in arms. I shall always stand with you."

They met Dales on his way back and sent him on his errand to Horse Guards. He told them that the scullery door was open and that a maid would guide them to the kitchens. The foot guards were in their guard room, all but two who stood sentry by the front doors. Their entry would not be challenged.

The scullery maid was small with a dirt smudged face and seemed terrified of the two officers and the darkly cloaked soldiers. She stared round-eyed at them with a hand to her mouth. He did not know what story Dales had told her but it was apparent she had not expected twelve heavily armed men. Chris took pity on her.

"Don't be alarmed, miss, we are on the king's business. He showed her Pitt's note with its embossed seal. It was unlikely she could read but the sight of it seemed to allay her doubts.

"Take us to the kitchens. I wish to speak with the head of the household servants."

The girl nodded and led them dumbly along narrow passages and up a flight of stone stairs to where candles were lit and pans clattered. In a side room sat a man dressed in livery taking his breakfast. The girl pointed and ran.

He sat up startled and dropped his knife. "Who be you and what do you want here?"

"What is your name?"

"My name, sir, is Machin and I am the under-butler to her Majesty Queen Charlotte."

Chris showed Machin Pitt's warrant but did not give him time to read it. "We are on the king's business and have been assigned to be here when he arrives. What time is His Majesty due?"

"You do not know, sir?"

"Only that it is to be this day and I need to position my men to best account. Now, sir, answer my question." Chris put an edge of anger in his voice. The man had to know who was in command.

It worked, Machin swallowed. "At eleven of the clock, sir and His Majesty is always punctual."

"We wish our presence here to remain confidential. Only you and your most trusted servants will know of it. The Queen is most definitely not to be disturbed on any account. However there must be some pretext that prevents any member of the Royal Family from entering the house grounds until after His Majesty has safely arrived. Can you devise such a stratagem?"

Machin thought for a moment and nodded. "It is a most odd request, sir but tis unlikely that any of their highnesses would venture abroad before such times. I shall let it be known that the courtyards are being cleansed and would not advise their presence."

"That is excellent on two counts," Chris said. "It will keep the family from those places and will allow my men to adopt their positions without question."

"Now, sir, if I may be so bold," Machin said, "what is the meaning of this? You did say that His Majesty has *safely* arrived. Is there any question that he may not?"

Chris gave him an approving smile. "You are very astute, Machin. There is a possibility, and this should remain confidential between us, that there may be a demonstration against the king's refusal to approve an Act of Parliament. I have men positioned along the Mall and those here are precautionary. We do not wish to cause undue alarm and the risk may be slight but we are not prepared to take the chance of anything untoward happening. Now you know as much as we. And I thank you for your aid in this delicate matter. I will ensure that the Household knows of it."

"If there is any other service I may perform ..."

Chris threw back his cloak and pushed Pitt's warrant into a pocket. "Finish your breakfast. There is yet time and perhaps you could furnish several of my men with household garments to cover their uniforms. Otherwise continue with your normal duties as if we were not here."

Machin's eyes opened wider at the sight of Chris's uniform. "You are the green coats of whom I have read in the *London Gazette*."

"We are the Corps of Riflemen and proud of it. We serve His Majesty and the country as best we may."

"Then, sir, you are welcome here. I shall ensure that those servants who may see their way to enquiring are informed that your men are labourers from the park engaged for the day to cleanse the courtyards. I have charge of below stairs this day and they will harken to me."

"Very well, Machin. You have our thanks. Now where can the major and I wait for His Majesty's arrival?"

"There is a room further along this passage with a view across the quadrangle where His Majesty will dismount his carriage and be received by Queen Charlotte within. Let me show you gentlemen the way."

Machin left them in the room and Henry, who had remained silent throughout the exchange, threw off his cloak and collapsed in a chair. "By god, sir, you do sail close to the wind. It is fortunate that Mr Pitt's seal does carry more potency than he knows of. It buttered our way into this house and without it we may have been in poor standing."

Chris grinned and untied his own cloak. "I believe that Mr Pitt is fully aware of the power of his office. I also believe his seal was given with just such intent. Mr Pitt is a wily animal and I am beginning to like him better."

"If you believe it so, then so must I. But what now, Lennox? What should we expect?"

"We should expect trouble to find us but hope it does not. For now, we wait."

54

King George III lived most of the time in his house at Kew and made the journey from the south of the River Thames to the Mall via Knightsbridge in a carriage with postilion outriders and a long guard of Life Guards, heavy cavalrymen commanded by a lieutenant with a corporal-major carrying a standard, a trumpeter and ten troopers. Although a popular king, not many subjects stopped to cheer or line his route as his passage was a common sight and unremarkable.

It was a dry day but presaged rain and the royal carriage was closed to the elements on a chilly morning. The King's normal troop of Yeomen from the Tower had been dispensed with on this occasion as they would slow his progress through the muddy winter roads and his escort commander did not give much thought to the small group of mounted lancers who replaced them and rode behind. It was a tiring journey for the soldiers whose horses followed the carriage at a slow trot and they welcomed the sight of the house at the end of the Mall when eventually it came into view.

Biggin eyed the royal coach and its escort as it passed him on the Mall. The Life Guards were covered in their long blue-grey cloaks with their shining helmets and white horse hair plumes twitching in the breeze. The lancers were just in normal uniform and seemed hunched in the increasingly cold wind. He thought it odd that they were not dressed for the weather but gave it no significance. The cavalry were a law unto themselves and loved nothing better than to preen in their finery.

He clapped his hands together and blew on them. The noise making the leading lancer turn his head to stare at him. He thought to give the man a wave but thought better of it. He glanced round in turn to cast an eye over the placement of his riflemen. They were spread in a long thin line of five pairs, some partly hidden in trees, some more openly on display stamping their feet on the cold turf. He faintly heard a church clock chime the quarter hour. Fifteen minutes to eleven on a November morning with nothing to show for a near sleepless night.

Edenderry heard the hands clap and glanced to his left to mark the man in the riding cloak partly hidden behind a tree. He looked further and saw others dressed similarly. He wriggled in his saddle and a wave of apprehension rolled up his spine. He was being stupid. How could these few men have any link to his plan? It was mere coincidence and nothing to concern him. The man he knew as Docherty who rode beside him gave him a sly whistle and nodded at yet another pair of men idling under the trees. He too had seen the unusual sight amid the bustle of normal traffic; the gentlemen exercising their horses who stopped to raise their hats and bow as the royal carriage passed and the ladies in their fine carriages who waved and gawked. It was business as normal so why did the sight of the men give him such cause for concern?

There was nothing that could now be done to stop him.

The small gates in the fence curving around the front of the house were opened by uniformed flunkeys as the carriage approached. The foot guards were lined up to the left of the drive and presented arms as it passed. The Life Guards wheeled to the right into the front courtyard as the carriage passed under the arch into the inner quadrangle with the six lancers following.

The lieutenant commanding the Life Guards turned his horse in time to see the lancers approaching the arch and yelled for them to halt but he was ignored. The foot guards commander raised his sword and stepped in front of the leading lancer who dropped his lance and pierced the officer through the chest. The man fell with the lance still in him its shaft pointing skyward.

Just for a second there was a stunned and hushed silence then the foot guards dropped their muskets from the present and broke ranks to charge at the rearward horses which were already passing through the arch.

The Life Guards were all still facing away and it took several seconds before the lieutenant could order them to turn into line. The mouth of the arch was filled with foot guards as they tried to advance but two of the lancers blocked the narrow gap with their horses. They pulled pistols from saddle holsters and shot into the mass of red coats.

Chris and Henry had heard the carriage approaching and made their way through a door into a corner of the quadrangle as the coach came through the arch followed by four lancers riding at a fast trot, horses' hooves skittering on cobbles as they turned to surround the carriage. Four explosions echoed from the archway and men screamed.

Two of the lancers skewered two of the three postilions from their saddles and the third jumped down to search for safety. The leading lancer grabbed the carriage horses' bridles and brought the vehicle to a halt.

Chris screamed at his riflemen to cover as he rushed towards the carriage drawing his sabre and his Dragon pistol. A third lancer spurred his horse towards him couching his lance and thrusting it forward. Chris threw himself to one side and rifle shots hit the horse in the belly as it passed. The poor animal screamed, contorted and threw its rider onto the cobbles. Henry was onto the man in an instant, hacking with his sword.

A fourth lancer had rounded the carriage and was leaning towards the door handle.

"Your Majesty, stay down," Chris screamed. The Dragon pumped shot into the man's back. The horse shied away and the man fell between the hooves and the carriage wheels.

Chris ran towards the carriage as the first two lancers were wheeling around, discarding their lances in favour of horse pistols. One fell as a rifleman blew him out of his saddle. The other swung down along his horse's neck and fired at Chris from beneath its head. The ball caught his left arm and swung him around. He felt the slam of the lead ball but not the pain. He spun and slashed at the horse's hamstrings and it went down with a shrill scream its rider leaping clear and rolling onto the cobbles.

Rifles cracked and the two lancers fighting the foot guards under the arch were thrown bodily from their saddles as their mounts reared and kicked in fright.

The lancer scrambled to his feet and Chris could see the cold eyes of Edenderry staring at him. He raised his sabre. "That's enough, my lord. It's finished."

"Not whilst I have breath in my body." Edenderry drew his cavalry sabre and made a move towards the carriage. Chris cut him off. Now he could feel his wound and the blood running from his fingers onto the cobbles. His eyesight was getting misty but he could see Edenderry's wicked grin.

"You are no match, sir," he said and lunged, the point of his sabre catching Chris high on the shoulder and he staggered back, tripping over the kicking legs of the felled horse.

Edenderry took another cut but the blow from his heavy sabre was stopped by Henry's sword which snapped off at the hilt with the force of the strike.

Edenderry slashed at him but missed as his eyes were watching the foot guards forcing the two horses under the arch backwards into the quadrangle and the riflemen closing in from all sides with bayonets.

One of the horses turned and he grabbed it by the bridle and saddle pommel, hauling himself aboard. The Life Guards were trotting their chargers into the quadrangle scattering the foot guards but his horse was nimble and he spurred it past the last trooper and into the outer courtyard. The flunkeys were closing the gates but the horse cleared the low fence. He pulled it hard left, away from advancing men drawn by the sound of gunfire. A rifle cracked and he jerked in the saddle but maintained his grip as the animal raced him away.

55

The quadrangle looked like a charnel house with dead men and horses littering the cobbles. Chris felt bad for the horses. Two of the animals were put out of their misery by the riflemen.

The king had been rushed into the house surrounded by foot guards and Chris was left facing the Life Guard's lieutenant who was bemused, suspicious and angry. His troopers had dismounted and were in a semi circle behind him all red in the face and muttering, their hands on their sabres still sheathed but at the ready.

Chris's left arm was throbbing. Henry had bound the flesh wound made by the pistol ball but, although his Kevlar vest had taken the brunt of Edenderry's sabre thrust, he was sure his collarbone was broken. He tried to keep the pain off his face as he answered the lieutenant's questioning look.

"Major Henry Wadman of the General Staff and Captain George Lennox late of the Corps of Riflemen at your service. Whom have I the honour of addressing?"

The lieutenant clicked his heels together and bowed. "Lieutenant Charles de Launcey, sir. Is there an explanation for this, this ...?" He waved his hand over the battleground where Machin and the servants were busying themselves covering the dead and washing blood from the stones with buckets of water and stiff brushes.

"I think the word you search for is atrocity, sir," Chris said. "It was an attempt on His Majesty's life the rumour of which we became aware of just this morning and hastened to this house to be of whatever service we may."

De Launcey relaxed a little although suspicion still showed on his face. "Why was I not informed? Why was not His Majesty's household informed? Good god, sir, there may have been a tragedy worthy of the Bard if you had failed in your duty."

"There was little else that could be done, given the late hour," Henry said. "It was but a rumour that had little substance. Were it not for Captain Lennox, naught at all would have been brought to my notice and the assassins would have carried out their evil intent."

"One did escape, de Launcey," Chris added. "You must ensure that the guards are reinforced lest he return for another attempt."

O'Dell, who had been eavesdropping on the conversation, butted in. "I believe I did wing him, beggin' your pardon, sirs."

De Launcey turned on him. "Hold your tongue. Speak when you are spoken to and not before or else taste the lash."

"Chris held up a hand. "My soldiers are free to speak their part when they have something of import to say. I would hazard knowing that the assassin Lord Edenderry is wounded has due relevance and Corporal O'Dell is right to speak out."

De Launcey glowered at O'Dell and turned back to Chris. "You have strange ways indeed in the Corps of Riflemen. It would mean fifty strokes of the lash for my troopers to speak without permission."

"And I would hazard again that you would miss many grains of truth and experience because of it. Now, sir, are we to sit here jawing all day or shall we enquire as to His Majesty's health?"

De Launcey nodded and waved over his corporal-major. "Sykes, send the trumpeter to Knightsbridge for more guards for the Queen's House. With all possible speed lest the blackguards return. Take command of the foot guards and set your piquets." He turned back to Chris. "And what of your green coats, sir? Are they also to be part of the king's guard this day?"

"They are so already, with honour, de Launcey. My two serjeant-majors will see to their deployment where they may be placed to the best advantage."

"You trust them?"

"With my life. We fought side by side in Portugal and they know their work. They need no further instruction from me."

"More and more curious but I recall now that the green coats did fight like demons at Ferrol and took the heights."

The trumpeter's horse clattered under the arch and brought de Launcey's attention back to the present. "Come, sir, I am negligent in my duty. Let us see to His Majesty's comfort."

Chris admitted to himself that he was more nervous of meeting the king than he was of facing Edenderry's Grey Wolves. That Coileán Leech and Edenderry were one and the same was not in doubt in his mind. The man was wounded and on the run but still could be a threat. London was riddled with French emigrés who had spies amongst their number reporting back to the French Revolutionary Council. There were powerful forces abroad in the city that Edenderry could call on for succour and that was a worrying thought.

He, Henry and de Launcey were admitted to the house where bedlam appeared to reign. Flunkeys were hurrying from room to room and they stood in the hall waiting to be noticed by someone in authority. Eventually an officer in uniform saw them and approached. Chris started, he recognised the king's equerry and Colonel-in-Chief of the Corps of Riflemen, Colonel Coote Manningham.

Coote Manningham's eyes opened in surprise when he spotted Chris's green uniform and opened even wider when he recognized Chris.

"Lennox, by god, sir, what are you about?"

Chris gave him a tight smile. "Hopefully saving His Majesty's life, sir. Is he unhurt?"

"Indeed, sir, he is, sir, quite unhurt but has lost his equanimity somewhat for the moment. The queen is comforting him. You are wounded, sir. Are you in pain?"

Chris lied and shook his head thinking of the morphine he had in his Bergen back in Downing Street.

Coote Manningham gave him a grim look. "Now, what is afoot? What has come to pass this day?" He ushered the three into a side room and found them chairs. "Now, sir?"

Chris explained everything he knew about Edenderry and the Grey Wolves, how he had been fighting them and tracking their movements on Pitt's orders. He glossed over Pitt's reluctance to act on his suspicions over the attempted assassination of the king and repeated what he had told de Launcey.

Coote Manningham listened gravely to the tale, stirring occasionally in his seat and shaking his head. When Chris had finished he pursed his lips and stood.

"An astonishing tale, Lennox, most astonishing. I will take your leave. Wait here until you are called for."

It was over an hour later that a page came for them and led them into a wide reception room. The walls were lined with courtiers and various members of the aristocracy and household. Two people were seated at the far end with a small group of ladies in waiting fussing around them. They were ordered to stand and wait.

Coote Manningham was alongside the king, bending over him and speaking quietly to him. Then he stood upright and beckoned the three forward.

De Launcey had removed his cloak and helmet and shone in his burnished breastplate. His gleaming black thigh boots and red tunic was in stark contrast to Chris's green and Henry's black General Staff uniform. He was the one who caught the king's eye first and was asked his part in the morning's affair.

De Launcey gave a deep bow. "There is little I can tell, Your Majesty. Twas, Major Wadman and Captain Lennox who did save the day."

Both Chris and Henry copied de Launcey's bow and waited for the king to speak.

Chris thought he was very like his portrait with his white powdered wig, full lips, slightly bulging eyes and round face. He looked careworn, not surprising, Chris thought, as his malady of twelve years earlier must have taken a lot out of him. The King's madness, as it was known, was, according to modern diagnosis, acute intermittent porphyria, a hereditary metabolic disorder. The malady was unknown at the time and his treatment of the times had been more damaging than the illness.

The king raised his hand. "Which of you is Lennox?"

Chris bowed again. "I am, Your Majesty."

"Come closer, Lennox. Let us get full sight of you. Coote Manningham informs us that you are responsible for saving our life. What have you to say. "

"I was but one small part, sir. Major Wadman and my chosen men from the Corps of Riflemen are all to be commended."

"Yes, yes, but was it not you who did deduce the threat from Edenderry and did act upon it on your own cognisance?"

"With the support of Major Wadman, sir."

"Dammit, fellow, are you to take no praise upon yourself? Did you, or did you not, deduce the plot to our life and act upon it?"

"Yes, sir, I did."

"And was that plot executed by Edenderry this very morn?"

"Yes, sir, it was."

"And did you not gain your wound in forcing Edenderry's flight?"

"Yes, sir."

"Are you aware that you are dripping blood on the queen's ballroom?"

Chris glanced down at his fingers where a drop of scarlet was dangling from his thumb. He looked at Queen Charlotte who was also staring in mute fascination at the blood.

"My apologies, Your Majesty." He summoned up the little German he could remember. "Wie gedankenlos von mir. How thoughtless of me."

He bowed and stuffed his hand into his pocket. The queen gave him a delighted smile and the king guffawed.

"Pon my soul, Lennox, gallant *and* courageous. I do swear we owe you a debt that is beyond repayment. Kneel, sir."

Chris gave him a puzzled look. "Your Majesty?"

The king tutted. "Come sir, do as your monarch bids you. Kneel. You, sir, Major Wadman give me your sword."

Henry turned red. "If it please Your Majesty," He drew the two inches of sword blade left from its scabbard and shrugged.

"Was that too broken in our defence?"

"It was, sir."

"Then you also must kneel. Manningham, your sword if you please.

The king stood and took Manningham's sword. "What is your Christian name Lennox?"

"George, sir."

"And yours, Wadman?"

"Henry, sir."

The king tapped them both on either shoulder. Then arise Sir George and Sir Henry, Knights of the Most Honourable Order of the Bath. By God's good grace you have this day saved your king and you have our eternal gratitude."

56

Although he was desperate to get back to Downing Street Chris allowed Coote Manningham to lead him and Henry back to the same side room where they had waited earlier. The Colonel had a huge smile on his face as he sat them down.

"By god, Gentlemen, knights of the realm both and well-earned. It will do the Corps of Riflemen no harm, Lennox and for that you have my gratitude.

"The king bids me to inform you that Edenderry's title and lands will be forfeit. He has a mind to cede them to you, Sir George, in payment for your loyalty and courage in his service. Edenderry has a large estate in Ireland that will be yours to do with as you wish."

"I cannot get used to the title, sir. As a friend you may call me George. I thank His Majesty for his generosity but I would rather be reassigned to the Corps of Riflemen as Lieutenant-colonel Lennox than to have any estate in the kingdom."

"Then I will see what can be done to give you both although I fear it will be in the hands of the First Lord of the Treasury and Horse Guards.

"Now, Sir Henry, tis a pleasure to make your acquaintance in such circumstance. Is there ought that you desire from His Majesty?"

"His Majesty has honoured me enough, sir. He must also be aware that the queen's under-butler, Machin, has been of great assistance."

"I will see to it that the king hears of it and that His Royal Highness the Duke of York hears of your service this day."

"I thank you, Colonel," Henry said.

Chris was fidgeting in his seat. "I worry that Edenderry is still at large. He may have friends and resources nearby. His Grey Wolves are a spent force but the French, whom I believe are behind his plotting, have many spies and agents in London. The king must be better protected until Edenderry is caught."

"The foot guards have been reinforced and there will be no further opportunities for Edenderry to strike at His Majesty."

"I'm gratified to hear it. However, Mr Pitt was concerned that the news of today's occurrence should not be allowed into the public domain. There was gunfire heard at the Queen's House which would have attracted attention in the Mall. Rumours could already be flying. Could I suggest that a statement is issued that a horse did go mad, injuring many and had to be brought down with musket fire. I know of a man who would publish such a statement in the *London Gazette* and would thank me for the task."

Manningham beamed. "Excellent, George. We cannot have such news as this abroad to foment ideas amongst the levelers and republicans. I will leave this with you and Mr Pitt but report your notion to His Majesty."

Dales was clucking like a hen on its eggs as Chris and he walked the short distance back to Downing Street. Chris had two thoughts in mind. One was to get his wound dressed and a shot of morphine to dull the ever-increasing pain and the other to brief Pitt and Lloyd in turn. They reached Number 19 and Chris sent Dales to find Lloyd at the Fleet Street pub with orders to stay until Lloyd showed up to receive the message.

Catherine heard his arrival and came in to greet him with Amelia. Her hand went to her mouth as she saw him struggle to get out of his bloodstained tunic. Both women rushed to help and he yelped as the cloth was peeled off. Catherine ripped his shirt up the sleeve and cast a judicial eye on the wound.

"Tis deep but merely a flesh wound, sir. It has furrowed the muscle and requires sutures to ease the bleeding. I shall summon a doctor to attend you."

"In good time, madam. Instruct Matthew to bring the box with the red cross that you found in my knapsack. It is on the bedside table."

Amelia curtsied. "At once, sir." She left in a swirl of silk skirt.

Chris was peeling apart the Velcro straps on his Kevlar vest and sweating with the pain. "Lend a hand, my dear. I think I have a broken collarbone as well as the wound."

"Oh, my dear. Whatever have you been engaged upon? It seems that you return with a fresh injury each time you essay from our home."

"I have much to tell you but it will need to wait until I have spoken with Mr Pitt and that can wait until I have properly tended my wound."

Matthew came in with his trauma kit and stood opened mouthed until Chris gestured for him to bring it over. He opened the box, took out a self-injecting morphine syrette and punched the needle hard into his thigh.

Amelia followed Matthew with a bowl of hot water and some towels. Chris held up a hand. He had no intention of letting contaminated water anywhere near his wound. His kit contained antiseptic wipes and he used these to clean off the congealing blood and fragments of cloth, then dusted the wound with powder before using a fresh wound dressing to cover it. Catherine helped him tie the knot to secure the bandage but had huge question marks in her eyes.

The morphine was kicking in, the pain was easing and with it the nausea that he was beginning to feel wash over him. It would keep him going until he had time to talk with Pitt. With Catherine's help he made a sling for his arm, pulled his tunic back over one shoulder and buttoned it at the neck. He kissed Catherine on the cheek and squeezed her hand.

He was feeling light-headed as he walked the short distance to Number 10. For once Pitt did not keep him waiting. It was obvious that he had already heard of the commotion at the Queen's House and was in want of information. He saw Chris's condition and drew a chair over to him.

Chris sat heavily and sighed. "Your servant, sir."

"You have tidings, Lennox? I see you have encountered some little difficulty this day."

"Indeed, sir. You may rest assured that His Majesty is in far better health than myself. We did prevent an attempt on the king's life and he is unhurt."

Pitt's normally serious face lit up. "That, sir, is momentous news indeed. What of the why and how of it?"

Chris ran through the story yet again but this time pulled no punches. "The king was in mortal danger, Mr Pitt and it was by sheer luck that we prevented Edenderry from carrying out his evil intent. The man is still at large, we were unable to prevent his escape although we did rid the world of five of his Grey Wolves.

"I would far rather have it that my warnings were heeded beforehand than having to prove my theories in conflict. I thank you for your warrant, it did me great service but nothing could make up for the lack of belief. It damn near cost the king his life."

Pitt nodded at the sling. "Yours too, I warrant."

"My life is of no consequence. I am more concerned of what the country may make of this happening."

Pitt jerked upright. "None of this must ever become public knowledge. It must be erased from the record as if it never occurred."

"My chosen men have already been sworn to secrecy. You must make your own arrangements with Horse Guards over the other regiments concerned. I have no doubt that they will concur that this must be kept completely confidential.

"The king has promised promotions to all who were present and that promise may be used to seal lips better than the threat of the lash.

"Others were abroad in the Mall and would have heard gunfire. I am arranging to meet with a representative of the *London Gazette* ..."

"Good god, sir, are you mad?"

"... to give him a version of events that, although far from the actualité, would explain much of that which occurred and would still any unfortunate speculation. Some may choose not to believe it but most could not conceive that an attempt to murder the king was possible."

Pitt relaxed and found another chair. "You continue to surprise me, Lennox. You have the makings of a first class politican. Your semantics do you credit."

Chris gave a pained grin. There are terms we use where I'm from. Spin doctoring and fake news. I believe I dabble in both here but in this day and age it does me little credit."

"Strange terms indeed, sir. He must needs go as the devil drives, as the Bard would have it. We live in hazardous times and must be wary of any action that may give succour to the king's enemies."

"Amen to that, Mr Pitt. Now if you would excuse me, I have much else to do."

57

The blond tousled head of Dales greeted him as he returned to Number 19. The lad had a grin on his face. "I did find Mr Lloyd for you, Colonel. He is in the withdrawing room enjoying your Madeira."

Chris found Lloyd, watched over by a concerned Matthew who had one eye on the Madeira decanter.

Lloyd stood as Chris entered and noted Chris's injuries with a quizzical eye. "Colonel Stewart, your health, sir. To what do I owe the pleasure of this summons?"

"Please be seated, Mr Lloyd. No doubt you have heard something of the commotion at the Queen's House this day?"

Lloyd nodded. "I have, sir, and did wonder of it. All London is abuzz with rumour."

"Then I may set the rumours at rest. You shall have the real story which is nothing more than a horse gone mad that did injure and kill some people. The sad fact is that more were injured when an attempt was made to put down the horse with muskets. I was caught by such a stray ball and the horse did break my collarbone as I fought to grip its bridle. The poor animal was then shot dead."

"And of the king, sir? I did hear that twas his carriage that was seen entering the Queen's House before the commotion ensued."

"His Majesty was within the house at the time and was not concerned with it. I do hear he expressed his sorrow over the injuries."

Lloyd sipped his drink and gave Chris a thoughtful look over the rim. "Pray tell, sir, why would you be within the confines of the Queen's House this morn?"

"Other business than does not concern you, Mr Lloyd."

"There is much that does concern me. I must be the judge of it."

"Then let me give you some news that will concern you. I promised you intelligence before others have wind of it. This news is to be embargoed until the day before the date I am about to reveal. You must give me your word on that."

"Is it of great import?"

"I believe so."

"Then I will gladly give it to steal a march on other scribes."

"It is now nearing the end of this year. As you will be aware, on January 1st 1801 the Act of Union, joining the Kingdoms of Great Britain and Ireland comes into force. Mr Pitt will fail in his attempt to gain emancipation for the Catholics as I am informed that His Majesty is implacably opposed on the grounds that it will be a violation of his coronation oath as head of the Church of England. I have it on impeccable authority that Mr Pitt will resign his position due to this impasse. That date is already marked as February 18th."

"Lloyd sat upright, his eyes round. "How the devil come you by this intelligence, sir? And how may I take it?"

"The how is not important, I shall not reveal my sources but you may take it as gospel."

"What credence can I give to it? I cannot publish without due diligence."

"Then I suggest you write as conjecture and be all the more applauded when it comes to pass. But there is more should you wish to hear it."

"Speak on, sir. I am all agog to learn more."

"Mr Pitt's position as First Lord of the Treasury will be offered to Lord Henry Addington, Viscount Sidmouth, who will be reluctant to accept the honour but will succumb. I have spoken with Viscount Sidmouth and believe I know his mind in this.

"Now remember, Mr Lloyd, you will not publish until February 17th at the earliest. It will give you the time to polish your prose. There will be more such as this at future times should you honour your word."

"Rest assured, Colonel, it shall be as you ask. News of this great import is worth more than jewels to a lowly scribe."

"You have been of singular help and I repay my debts in full. Now as to future meetings. You will not come here again. Messages will be carried to you by my man Dales who called upon you this day. They may be proxy messages from a friend called Sir George Lennox as I am recalled to my duties with the Corps of Riflemen at Shorncliffe. Pay as much attention to those despatches as you will to this story and you will be well rewarded in your occupation."

Lloyd stood to leave and turned as he reached the door. "I hear tell that a musket was discharged at a horseman leaving the Queen's House. Is there any substance to the rumour?"

Chris hid a smile. He had been half expecting this from a dyed-in-the-wool reporter. "The rumour is correct, Mr Lloyd in all but one case. It was a rifle that was discharged and not a musket. The rifleman concerned, on hearing gunfire from the house and on seeing the rider leave in haste, wrongly assumed the messenger to be a miscreant making good his escape and fired on instinct without due care. There was no cause to suspect injury and the rifleman has been reprimanded.

"Now, Mr Lloyd if that is all?"

As Matthew showed Lloyd out Catherine joined Chris in the drawing room. She held out both her hands to him and he took them in one of his. She stood on tip-toe and kissed him on the lips. "How is my wounded warrior?"

"All the better for your tender ministrations, Lady Lennox?"

"Lady …?"

"The king himself created both Henry and me Knight Commanders of the Bath for our endeavours this day."

"Henry? Is he also wounded?"

"No, dear one. He is perfectly well. I will tell you everything over dinner. Much of my work has been done and, but for a small loose end, I shall be free to escort you around the salons of London this Christmastide."

Chris could not sleep that night due to the discomfort of his wounds. Catherine had teased him over his inability to make love until he had suggested she ride on top. Her eyes had opened wide at the notion but agreed and after it was over she gave him a triumphant smile of sheer pleasure.

"Where, sir, did you learn of such tricks?"

Chris squirmed a little. His inability to tell Catherine of his real life troubled him more and more. That his past girlfriends had no qualms about sex before marriage was something he did not want to mention as he was sure it would scandalize his lovely wife.

"It was a book I read from India called the Kamasutra. It did suggest such alternatives for medical reasons." It was not a lie. He and his classmates had giggled over the book in their schooldays as a teenage rite of passage.

Disingenuous, perhaps, but something he could live with for now.

Catherine had rolled over and was lying beside him, one slim finger to her lips. "It occurs to me, George, that I must procure a copy of this tome, for medical reasons, of course."

Chris nearly choked. "I believe it is an ancient book and out of print. I came across it by chance."

"Were there other tricks to learn from it?"

"Some, I believe. From what I can remember some that would be unbecoming for a lady to perform."

"Then you must teach me those which you can remember that are not unbecoming."

Chris put his good arm beneath her and pulled her to him. "It shall be my delight once my arm is mended. Let us hope we have many more nights such as these to enjoy."

The thought brought his current situation into sharp relief. When he compared his life in the 21st century with his existence in 1800 he knew where his real sympathies lay. To a certain extent he missed modern technology, mobile phones, radio contact, the ease of travel, flush toilets and clean water. His accomplishments were few. A second class degree in history at Oxford, being a possible Olympic hopeful for the British Pentathlon Team and gaining his commission after eighteen months at Sandhurst.

In his present incarnation he was playing a huge part in these roiling brawling times of political upheaval where his presence and influence had made a real difference. He had one nagging concern that saving the king's life had landed the country with centuries of Irish unrest. But for his involvement, King George would probably be dead and Pitt would get his Act of Catholic emancipation through

Parliament, thus removing the poison from that particular chalice.

He had been in the past almost a year. It had been a year the first time before he was blown back to his own period. Then his mission to the past had been completed with the raising of the Corps of Riflemen. Now the defeat of Edenderry and his Grey Wolves made him feel it ever more likely that his time would soon be up and he would lose Catherine forever. He loved her so deeply it caused his chest to ache and his arm to tingle whenever he thought of her. Her wit, her impish sense of fun and adventure, her beauty and her unadulterated love for him would leave him completely bereft without her.

He had found his preferred place in time and it seemed like a version of paradise. Would it, all too soon, be paradise lost?

58

At breakfast the next morning Chris received two notes. One from Pitt and another from Horse Guards, both requesting his presence. He sighed, excused himself and wrote replies to both, sending Dales off to deliver them.

Catherine had also received a letter from her father and gave a small squeal of delight as she waved it at Amelia.

"Papa and mama have given their blessing for Mary to join us and all three will be travelling to be with us this Christmastide.

"I know I made a promise to George that I would be circumspect with my household allowance but we must ensure we have the very best of Christmases here in Downing Street."

Chris came back in shrugging into his cloak with Matthew's help. "Good news I suspect."

"Mary is to come to be with us. Oh Matthew, we are so pleased for you."

Matthew gave a broad smile. "Thank you, your ladyship, that will be the best Christmas gift a man could want."

"As good as it is, I hazard a guess that is not all the news you have," Chris said.

Catherine pulled the letter to her breast. "Oh, sir, mama and papa wish to come for Christmastide and we must make them welcome as best we can."

Chris smiled. "Indeed we must. They have been so very kind to me. They have given me their beautiful daughter and their blessing. We must ensure they have the best of everything."

Chris went first to Number 10 where Pitt kept him waiting his customary half hour. He had allowed for it and made his subsequent appointment at Horse Guards for past eleven. He sat on a chair in the hall until he was ushered into Pitt's office. Pitt looked up from a document he was reading and waved a hand at a seat. "My apologies, Sir George, my correspondence must take precedence but I will not keep you for much longer."

Chris smiled. So the news of his knighthood had reached Pitt and he had made a point of it. He wondered why Pitt had summoned him. News of Edenderry's whereabouts he hoped, so that he could finally put a lid on the Grey Wolves. He hated leaving such a loose end.

Pitt was looking older than his years as he pored over his papers in the dim light from his casement window. He had candles burning on his desk and, as weak as these were, they still threw shadows. Pitt sighed and signed one document with a flourish, sanded it and rang a small bell. His secretary came in and removed the papers with a slight bow.

Pitt sat upright and stretched his fingers. "Now, sir, what have we to make of your advancement?"

"At His Majesty's pleasure, sir."

"I have heard both you and Major Sir Henry Wadman acquitted yourselves well."

"We had the support of my chosen men and aid from the household. We did but put up the fight to see the Grey Wolves done down."

"Except for Edenderry, whom I suspect of being the evil Coileán Leech."

"That, is also my belief. I thought as much as soon as I laid eyes on him."

Pitt picked up his quill and twirled it before looking Chris in the eye. "His Majesty has taken Edenderry's estates as forfeit and wishes to cede them to you."

"That is my understanding but I cannot surmise what I would do with such a gift."

"His estates provide income in the region of £15,000 per annum. He has two thousand acres to the west of Dublin reaching to the slopes of the Wicklow Mountains. Rich farmland in the main with grazing for sheep and cattle. I should say it would suit your circumstance well."

"What of his kin?"

"There is none. Edenderry's wife died of the cholera some years ago and there was no issue. His estates are managed in his absence and his house kept closed and shuttered until such times as he would return. He is an only child and his line will die with him."

"You are suggesting that I take this estate?"

"No, sir, I demand that you do. Edenderry is a traitor and will be tried as such when we have him. His lands and inheritance are forfeit and in His Majesty's gift. Your knighthood has raised the name of Lennox into public notice. I did inform you that I wished no such thing to occur and it would suit me well to have you rusticated to Ireland until your name is no longer on knowledgeable lips."

"And when should this take place?"

"As soon as the warrants are made. These will needs be nailed to Edenderry's doors before you may take possession of the property. I dare say that you will not be made welcome at first but the Irish lords will soon see the sense of it and take it as a warning not to involve themselves in treachery. Should you need it, the Dublin garrison will provide a piquet betimes."

Chris grimaced at the mental picture Pitt painted. He knew too much and was being side-lined, that was obvious, and was being banished to where he could do little harm with loose talk. "I ask again, sir. How long will this take?"

"Not until the New Year is upon us. The wheels of government and the law grind slowly in such cases. You shall have Christmas in Downing Street but I warn you, sir, to keep your own counsel betimes."

"Is there news of Edenderry's whereabouts?"

"Last seen riding towards Cheapside but there is yet no news of him. We have let it be known that a dangerous felon is abroad with a reward for news of his whereabouts. He will be given up before the week is out."

"I should like to be there when he is arrested."

"And so you shall, Lennox. I shall insist upon it."

Henry greeted him at Horse Guards with a handshake and a big smile. "Come to my room, George. I have much to tell you before your audience with His Royal Highness."

"I hope the news is good, Henry. I have had a disquieting interview with Mr Pitt this morning."

"My news is good. I have been promoted to colonel with effect from New Year's day. My income is increased and I shall be able to afford to take a wife."

Chris grinned. "Do you have anyone in mind?"

"There is a lady of my acquaintance who may not be averse to an approach on the question of marriage."

"Then I am extraordinarily happy for you and hope to dance at your wedding."

"Ha, sir, I have seen you dance and you should not threaten me with such an exhibition."

Chris laughed. "I am learning and I have an excellent teacher in dear Catherine."

"Indeed, none better, she dances as light as a fairy on dew. Now, sir, what of this interview with Mr Pitt?"

"I'm to be banished to Ireland on Edenderry's estate. I should not look such a gift horse in the mouth for the income is substantial. However, I would rather it was run by managers and Catherine and I stay in London. Mr Pitt is adamant that I go in the New Year."

"For what reason? None that I can deduce to be sure. You have given him great service in preventing Edenderry's foul plot."

"There is more to it than I am at liberty to divulge. I shall ponder on it, Henry and maybe I can dissuade him from his decision."

Henry pursed his lips. "You will not receive such a warm welcome. I fear that the Irish will demonstrate against you."

"As do I and I've a mind to leave Catherine here in London until such times as I deem it safe."

59

The Duke of York greeted Chris with a beaming smile and waved him forward as soon as he entered the room. "I hear we are greatly in your debt, Sir George."

"I did my duty, Your Royal Highness."

"With great valour I did hear."

"Nothing that any officer would not do in my place."

"Your modesty becomes you, sir, but we know of your true mettle. It has been proven in the past with your expedition to Portugal and leading the attack on Ferrol. His Majesty is most inclined to reward you, sir, but is there any favour that we may add?"

"I should like to rejoin the Corps of Riflemen, sir."

The duke's face dropped. "Alas I fear that is impossible. We will return you to your rank of Lieutenant-colonel but there is no longer a place for you at Shorncliffe.

"Mr Pitt is determined that you be kept at his disposal else we would have you on the general staff. Sir Henry Wadman tells us that you did divine Edenderry's plot and put in place your plan to prevent it on your own cognisance and authority. Pray tell was Mr Pitt privy to this?"

"Mr Pitt did issue me with warrants to effect arrests but was unable to summon any further aid due to the lateness of the hour and lack of corroborating evidence."

The duke gave a grim smile. "Now we see the why, where and how of it and you are to be commended even more for your perspicacity. We may be of little aid in your present circumstance but be assured we will not forget. We shall ensure that your rank is made permanent and it will be gazetted. Now, sir, we have much with which to concern ourself. Be so kind as to inform Sir Henry that we wish his presence forthwith."

"Copenhagen again, sir?"

"By god, sir. How the devil do you do this? Do you have gypsy blood in your veins or a talent with tarot?"

Chris grinned. "Merely a reading of the runes, sir. At our previous visit to Copenhagen I did remark that it would not be long before we were forced to return to read the Danes the riot act."

"Ha! Lennox, read the riot act, you do amuse us with your turn of phrase. You are correct. The French once more have persuaded the Danes on their Northern Alliance and we must show them the error of their ways. Our fleet under Admiral Parker will set sail in March once the weather has abated."

"I would be honoured to be part of the expedition, sir. With my chosen riflemen who currently languish at Knightsbridge with little to occupy them."

"If we can but prise you from Pitt's grasp then it shall be so. Your knowledge of the Dane's defences could prove valuable."

"I hope to be free of Mr Pitt's clutches before long, sir, although he has hopes to rusticate me to Edenderry's estate in Ireland."

"Then go, do as you are bidden but be assured you will not rest there on your laurels for long."

1800 had been a dry summer after a long cold winter but at its close London was now experiencing some wet weather. Chris turned up the collar of his cloak and pulled on his cap for the short walk back to Downing Street. It seemed he was to be unemployed for some weeks which suited him. It would give his arm time to heal and allow him time to put some of his own plans in place. He had mixed feelings about Edenderry's estate. The income would mean that Catherine would never need to worry about money, the duke had made no mention of reinstating his former income with his rank and he was still on half pay. The downside to his Irish question was having to travel there and face the animosity of the locals until time cooled things down. He had little doubt that his occupancy of the estate would be met with a great deal of hostility.

He knew that Pitt's tenure at Number 10 would be short lived and he would be able to return at the end of February in time to prepare the men for the expedition to Copenhagen. He would write to Biggin and Pocock to ensure that his training regime was kept up, with the promise of action in the near future if all went well. In the meantime, the men should be released to enjoy their Christmas and, as Henry had informed him, the extra pay their promotions had brought them. Biggin and Pocock themselves had reached the top of their particular promotion ladder and were happy to receive a week's pay in lieu. The king had kept his promise to the men who had helped to save him and it pleased Chris more than his own rewards had.

Matthew met him at the door and took his wet clothes. "Her ladyship and Miss Wadman are abroad, sir with the intent of acquiring the means for a Christmas to be remembered."

Chris grinned. "They've gone shopping, Matthew, that's what we call it."

Matthew ducked his head and smiled back. "As you say, Sir George."

"Is Dales in the house?"

"In the scullery, sir."

"Send him to me, I have an errand for him."

Chris sat and wrote his note to Biggin and Pocock. He knew Biggin could read but wasn't sure that Pocock could. It was only polite, he thought, to include the mans's name on the orders. It occurred to him that all his soldiers should be taught to read and write and not just Dales. It was something he would look into after the Christmas holiday was over.

There was a knock at the door and Dales stepped smartly inside. He tried to keep his face serious but could not help a smile flutter on and off his lips.

"You are happy, Corporal Dales?"

The phantom smile widened into a grin. "Indeed, Colonel, thank you. A corporal and not yet eighteen years. I do wish my ma and pa could see me now."

"Then you shall have leave to visit them. He sealed the note and handed it over. "Dales take this note to Serjeant-major Biggin at Knightsbridge. Await any reply and once you return you may take until the second of January to be with your family. You must return on that day as I will have need of you."

The grin had never left the boy's face. "Thank you, Colonel. I shall be back on the dot of noon on that day."

"Off with you now. Oh, Dales, you may now continue to call me colonel with accuracy."

Dales left at the run, happy with his news. He left without his cloak in all his excitement wearing his green tunic. He did not notice the man who stopped in his tracks to watch him pass and then swivel back to note the house from which the boy had left. He gave a nod of grim satisfaction.

Edenderry was badly wounded. O'Dell's rifle ball had entered his lower back as he bent over the horse's neck and had travelled through his body to lodge below his left clavicle. He could not remember most of the ride across London Bridge to the stews of Southwark doubling back and fourth in a red mist of pain in order to throw any pursuers off the scent and mask the final direction of his flight. He had enough sense to know that his lancer's uniform would be remembered so at the first opportunity he stole a threadbare cloak from a washing line and draped it across his blood soaked shoulders. The act took nearly all of his remaining strength and he was nearing unconsciousness when he pulled the horse into a decrepit yard near the cathedral and slid gracelessly from the horse's saddle into the mire of manure and old straw that lined the dirt floor.

Two men rushed out of a nearby stable door to turn him over and peer at his face.

Edenderry moaned and his eyes flickered open. "Je suis Coileán Leech. Aidez moi."

One of the two nodded to the other and ran off towards a nearby house. Edenderry knew none of what followed until he awoke three days later laying prostrate on a truckle bed with his face buried in a straw stuffed pillow. He groaned and tried to roll over.

"I would not try to move, Monsieur." A voice said in accented English. "I had to delve deep to remove the ball from your back and it will be some time ere you recover sufficiently to use your arm. Stay and I will aid you to turn."

"Who are you?" Edenderry muttered from the side of a mouth that was as arid as the bed of a dried up stream. "I need to drink."

"One thing at a time, monsieur. I am Michel Levarre. I was once a surgeon at the Sorbonne. Now I ply my trade with the emigrés here in this city. I ask no questions and I am told no lies."

Edenderry gave a rasping cough. "But you wonder about a man with a ball in his back?"

"I do not wonder of anything, monsieur. I have seen too much and suffered too much to have cause to question the suffering of others. Now sir, prepare yourself for the pain as I turn you over. It will not be a pleasant experience."

The doctor was not lying and Edenderry could not help a squeal of pain squeeze through his clenched teeth. The doctor propped him up and the pain eased to a dull throb.

"Thank you, Doctor Levarre. Now may I have that drink?"

Levarre poured a mixture of rum and water from a pitcher on the floor and handed over the leather beaker. "It is grog, monsieur. The water it is mixed with has been boiled to the point of steaming away. It would not do for my patient to succumb to poisoning after my efforts to retrieve his soul from wherever it was destined."

Edenderry grunted. "Save your wit, doctor for one who would appreciate it. Who is the proprietor of this establishment?"

"I only know him as Jean."

"That is the man I wish to see."

"Very well, monsieur. I will have him come to you."

60

Edenderry was sitting up in bed, his face the colour of flour. The doctor had been gone several minutes before the stairs creaked and a well-dressed middle-aged man entered.

He held a handkerchief to his nose in a foppish manner before waving it.

"You called for me, sir?"

Edenderry gave a tight grin. "Monsieur le Comte."

"Jean Gabriel Rocques a votre service."

"The Comte de Montgaillard. I am surprised you still live."

"Survival, sir, depends on giving the victor that which he requires. I served the Bourbons and now I serve the First Consul. I give Bonaparte that which he seeks and serve as best I may."

"Tis a fine line you walk, Jean Rocques."

"Maybe so but tis one that, with God's assistance, will see me die in peace and comfort." Rocques was one of nature's survivors. He had been friends with Louis XVI's nephew whom he met at a military school and had served the French monarchy in the West Indies before the revolution; reaching London and then Paris on his return. He had used his diplomatic skills for the directorate and had then persuaded Bonaparte to return from Egypt and take control of France. Although not altogether trusted he was now paid to spy for the French and give diplomatic advice when needed. This was his second visit to London where he was quietly gaining influence amongst the levellers. He was not pleased by being saddled with a rogue Irishman, who, if the rumours could be believed, was wanted as a common criminal by the British authorities.

Edenderry was studying his face and broke the silence. "You have heard the news?"

"What may that news be, if I may so bold as to enquire?"

"The king still lives. Our plot has failed due to the green coats."

"I have heard nothing of it, sir. There has been no word on such an attempt on King George's life."

"Then they are keeping it from public knowledge lest others are encouraged to follow the example."

"I have only your word on it, sir. I am told you are Coileán Leech and that you require the aid of our small band. We acquired the services of the doctor who has kept you alive with his ministrations. It has cost six guineas which we did take from the purse around your waist."

Edenderry's face darkened and flushed away the pallor. "You have taken my money?"

Rocques angled his head. "Only that which was owed. We are not thieves."

Edenderry grunted as if he disbelieved the statement. "I was given your name in Paris and how to find you here before I departed to these shores. I was assured you would give me shelter and succour should I need it."

"That is so, monsieur. But I hazard that would have been in the case of success in your plot. I thought the notion ill advised and did let the First Consul know that was my opinion. Now I hear that it has ended in failure. I am honour bound to give you whatever assistance I may although it may place my own plans in jeopardy should you be found here."

"I see then that I am an unwelcome guest and you want rid of me."

"One can but hope that your wound will quickly heal, sir."

Rocques turned to leave and then paused. "You mentioned green coats. There has been an instruction from Paris to pass on any sightings of men in green. It so happens one was seen these two days gone in Downing Street and we have a watch on the place."

"Then I must know more of it," Edenderry begged. "Apprise me of what is discovered for I have a score to settle."

It was now four days since Edenderry's disappearance and the threat to the king seemed to have receded. Chris felt that maybe Edenderry had made good his escape and was probably back in Paris licking his proverbial wounds.

For the first time since his association with Pitt he felt able to relax. Catherine's plans for Christmas were advancing daily. She had sent out invitations for a soirée on Boxing Day to those she knew and whose acquaintance had been made on her various shopping forays. Covered wagons were pulling up outside daily with men carrying various items into the house. Chris made himself scarce during these operations and kept himself busy sketching out plans for a Martini action breech loading rifle. He had an idea that Ezekial Baker the gunsmith, whom he had met during the rifle trials at Woolwich, may be interested in the designs and wrote him a letter to test his interest in breech loaders. It was something for his bottom drawer and a later date as first the combined cartridge and bullet had to be developed. He kept a 9mm round permanently on his desk as a reminder until he could figure out a way to interest someone in producing a proper bullet. He resolved to make enquiries at the Royal Society when he had the opportunity.

For now it seemed no more than an intellectual exercise as the need to increase his income had been solved by the ceding of Edenderry's estate. When and how the money would be made available he had no idea but he hoped his £2,500 would cover the bills that Catherine was racking up. The first of his wagers were due to come to fruition in February and that would help fill any gaps.

He smiled as he thought this but grimaced as he twinged his arm. True to her word, Catherine had brought in a doctor who had stitched the wound with cat gut. Chris had taken the precaution of dosing himself with morphine first. The doctor had been impressed by his stoicism but it now ached worse than before and the stitches pulled if he moved too quickly.

He had banned the use of water for drinking or bathing unless it was boiled for several minutes beforehand. He was determined to introduce 21st century ideas of hygiene into his household and a copper of water was always kept simmering on the range in the kitchen.

Catherine had queried his toothbrush one night. She invariably used crushed shells on a finger to clean her teeth. He found that toothbrushes were made in London by a man called William Addis and bought one for her. It was crudely made with hog's hair bristles but was better than nothing. His own toothpaste, like the morphine, never seemed to run out and he shared it with her. Next on his list of inventions was going to be a working shower, a flush toilet and central heating. If the Romans could have it, he could see no reason why he couldn't.

After a couple of days his bureau was covered in pen sketches. It kept him amused but he had little idea how to progress the ideas as some of the technology he needed was still decades away.

He decided to put all his drawings into escrow at his bank until he needed them. He didn't know why but he also decided to cut a lock of Catherine's hair and a lock of his own, put them into a locket and keep it with the drawings. It seemed a strange thing to do but Catherine was charmed by the idea that their hair would be entwined forever. She bought her own locket, put two more samples into it and hung it around her slim neck where it rested over her breast.

The weather was still dull but the rain had stopped. He decided to walk to Coutts Bank. He still couldn't ride and Catherine and Amelia exercised the geldings in the park every morning. As was usual he took his sabre and the Glock pushed down inside his waistband. It was unlikely he would need it but its presence was comforting all the same.

Downing Street was as busy as usual and he did not notice the two men standing outside the pub, one of whom turned to follow him.

61

Just before Christmas, Chris received a summons to Kew Palace and an audience with the King on New Year's day. He was unsure of the protocol so asked Henry what would be expected of him. Henry smiled and showed Chris his own summons.

"Tis the investiture, I'll warrant," Henry said. "We shall receive our decorations so you must appear in your green, sir."

"Will Catherine be welcomed?"

"Twould be impossible to keep her from your side on such an occasion. As your consort she will be made welcome at the court."

"And your intended?"

Henry pulled a wry face. "Alas no. Matters have not progressed so far. I have not yet found the time to ask for the lady's hand."

"Don't let the grass grow, Henry. Life is too short as it is."

"Wise words, sir. I find I am much occupied with Horse Guards business and it would seem churlish to consider marriage when I can spend so little time at it."

"That sounds like an excuse, sir. The lady may tire of waiting and you will be left a lonely bachelor to the end of your days."

"The lady does not yet know of my intent. I had thought to surprise her with it."

"Has she any idea how you feel about her?"

"We have passed times in agreeable companionship and I am sure she is aware of my regard for her."

"Henry, you do surprise me. I had not thought you so reticent. You must take your opportunities when you can. If the lady is worth your attention then others will think so too and beat you to the question. If she has no inkling of your intentions then there is nothing to prevent her from accepting another's proposal."

"For one so young, Lennox, you are full of sage advice. You no doubt speak from the experience of a deeply happy marriage and see things with a rose hued glow. For me, there is the question of suitability and whether my proposal would be acceptable to the lady and her family. She is the widow of a young officer and has an estate in Surrey."

"That wouldn't be the young officer whose geldings I bought, would it?"

"It would, sir. It was over the geldings that I was able to make her acquaintance. She is still in mourning and I do not want to be seen as too forward or too self-serving in this."

"You are the heir to an estate at Imber and your father's baronetcy. Your grandfather is an earl. You have been awarded a knighthood in your own right. I would consider you qualify on all counts. Make your intentions known to the lady but do not press her for a decision until she feels more able to accept a proposal of marriage."

"You have lightened my load on this matter, Lennox. You have my thanks for your wise counsel and I shall do as you suggest."

"Why don't we invite the lady to Catherine's soirée? It may help to break the ice."

"I fear, sir, at this late hour she may already have an engagement."

"We can but try, Henry."

"Now, sir, this royal summons must delay your departure to Ireland."

"Mr Pitt is determined that I should go as soon as possible but you are right. I can't go until after the investiture. Sometime in early January should the weather permit," Chris said.

"His Royal Highness has written letters of introduction on your behalf so that you may be welcomed to the homes of loyal Irishmen. You must first visit Dublin Castle and make the acquaintance of Sir Charles Cornwallis, the Lord Lieutenant of Ireland, who will render you some aid and intelligence."

"His Royal Highness is too kind."

Henry smiled. "He does not wish to see you languish too long there and wishes to speed your return however he may, without appearing to tread heavily on Mr Pitt's toes."

Chris returned home with a vague feeling of unease. It wasn't about money matters, as yet another wagon was unloading goods into the cellar, but it was his general acceptance of his life. He was making plans for the future as if he were in the early 19th century forever.

He was making a success of it, mostly due to his foreknowledge of events but he was also creating a hole for himself. His feelings for Catherine were so strong he doubted his grip on sanity could be maintained should he be thrown back into his own time. And what if this was nothing but an illusion? He could feel the weight of doubt crowd his mind.

His wounds were real, he was sure. He could feel the ache in his collarbone and the pull of the stitches in his arm. The scab had dropped off his ear leaving a short flat area where the top had been sliced off. So much detail, surely he couldn't be dreaming this. He could feel the nap and texture of his clothes, he could taste his food and drink, he had met people who he never knew existed. People who could not possibly have been dredged up from his subconscious. It beggared belief that he was not actually in the past. It beggared belief that he was not actually married to Catherine. Her scent, her touch, the feel of her body next to his, the taste of her lips. All he would lose. Then it hit him he was a loser either way. If he were truly in the past he would lose when sent spinning back to the present. If it were a dream he would lose it to reality. His only hope of true happiness was to remain in the past for the rest of his life and that, it seemed, was in the hands of fate.

It was not a happy thought but he smiled a cynical little smile. He prided himself on being a realist. A realist who was so willing to believe he was actually a time traveller.

"Buck up, Lennox," he said to himself. "You have two lives to live and you'd best make the most of it. Whether real or imaginary, you've been given a gift. Be thankful for it and take whatever gets thrown your way."

He felt better for giving himself a verbal kick but he still found Catherine and put his arms around her. She swivelled in his grip and cupped his face with both her hands.

"What is it, dearest? You seem disturbed."

"It has come home to me how grateful I am for what I have for however long I have it. I cannot but feel that the life I can give you will be fraught with sadness. I will soon be departing to Ireland to take possession of the property His Majesty has ceded to me. I fear I will not be welcome there and therefore will be travelling alone. I know too that I may be returning to Copenhagen at some time. It occurs to me that I lead a selfish life that puts my wishes above yours and perhaps it should be otherwise."

"You have chosen the life of a soldier with all the dangers that entails," Catherine said. "I have thought upon it and resolved that I must be grateful for the time that we have together, be it long or short. It is my desire to be with you always and I will not dwell upon what may or may not be." She gave him her look that could melt glaciers and kissed him on the lips. "Now come, sir. Christmastide is almost upon us. Mama and papa will be arriving on the morrow and we shall make merry."

He pushed her gently to arms length. "Which reminds me. We should invite a lady of Henry's acquaintance to your soirée."

"A lady? Of Henry's acquaintance?"

"He is resolved to make her an offer of marriage and I thought that perhaps we should help to grease the wheels of his proposal."

Catherine's face lit up. "Tis time Henry did consider taking a wife. He has been a bachelor far too long."

"She is Lady Maria Burgess, recently widowed, and Henry does not wish to appear insensitive to her state. She has a house in Mayfair."

"Then I shall write a personal invitation and hope that Lady Burgess has no prior engagement to entertain her."

He kissed her on the cheek. "You are an angel but your halo is in danger of slipping."

"How so, sir?"

"There is yet another wagon delivering. It seems our larders are beyond bursting."

A frown puckered Catherine's smooth forehead. "I had thought that all deliveries had been made. No matter I am sure every bit will make the days the merrier. Now, sir, tis time you changed your everyday garb as supper will soon be served."

She ran her hands down his back and felt the hard shape of the Glock. She put her head on one side with a question in her eyes.

Chris sighed. "It's another invention from the place I come from. I fear it's ahead of its time. I will show you later what it is and how it can be used but you must promise me never to tell a soul about it."

"I would so promise but why the need?"

"It is an invention that might change the balance of power in the world. I'm not sure this world is ready for it."

62

Edenderry was out of bed but in great pain. He seethed with anger at the memory of his doomed attempt on the king's life and the hatred he felt for the man who had prevented his success. Captain Lennox, the man had called himself and he wore the green of the German Jägers. Professional hunters. His sources told him it was now the uniform of the British Corps of Riflemen who had also thwarted Bonaparte's attempted invasion of Southern Portugal, hence the French First Consul's interest in their whereabouts; hence the order for the Irish and the emigrés to be on the lookout for them.

It was his fortune that one had been spotted leaving a house in Downing Street. It was his fortune that enquiries at the nearby inn had gained the intelligence that a Colonel and Mrs Lennox had recently taken up residence. The watchers had reported back to Rocques who had passed the news to him.

Now he had a target for his retribution and a plan. The watchers had reported wagons delivering goods at regular intervals and this had given him the idea. Rocques raised his eyebrows at the sheer audacity of it and wished to be no part of it but had arranged for men to visit Edenderry and take his orders. These men were revolutionaries who had smuggled themselves to England amongst the escaping emigrés, men who were loyal to the revolution and who spied for the French Directorate, fomenting whatever dissatisfaction they could amongst the levellers and closet republicans of the hated British. These were men who would do anything to disadvantage the British. Tough men, some would call them evil men, others that they were the heroes of the revolution fighting for France and a just cause. To Edenderry they were useful fools. He cared nothing for the French revolution or for the mountebank Bonaparte who had overthrown the ruling Directorate and assumed the title of First Consul. He cared for the money they contributed to his cause and for the succour they gave to men such as he when they needed sanctuary. And for the aid they were now supplying.

Under the guise of tradesmen, two of them had smuggled a barrel of gunpowder, pistols and ball into the house in Downing Street and secreted them in the basement. He had hoped to be able to complete his plan of revenge before Christmas but his wounds were too severe for him to contemplate leaving the room that had become his prison. Every move was agony and the thought of braving the stairs down to the ground floor too much to contemplate. He was assured that the gunpowder and arms were so well hidden they would not be discovered and he had the time to lick his wounds, regain his strength and wait for the New Year.

Chris spent Christmas Day with the Wadmans. They had not just brought the maid, Mary, with them but also Amelia's amour, Charles Dean who had proposed to Amelia and been accepted and it was a happy gathering that made their way to the service in St Martins in the Fields which, despite its name, was crowded in by houses and faced a watch house and sheds on its west frontage.

Although something of an agnostic, Chris admired the genuine faith of the people of this age. It was simple and true without any of the misgivings that plagued later generations. He was pleased to take part and sing the carols as lustily as anyone in the congregation. He had a good voice and, as he sang, noticed with his peripheral vision that Catherine was smiling up at him. He felt her hand slip under his arm and she hugged herself to him. His day was complete right there. Her touch always sent a shimmer, a frisson of energy, up his back. It was almost an electrical impulse and he had no explanation for it. It was outside his experience and had never felt the same sensation with any other person. Maybe it was the memory of Cat Dean and her defibrillator that had shocked him back to life alongside the cold monoliths of Stonehenge that summer's morning. Maybe it was the genuine and overwhelming feeling of love that he felt.

It was later, back in Downing Street that he missed his own family. His parents and younger sister Chloe who was studying at Cambridge. They would be together at the family home near Carlisle and he would normally be there with them. It disturbed him that he had not given any of them a thought before now on his two trips to the past.

Chris shook off the sadness and decided to bring in a tradition that the British army had continued for many years and serve the servants their Christmas supper.

Catherine, Amelia and Charles followed him to the kitchen where the servants were gathered. They all stood as the group entered but Chris told them all to sit. They looked uncomfortable as he outlined his plan.

Matthew stood again. "No, sir, tis not our place to be served by you. Tis not the right order of things."

"Please sit, Matthew. This is a tradition where I'm from. It will be a rare time Lady Lennox or I will venture into your domain below stairs but you will succumb to it each Christmas Day while I am master in this house. Now, cook, where is your food?"

The cook pointed to the range. Both Catherine and Amelia dished up and Charles helped serve the portions. Chris found two unopened bottles of port and placed them on the table. "That is for you to share. You all have the rest of the evening off until the family retires when they may require your usual services. Lady Lennox and I will see to our own comfort. It will be a busy day for you all tomorrow preparing for the soirée so get your rest while you may."

As they left all the servants stood and raised their glasses. "A merry Christmas to you Sir George, to you Lady Lennox, Miss Amelia and Mr Dean," Matthew said.

Back in the drawing room Catherine gave him one of her familiar quizzical smiles. "Sir George Lennox, I do believe you are the strangest of creatures upon this earth. On one hand you have embarrassed the servants beyond endurance and on the other you have made them your loyal servants for life. I do swear that no other man is like you in all of Christendom."

"I do believe you are quite correct in your assumption, dear one. I am unique and admit there is no other like me."

Catherine tutted and tapped him with her fan. "You are making merry again, George Lennox but I do believe there is an iota of egotism in your reply."

Chris grinned. "If one has it, one should flaunt it, or so it's said."

"Henry came over with a sherry glass in either hand and presented it to them. "I hear you have given the servants time to refresh themselves and so I am bound to serve you myself. Tis not a tradition I should like to encourage in my own household."

Chris raised his glass in a toast "Then let us drink to the tradition finding a home in the British army where officers will serve enlisted men on Christmas day."

Henry snorted. "You, sir, are a leveller at heart if but you would admit it."

"Not so, sir. I am for king and country and for the status quo. I do think that some humility amongst the ruling classes would not come amiss. One day each year when they may follow Christ's example and serve those who serve them. Did he not wash the feet of his disciples?"

"I concede you have a point there," Henry said, "but I cannot see it taking root amongst the aristocracy or indeed within the soldiery."

Chris smiled. "Perhaps one day, brother Henry, you may be surprised."

Henry raised his glass. "I would not wager against you. There have been too many occasions when you have been proved correct. I shall keep my powder dry on this."

Catherine, who had been listening to the exchange with an amused smile sobered a little and said, "Henry, I have received a reply to my invitation from Lady Burgess. She is unable to attend our soirée but has given most gracious thanks for our kindness in having her in our thoughts. It seems she is to go to Surrey this Boxing Day."

"Then we shall all bear the loss," Henry said. A sad look crossed his face. "You must excuse me, I must write to Lady Burgess to express my sorrow at her absence."

As he left Catherine said, "he is so disappointed."

Chris nodded. "The lady has an estate in Surrey and must have good reason to go there. It is a blow but her reply was very cordial and we have marked her card for the future. She now knows Henry and his family have a thought for her comfort and that will stand him in good stead."

Catherine gave him one of her looks. "I do believe I am beginning to understand what it is that has placed you in such good odour with His Royal Highness. You, sir, have a devious streak in your make up that you can concoct such seemingly innocent stratagems with such hidden motives. You must be the equal of Signore Machiavelli."

"A name synonymous with the devil. I don't think I would be that highly regarded and I certainly have no evil intent. No, madam, I submit I have more in common with Sir Francis Walsingham who did protect Queen Elizabeth so well."

63

The soirée and the investiture passed off with much celebrating. The Wadmans and Charles Dean left for Imber on the morning of January 2nd, which was the day that Dales returned from Lincoln and Chris decided it was time to leave for Ireland. It was a major operation that involved a mail coach journey to Liverpool and a packet boat to Dublin. There he would need to hire or borrow a horse to take him to Edenderry's estate further to the west.

As soon as the boy arrived he sent him out to purchase tickets for the mail coach. Dales was followed without him realising it. The weather had turned stormy and he kept the hood of his cloak over his head and his eyes down on the road for fear of stumbling into a deep puddle. His follower overheard the transaction at the coaching inn and hurried to Southwark to pass the news to Rocques who in turn passed it to Edenderry.

In the days since Christmas Edenderry's health had improved enough for him to brave the stairs and he could now raise his left arm above his shoulder before the pain became too great to bear. He heard the news and knew that his time to act was running out. He called for the two men who had hidden the powder and weapons and looked them both in the face. "There is work to be done, messieurs. Hard and dangerous work for the benefit of the Republique and of your pockets. Are you with me?"

One looked at the other and grimaced. "What is this work, monsieur?"

"A blow for France and death to her enemies. We must kill a British agent who plots against us. I will pay fifty sovereigns to the man who kills him."

"Who is this man, monsieur? And where may he be found?"

"At the house where you secreted the powder and weapons. The man is named Lennox and he wears the green coat of Bonaparte's enemies."

The second man looked at Edenderry through narrowed eyes. "I have heard of these green coats. It will be no easy task and the price will be fifty sovereigns each man. There will be three of us."

"Four," Edenderry said. "I will be with you. I have to see the man killed with my own eyes. It is a matter of honour."

The first man spat on the floor. "Honour? Tis of little consequence to us. Killing a British agent is a matter of duty and the money will be for our expenses. Come if you wish but we will move swiftly and will not be beholden to your safety. If you lag behind you will be left to whatever fate befalls you."

Edenderry's face hardened. "Do not let my bent body mislead you. I have the strength and the will to do what is required and I will not need your aid in this. Lennox's death will speed me on."

"When is this to be done?" the second man asked.

"Tonight, monsieur, or else our pigeon will have flown the coop. Lest you prefer a highwayman's act upon the mail on the morrow."

"To face blunderbusses and Dragons, I think not monsieur. How well is this place in Downing Street attended?"

"Not at all. There is one young soldier as well as Lennox. One male servant and the rest are women. There should be no resistance worthy of the name. The danger lies in making good our escape as a hue and cry may be raised should we act carelessly."

"Very well, monsieur," the first man said. "We will lay plans to enter the house at the dead of night when all are sleeping. We will carry no weapons save our cudgels should the watch stop us and will use those that were left in the house should the cudgels not prove sufficient to the task. Be in Downing Street as the clocks strike the eleventh hour."

Candles were still burning, the dull glow glimmering through the fanlight above the door of Number 19. Edenderry heard a church clock strike the half hour and shivered in the cold wet night. The Frenchman alongside him stamped his feet and Edenderry gave him a sour look and whispered. "Tis time we made our move afore the watch does challenge us."

The man grunted his reply. "There is still movement in the house, we should wait until all are abed."

"The torches in the sconces are burned low ere the watchman returns to rekindle them, we should not be seen."

Edenderry felt rather than saw the man's nod of agreement. "As you wish, monsieur." He gave a low whistle and two others emerged from the deep shadows where they had hidden and all four sidled along the railings. A flight of stone steps led down to the cellar. One man pulled a short crowbar from under his coat and forced the door with a sharp crack as the wood gave. Each man froze for a few seconds, listening, but heard nothing, the noise perhaps mistaken for timbers settling in the cold. Edenderry drew his sword and waved them into the cellar which was used as a storeroom. In one corner was piled wood for the stoves and lamp oil in spouted tin containers with ale kegs stacked in another corner old and covered with cobwebs. One man put his hand behind the pile of kegs and came out with the barrel of gunpowder. Another delved deeply into the wood pile for the cloth-wrapped pistols, pistol balls and priming flasks. Working by touch and what little light filtered down from the dying torches on the walls outside, the three Frenchmen loaded their pistols and put them on half cock.

"We are ready, monsieur."

Chris had been about to get undressed when he heard the crack from below. His preparations for the journey had kept him up late and he was in his shirtsleeves and breeches.

He had also been writing mischievous letters. He had received a reply from Ezekial Baker about his suggestion for a breech loading rifle. Baker had declined to invest in the idea, quoting the fact that the army had experimented with them in the Americas and had abandoned them in favour of the reliable Brown Bess musket. One letter he had written to an uninspiring ten year old schoolboy called Faraday to help stimulate his interest in electricity and another to a Edward Howard, younger brother to the Duke of Norfolk, with the chemical compound for Fulminate of Mercury, $Hg(ONC)_2$, which was made from mercury, nitric acid and alcohol, in the hope it would beat the French in producing the first viable percussion cap. He knew that Howard would become famous for his discovery in making the powerful primary explosive.

He left the letters on top of his bureau for posting. He had still been smiling at the thought of his effect on history when the noise from below startled him and he froze.

Catherine noticed his sudden immobility and sat up in bed. "What is it, dearest?"

"Maybe nothing. Perhaps one of the servants dropped something."

"The servants are all abed, sir. They have been for some time."

"In that case I'd better check to see if a door has been left unlatched. I'll be just a minute."

His sabre was propped against a wall and he picked it up on his way out. He tried to hide it but Catherine had seen him take the weapon. She slid out of bed and pulled on a dressing gown.

He made his way down the curving staircase to the ground floor. A shape loomed at him from the kitchen entrance and he flipped off the sabre's scabbard and turned.

"Hold, Colonel, tis me," Dales said in a choked whisper. He had his sword bayonet in his hand.

"You heard it too?"

"Aye, sir. I am but a light sleeper and it did startle me. Tis nothing on this floor to cause alarm."

Chris took a deep breath. "The cellar then. Bring a candelabra from the withdrawing room we need to see what we are about down there, keep close behind me and be careful where you place the point of your bayonet."

Chris thought he heard Dales chuckle but the boy quickly returned with four candles burning which threw shadows on the walls behind them.

"Do you hear anything, Dales?"

The boy cocked an ear. "Whispered converse, I believe, Colonel. Ne'er-do-wells are below."

Catherine had crept down behind Chris and now whispered. "What is afoot?"

"Catherine, you should not be here," Chris said in a hoarse whisper, "return upstairs and rouse the servants. We do not yet know whether we have burglars or other miscreants and they should be prepared for whatever befalls us. Matthew is to take personal charge of your and Amelia's safety. Find my Dragon in the drawer in the dressing room and give it to him. Quickly now."

Dales watched her go. "She is safely away, sir."

"Then let's see what the future has in store for us."

64

Catherine found the Dragon and also Chris's Glock. She thought for just a second before picking up both, running to the servant's quarters on the top floor and banging on Matthew's door.

"Waken, Matthew, we are invaded. I shall leave a Dragon by your door. Guard Miss Amelia and the servants with your life." With the Glock in her hand, she turned and raced back down the stairs in time to see the candlelight fade down the hall into the cellar.

Edenderry and the three Frenchmen were about to climb the stairs when they heard the banging and noise from the top of the house. Then candlelight reflected off the walls from the doorway at the cellar's entrance.

"We are discovered," Edenderry said. "Prepare yourselves."

Chris had taken the candelabra from Dales' hand and he held it at arm's length as he put one foot in front of the other in a slow descent. The staircase was curved and he still did not have sight of the room below. He took a firmer grip on his sabre and took a deep breath.

The first Frenchman took up a position between the kegs and sighted along his pistol's barrel. There was a small foresight and he aligned it on the candles' glow as it brightened. There was the crunch of a footstep on the stone and he put his hammer on full cock. The candelabra came into view and he pulled on the trigger. A flash in the priming pan and a loud bang sent the ball flying across the room.

Chris saw the sudden flash and dropped to his knees as the ball smacked into the brickwork above his head. Dales screeched a battle cry and pushed past him, jumping the last four steps in one leap and hurtling across the floor towards Edenderry.

A second Frenchman raised his pistol and stood up from where he had been kneeling. Dales saw his dark shape loom in his peripheral vision and swung his bayonet. It was a lucky blow and the pistol clattered to the floor as the man screamed.

Edenderry took a pace back and thrust his sword into Dales' body.

Dales had taken Chris by surprise but he reacted quickly, dropped the candelabra and followed the boy down. He saw Dales stagger and fall and glimpsed Edenderry pulling his sword free. He made a lunge for him and his sabre thrust was parried.

The third Frenchman took aim. He was so close he could not possibly miss and the thought of victory was already bringing a sneer of triumph to his lips as Catherine fired the Glock from the steps. Chris had shown her the workings but had not prepared her for the recoil and the pistol jumped from her grip. The bullet hit the Frenchman in the head. His pistol discharged and he fell, knocking the gunpowder barrel onto the floor where the dry wood cracked open and spilled its contents on the stone flags.

Chris was getting the upper hand with the wounded Edenderry but the first Frenchman pulled his cudgel and lashed at him with it. The blow hit his shoulder and he staggered back, allowing Edenderry to attack.

Chris's arm was numb and he could barely raise his sabre in defence as Edenderry launched a frenzied attack. He backed away but the cudgel swung again on his wrist and he dropped the sabre. Edenderry advanced on him, his sword point held at Chris's throat.

Chris backed further and felt Catherine on her knees behind him. She pushed the Glock into his good hand. He caught it by the slide but could not turn it to get a finger on the trigger. Edenderry lunged and Catherine screamed.

The sword tip pierced Chris's chest below his broken collarbone and he dropped to his knees. Edenderry had the light of victory on his face as he raised the sword again.

The Glock was on the floor and Chris spun it until he managed a hand on the pistol grip. As Edenderry launched his thrust he pumped rounds into him. Edenderry fell and the Frenchman roared and raised his cudgel for a killing blow to Chris's head.

Catherine screamed, "George!"

Dales wasn't dead. He watched the fight through waves of pain and a red mist before his eyes. His hand touched the second Frenchman's dropped pistol and he clawed it to him, pulling back the hammer with his chin. As the Frenchman swung his cudgel he fired. The sparks from the muzzle ignited the powder keg and it exploded with a sharp crack.

February 18th 1801

Pitt looked across Downing Street at the remains of Number 19 and filled a glass from a brandy decanter. The explosion had caused a fire amongst the wood and lamp oil in the cellar which had eventually gutted the building. Amelia Wadman and the servants had survived unhurt but of Lennox, his wife and aide there was no sign. Either blown to pieces by the explosion or buried forever in the rubble.

He was clearing his desk. He had resigned that morning and his friend, Henry Addington, Viscount Sidmouth, had reluctantly agreed to take on the position of First Lord of the Treasury. It would be an arduous task, Pitt knew.

Due possibly to the attempt on his life which had so unsettled him, the king was having another of his attacks of madness, and was therefore unable to ratify any change of government. Perhaps that also explained his rush of blood to the head in knighting Lennox and Wadman so precipitately. The Order of the Bath was within his gift but rarely ever granted without much deliberation. He fervently hoped the king was not shaking hands with trees again in the mistaken belief they were visiting envoys.

The country's enemies were gaining in strength abroad and it was a bad time but he felt honour bound to resign after the vote on Catholic emancipation went against him. Because of the king's illness, he would stay in office until Addington was confirmed but he was tired. Tired of the burdens of office that were turning him into a man older than his years. He would enjoy a brief respite when he could. He swallowed the brandy in one mouthful and refilled the glass. It was his only solace.

April 2nd 1801.

Colonel William Stewart folded the copy of *The Times* he was reading and looked across at his companion. "Well, your grace, what make you of the news that Tsar Paul of Russia has met his fate at the hands of assassins?"

"Sad news, indeed, sir," William Cavendish said. "But it has reminded me that the sad end to George Lennox did trouble me more."

"Indeed, your grace. A fine soldier and a fine man, laid low by thieves and scoundrels."

"He did forecast the Tsar's demise you know," Cavendish mused.

Stewart raised an eyebrow. "Now how the devil would he have known of that?"

"Fey fellow but, as you say, a good man. He also rightly predicted that Egypt would fall to us. There is ten thousand pounds to his account for wagers levied against him."

"Indeed, sir, a great sum of money. To what end will it be put now that he is no longer alive to collect it?"

"He has an account at Coutts Bank that I know of. I shall have the money deposited there. He has no heirs but may have family who would be glad of it."

"Chris!" A women screamed. "Wake up, dammit, wake up, speak to me."

He forced open his eyes. "Catherine?"

"It's Cat, Cat Dean. The scanner just exploded. You've been injured and we're taking you to casualty."

"How bad?"

"You were hit on the head by debris, you have a wound and metal in your left shoulder, I think your collarbone is broken and your right wrist. The top of your ear is missing and you have a nasty gouge in your left arm. I think you'll live but we're concerned about the effects of the blast and the head wound. We'll get you stitched up but it will be the IC room for you for a couple of days."

Epilogue

Three Years Later

"Well, Mrs Lennox, shall we?"

Cat looked at him and chewed her lip. "Are you sure you want to do this, Chris?"

His reply was a little hesitant. "Why else would we come out to a cold and frosty Stonehenge at the crack of dawn with a couple of spades and an intent to commit trespass?"

"It may prove it was all in your head."

Chris smiled at his new wife. He had told her the complete story of his 'imagined' time in the past and how it felt so real he believed it had actually happened.

Cat had helped him through some troubled times, first with his injuries and then through a near mental breakdown at Catherine's imagined loss which saw his army career finish. He still suffered from headaches, the fragment of dark energy remained in his brain, but doctors could find no reason for them. X-rays had proved inconclusive and Chris would go nowhere near any magnetic scanners after his second near death experience. No one had discovered what had made the scanner explode even though it had been forensically examined, piece-by-piece. A power surge was blamed and Chris had declined any compensation for his injuries; the NHS was strapped enough for cash in his opinion.

He had taken a teaching course and was now encouraging a love of history at a local comprehensive with little apparent success amongst the students but he was enjoying the work. He had a reputation at the school for speaking about Georgian times as if he had really lived them.

It was the Christmas holidays and they were on the first week of their honeymoon. They should have been sunning themselves on a Caribbean beach but this was something that had been on Chris's mind ever since his accident had brought him back to the present.

Cat gave a resigned nod. She wasn't sure whether this would prove a good or a bad thing for Chris's mental state. She was convinced he had dreamed it all. People only travelled back in time in science fiction. If he discovered that his stone jar, buried in the centre of the henge, did not exist she didn't know how he would react. But it had intrigued her that his imaginary wife Catherine was so like her and she believed it was her image he saw in his dreams and it was her he was deeply in love with. The final answer might convince him but, if the truth be known, she preferred to let that sleeping dog lie.

He gave her a leg up over the chain link fence and vaulted it himself. They walked to the path which surrounded the stones and stopped. Chris fiddled with the shaft of his spade. "Seems a bit like desecration now."

"Are you having second thoughts?"

"Yes. I'm asking myself do I really want to know. I have such glorious memories that I've only just realised it would kill me to know they were fake. You've helped me so much. I love you so much, it would now seem like a betrayal of our life together before it's really got off the ground. But you are so like Catherine …"

"Your dream girl," Cat said with only the slightest trace of bitterness.

He took her hand. "You are the girl of my dreams. Come on, let's get out of here. We may be able to get a late booking to Barbados."

The chief accountant at Coutts Bank scratched his head. "We've just unearthed some accounts from a couple of hundred years ago. God knows how they slipped through the net. Look at this one. £11,000 deposited in 1801 and look what it's worth now. £895,721 with interest. There was an escrow account attached and a box with some withered pen drawings of rifle workings and flush lavatories together with notes on buying certain parcels of land in London, I think where the Savoy Hotel is now situated in the Strand, at the corner of Green Park where the Ritz stands and land that Euston and St Pancras stations now occupy. And there was this gold locket with hair in it."

"It seems our account holder had an eye for the future. He's pinpointed some prime real estate. Do we know if there are any descendants," the manager asked.

"None that we have been able to trace. The account was in the name of a Lieutenant-colonel George Lennox but that is all we know."

"If we don't find anyone to inherit the government will scoop the money. Have another try to find someone. We could put an ad in *The Times,*" the manager suggested.

The accountant nodded. "I think it's a foregone conclusion that no one will take the bait but if anyone does try to claim it we can test their DNA from the hair in the locket. That will be the acid test. For now we'll lock everything away and keep our fingers crossed for the future."

THE END.

Author's Notes

As you might expect there was a great deal of historical research that went into this book. Much of what is depicted actually happened in the years 1800 to 1801. Wherever possible to ascertain, the names of military personnel, diplomats and politicians mentioned in the story are real people.

Theobald Wolfe Tone was executed for treason in 1798, he is commemorated on a wall in Dublin. Jean Gabriel Rocques was an untrustworthy spy in the employ of the French Revolutionary Council. He first served the monarchy and later Bonaparte and was adept at changing allegiances. He visited London for six weeks on his return from the West Indies but it is speculation that he returned at any other time.

Lacey Yea of the 7th Fusiliers wasn't actually born until 1808 but he rose to command the regiment and was killed during the Crimean War in 1855. The Royal Fusiliers (City of London Regiment) were called the Shiny Seventh due to a polished brass '7' worn on their epaulettes.

Lord Whitworth, Vice-Admiral Dickson and the British charge d'affaires in Copenhagen at the time, Sir William Drummond, were all involved in the *Freya* affair and the outcome of negotiation with the Danish is accurately depicted. However, to my knowledge, there was never any attempt made to assassinate Lord Whitworth.

The Grey Wolves are figments of my imagination although there was an attempt by United Irishmen with French support to burn Bristol which was swiftly put down. Lords Edenderry of Tullamore and Cavan of Kildara on the other hand are fictitious characters.

Number 19 Downing Street never existed. The numbers ran from 18 to 20, both of which were occupied by government offices. The rest of the details are historically correct. There was a pub in Downing Street called the Rose and Crown during that time and the road was a public thoroughfare.

King George III did succumb to another bout of 'madness' in 1801which delayed Sidmouth's appointment but it is highly unlikely that it was brought on by a failed assassination attempt unrecorded by history.

A second fleet was sent to Copenhagen in April of 1801 where Nelson distinguished himself in a naval battle against the Danes.

The very unpopular Emperor of Russia, Tsar Paul I, was assassinated on Monday March 23rd 1801 in St Petersburg by General Leo Bennigsen and Count von Pahlen who battered him and throttled him with a scarf.

In early 1801, the British Army Expeditionary Force of 30,000 men embarked to liberate Egypt. The commander of the expeditionary force, General Sir Ralph Abercromby, received orders to prepare his army for an amphibious assault in March of 1801. The Egyptian campaign is often forgotten as the British Army achieved more impressive successes in the Napoleonic Wars but they fought and cleared Egypt of French troops, who had been abandoned by Bonaparte, in a very few weeks. (Bonaparte had received a letter from Jean Gabriel Rocques urging him to return to Paris to take control of France). Abercromby was shot in the thigh in the Battle of Alexandria and died during the campaign.

There is a mention in the book about American Independence not being an issue in 1800. To clear matters up, the Declaration of Independence wasn't made until

1819. There were several presidents before that time starting with Washington in 1789. Although the colony enjoyed a certain amount of autonomy and had fought several wars against the British, including the most decisive in 1812, independence was not on the political horizon in 1800.

The characters from the previous book, *'To Fight Another Day',* Colonels Coote Manningham and Charles Stewart, are real people. The Deans and Wadmans, (who are named after family's that actually lived in Imber in Wiltshire) are themselves, and their part in this story, purely fictitious.

A final note: William Addis (1734–1808) was a former convict turned entrepreneur who made the first mass-produced toothbrush in 1780.

Under the trade name Wisdom Toothbrushes, the company now manufactures 70 million toothbrushes per year in the UK.

Ed Lane,
Lincolnshire 2017

About the Author

Whilst studying at the University of London Ed joined the Officers Training Corps and was commissioned into the Royal Regiment of Fusiliers before eventually joining The Parachute Regiment TA.

In civilian life, he founded a graphic design company where he honed his writing skills on marketing campaigns for national and multi-national companies.

Ed is the holder of three gold medals gained in national Sport Rifle competitions and has represented Lincolnshire over several seasons as a member of the County Lightweight Sport Rifle Team.

He took early-retirement which enabled him to devote more time to writing and lives in the Lincolnshire Wolds with his wife Barb.

His novels are a personal salute to the courage, dedication and professionalism of Britain's armed forces and are written specifically to raise money for deserving military charities. Hundreds of pounds from book sales have already been donated to such causes as the Royal British Legion, Help for Heroes and Spartan Warrior.